DEAD LETTER
DOUGLAS CLARK

Also available in Perennial Library by Douglas Clark:

DEAD LETTER

DOUGLAS CLARK

PERENNIAL LIBRARY
Harper & Row, Publishers
New York, Cambridge, Philadelphia, San Francisco
London, Mexico City, São Paulo, Singapore, Sydney

First PERENNIAL LIBRARY edition published 1985.

Library of Congress Cataloging in Publication Data

Clark, Douglas.
  Dead letter.

  I. Title.
PR6053.L294D4   1985   823'.914   84-48586
ISBN 0-06-080753-9 (pbk.)

85 86 87 88 89 10 9 8 7 6 5 4 3 2 1

DEAD LETTER

— 1 —

Detective Chief Superintendent George Masters was at ease. With no major case on his hands for more than a week, he had been able to break the back of some of the minor problems in his particular pipeline and, best of all, he had been able to return home at a reasonable hour each evening for some days. A rare treat for him and for his wife, Wanda, whom he could hear, upstairs, singing a nursery rhyme to their toddler son. It was bath and bed time for Michael. Masters had one ear cocked for the end of 'Lavender's blue, dilly dilly', as that would be the signal for him to go up to say goodnight—usually a slightly protracted ceremony on the comparatively few occasions when he was home in time to attend it.

He was in an armchair, in slacks and sweater, comfortable shoes, pipe alight and drawing well, with a folded newspaper on his knees. Had he been asked, he would have confessed that he was not engaged in thinking about anything in particular, but rather that he was just happy to be letting his mind wander, pleasurably, over enjoyable trivia. Had he not been awaiting the expected signal he might have snoozed in the warmth and comfort of the little sitting room.

The telephone in the hall rang to bring him back to complete wakefulness.

Bill Green. Detective Chief Inspector Green, now kept on at the Yard as SSCO, with his former duties virtually unchanged.

"George."

1

"Bill! I haven't seen or heard from you for days. What's going on?"

"I've been around."

"Are you at the Yard now?"

"At home."

Masters waited. Green was being laconic and untypically hesitant.

"You still there, George?"

"Yes. I'm waiting to hear why you called me."

"There's something I want to show you."

"Official business?"

"It could be, but at the moment it's more by way of being private. That's why I didn't see you in your office."

"You said show me, not tell me?"

"It's a letter, actually."

"Addressed to you?"

"Yes."

"In that case, Bill, why don't you and Doris come here this evening. Wanda and I will wait supper for you..."

"If Wanda's already got the meal ready..."

"She hasn't, and you know she's always delighted to see both of you. Tell Doris to get her bonnet and earrings on and get over here in time for a drink before we eat. Wanda's upstairs with Michael. I'll go up and tell her you're coming."

"You're sure she won't mind?"

"I don't have to answer that, Bill. But I'll say just one thing. You don't sound your usual self. So if whatever it is you've got to show me is worrying you, don't let it. To use an old cliché, let me remind you that a trouble shared is a trouble halved. We'll do better than that. We'll damn' well tear it in shreds."

"Thanks."

"See you, Bill."

After ringing off, Masters made his way upstairs.

"Who was it, darling?"

"Bill. He's got a private problem. I've invited him to bring Doris over for supper so's we can talk it over." Masters picked up his young son and lifted him high in the air as a prelude to a few minutes of pre-bedtime fun.

"Don't excite him too much, darling. I'd like him to get off to sleep quickly if Doris and William are coming."

"Right. Can I do anything? Peel a few more spuds or lay the table?"

"No, thank you. I'll just finish tidying up here and then I'll go down. The capon is in the oven so it'll just mean getting a few more sausages out of the freezer. We're having green beans, and they cook straight from frozen. Carry Michael through to his cot, and I'll join you in a minute."

When the Greens arrived, three quarters of an hour later, all was ready. As Masters handed his guests their drinks, he said: "Do you want to get down to cases straight away, Bill, or would you rather wait till after supper?"

Green took a long white envelope from the inside pocket of his jacket and handed it to Masters. "Read it for yourself, George. It's been tested for prints."

Masters scanned the envelope first.

Private and Confidential.
W. P. Green Esq., CID.
Scotland Yard, London S.W.1.

Then the postmark.

"Posted here in London," he said. "On the ... Bill, you must have had this for three or four days, unless it was seriously held up."

Green nodded. "Four days," he admitted.

Masters looked at him. "Is this why I haven't seen you recently?"

"Partly. Read the letter."

Masters did so.

Dear Sergeant Green,
 Forgive me for addressing you as Sergeant Green, but that was the rank and name I knew you by in the old days when you weren't a policeman but a Gun No. 1 in the RA. Of course I knew you were a policeman before you joined the army and again after you were demobbed. Indeed, I have seen your name more than once in the newspapers and I recognized you, despite the ravages of the years, when you appeared briefly on television in

3

connection with some murder in London not too long ago.

Masters looked up. "This bloke's a bit flowery, isn't he?"

"A bit," admitted Green. "But you'd better read on."

Masters did so.

I am, I believe, somewhat older than you and have been retired for more than a year. In preparation for my retirement, being sound in wind and limb, I took care, over the last decade, or so, to immerse myself in, and to become proficient in, a hobby. This is what the pundits recommend in order to combat the stultifying effect of any idleness of mind and body that can ensue when one comes to the end of one's active working life. I must say I agree wholeheartedly with the experts. So much so that I have come to embrace not only one, but two hobbies, namely photography and astronomy. Indeed, one could almost say I now have three great interests, because in connection with my photography, I have become quite fascinated by bird studies and have learned to recognize many of the types and species that are indigenous to, or honour us by visiting, our country.

"Cor!" said Masters extravagantly. "He's a bit much, this one." He handed over to Wanda the sheet he had finished reading. "Just read that, my poppet."

The second sheet.

I have mentioned my hobbies because they figure importantly in what I am now about to relate to you. My reason for approaching you is that I have witnessed a serious crime. A dastardly murder to be precise. Murder, followed by burial of the body within a very few yards of where I lay hidden, thankfully out of sight of the murderers, otherwise, I fear, the same fate would have befallen me as befell the poor wretch whom I saw slain.

Masters looked up. "Is this friend of yours an honest sort of chap? Not the sort to hallucinate?"

Green looked worried. "That's part of the trouble, George. I don't know who he is. He didn't sign the letter. Not with his name, that is. But if you push on, you'll see what I mean."

Masters raised his eyebrows in surprise, but passed no comment. The letter continued:

I was out with my impedimenta two nights ago, when the moon was full. I had my binoculars with me for scanning the sky and my camera because I thought that from the spot I had selected I should be able to get a shot of the full round moon low in the sky, laying a golden carpet across the water. I estimated that I ought to be able to obtain one of the classic shots beloved of photographers: that taken from the near end of the long reflection on a clear night.

I had chosen my spot carefully because I hoped to silhouette against the cloudless sky the black shape of a ruinous building and the stark outline of a very fine tree not yet in leaf. My hide would have made a good observation post in the old days, had the water been sand, the building one of those desert tombs and the tree probably the outpost of the palm grove at Jerabub. It was on the backward slope at the top of a small rise. Just to my left was a hedge junction. At this point, the hedges are built up on dykes, some of them double for the purpose, I believe, of denoting some old property or parish boundary. My spot was at a small gap where I could lie comfortably on the backward slope of the dyke, to rest my camera on a very small tripod on its ridge, and to face out over the short intervening distance of land that lay between me and the water. So I was virtually hidden from anybody who might happen into the area between me and my intended subject.

To my intense chagrin, after I had been installed for a full quarter of an hour—because I believe, as Nelson did, in being early for every appointment, even if only with the fickle moon—I was disturbed first by the noise and then the appearance of a group of men. There turned out to be four of them. I learned this because they halted within earshot of the spot where I was waiting: I was hidden from them by the bank on the reverse side of which I had chosen to lie, but I had all four in view even though it was night and the moon not yet risen.

I soon realized that I had been wise not to make my presence known. The fact is, the men were quarrelling, cursing and swearing, and it was obvious I would not

5

have been a welcome intruder. I do not know the nature of the quarrel, but I could make out from among the oaths, two names. One sounded like Drinkall or Drinkwell; the other like Slob or Squob. I began to suspect that these two were allies, with Drinkall being the leader. Of the other two, one man seemed to be the object of Drinkall's wrath, while the fourth man stood by contributing little.

The moon seemed to burst over the horizon. At any rate the scene brightened and I could get a view that improved with every minute that went by. Of course, I could not use my camera for fear the noise of it should advertise my presence. And it was as well I took such a precaution, for, to my horror, and full in my view, the one called Slob took out what I can only assume was some form of commando dagger and thrust it, with an upwards movement into the back of the man with whom Drinkall had been quarrelling. I believe the blow must have been skillfully delivered and that it must have penetrated the heart, for I think the victim died almost immediately. At any rate, by the time he had slumped to the ground, the fourth man said quite loudly: "By God, you've killed him."

Drinkall said: "That's right. And now we're going to bury him, and you are going to help."

Then followed the strangest thing of all. You can imagine that I expected them to go off for spades and other tools and I reckoned I could then slip away in the opposite direction. But I was mistaken. Those two men, Drinkall and Slob, already had a grave prepared. Under one of the hedges I mentioned and not a dozen feet from where they had killed the man. Then, of course, I knew they had led him to the spot for execution, all well planned in advance. Slob fished up two spades from the bottom of the slit trench which I had overlooked in the shadows of the hedge running at right angles to mine, between me and the sea path. There was some fumbling with the body. I assume they were rifling the pockets. Then the dead man was unceremoniously dumped in his grave. My impression was that the trench was deep for I can swear I heard him fall to its bottom, and the refilling took an appreciable time even with two men working. Drinkall stood by, directing operations and, after the soil had been tamped down, instructed Slob to find some rubbish to camouflage the scar. An amazing amount of hedge rubbish, tins, cartons and the like was, apparently, to be had close by. Slob dumped it as directed and then, to make the spot even more unattractive to both humans and animals, Drinkall broke, on the spade, a couple of bottles from among the rubbish. He scattered the broken glass around as a deterrent to inquisitiveness.

After that they went, presumably to a car parked not too far off. Slob carried the spades. I let a safe interval pass, straining my ears to catch the sound of a car, but not succeeding. Then, collapsing my small tripod, I collected my camera and binoculars and left the scene, quietly, by another way.

And that, Sergeant Green, is the story of my escapade. I did not go to inspect the grave, and I did not take an exposure film of the business that went on there, or even of the full moon. Not a very gallant effort, perhaps, and I know you are wondering why I am writing to you instead of approaching the local police. Alas, this course is denied me, because I recognized the fourth man in the party as a senior member of our local constabulary, and when I say senior, I am not talking about a sergeant or a one-pip wonder (as we used to call them). How far would I get were I to report to a man his own crime? How long would I live if Drinkall or Slob were to hear of such a report—as indeed they would?

I didn't need to think for too long about what action to take. I suppose that, like me, as you grow older, you become more prone to nostalgia. Particularly since my retirement, my mind has recalled the old days more and more frequently. The memories are peopled with very real characters. You have figured among them. So you see, you were not all that far from my thoughts when I knew I had to have somebody to tell this story to. You were the obvious choice.

I feel also, for my own safety, that I must not tell you where this murder occurred. You see, if whoever is reading this is not the Sergeant Green I knew of old, then unwise communication by another with the police in this area could jeopardize my life.

In the old days, we used to use the phrase "I say again" in clear, or "Ink Monkey Ink" in morse, when we wished to stress any part of a wireless message. May I do that again now? May I repeat that every word I have written to you is the truth? Should you believe me and wish for further information, please insert a message in the personal column of the *Daily Telegraph*. Only Sergeant Green will know the name to whom to address it. It will be the name painted on his 25-pounder in the desert. The signature at the end of the message will be the name of Sergeant Green's gunlayer (No.3) at Mareth. (At Mareth, not before then, not later.) The message itself will obviously be of your choosing, but I hope I shall be able to understand it.

Yours sincerely,
T. A. LAMIEF

Masters finished reading the last page and handed the sheet over without comment to Wanda who said: "You can start carving, darling. This won't take me long."

Masters ushered Doris and her husband through to the tiny dining room and seated them before passing through the alcove that led to the kitchen. He had taken the chicken from the oven and had sharpened the carver on the steel before Wanda joined him. Neither said a word as they busied themselves with getting the meal on the table.

"Sausage, Bill?"

"Just two or three, ta," said Green abstractedly.

"Bill!" His wife sounded outraged.

"What, love?"

"You can't ask for two or three sausages. George asked if you wanted one with your chicken."

"Sorry, George. I wasn't thinking."

"That's just what you were doing, Bill." Masters handed to Wanda his colleague's plate with three sausages nestling alongside a thigh of chicken. "He loves roast potatoes, darling, don't forget."

A moment or two later they were all eating. Wanda asked: "You said the letter wasn't signed, William. At least not with the man's real name."

"That's right, love."

8

"But you also said you didn't know who had written it."

"True."

"Then how do you know that T. A. Lamief is not the author's real name? Are you just saying so because you don't recognize or remember it from way back?"

"Oh, I recognize T. A. Lamief all right, love."

"Ah!," said Masters. "I guessed you had, otherwise you wouldn't have been so sure it wasn't a man's name. So what is it? A mnemonic of some sort? Something that any old gunner from those days would know so well at the time that he would still remember it after forty years?"

Green nodded. "Not a mnemonic, if by that you're talking about something like Every Good Boy Deserves Favour—you know, the musical thing."

"Some sort of memory aid, though?"

"T A L A M I E F is just the sequence of the initial letters of fire orders for laying guns. It was vital always to receive them in the same order, so everybody knew them as well as they knew their own names. Target, ammunition, line, angle of sight, method, interval, elevation, fire."

"I'll take your word for it," said Masters, "because quite frankly you are spouting Double Dutch as far as I'm concerned and I'm always at a loss with acronyms, anyhow."

"You're not cross, are you, George?" asked Doris. "You sounded a bit put out just then."

"If I did, I apologize, my dear. I certainly have nothing to be cross about."

"Good. Because it's not like you, but for a moment I thought perhaps..."

"Perhaps what?" asked her husband.

"That George thought you ought not to have kept the letter to yourself for so long."

Masters laughed. "Had I been in Bill's place, I should have done exactly the same. We get a lot of anonymous letters at the Yard, so we don't get too excited about them although, in our own defence, I must say we do try to weigh their value just in case they contain genuine and

9

useful information. With this one, Bill is in a slightly strange situation, because not only is it addressed to him personally, but it purports to come from an old friend or acquaintance of his. That being so, Bill quite rightly feels that if anybody should be able to vouch for its contents or authenticate it in any way, he must be the one. But we are forty years on from the time when his correspondent claims to have known Bill. That's a very long time to remember anything about another person, particularly when the other person gives neither his name nor any other clue as to his identity. So, even a man with a memory as good as Bill's will need time to think, as think he must, because that letter claims that not only has murder been done, but that a senior police officer is involved. The former is serious enough. The latter, quite frankly, is enough to cause any policeman to stop and think before he rushes into any action which may cause an unholy row. Don't misunderstand me, Doris. Bill would not want to shield any man who had committed such a crime, but he would want to try and make sure that the facts were true before starting anything, because the letter came to him from a one-time friend, and no matter how much he may disclaim it, he will be regarded as the instigator of any steps that are taken." Masters turned to Green. "I suppose what I have just said is, in essence, the reason why you have not been available for the past few days?"

Green nodded and then, inconsequentially, he said: "These spuds are good. Roasted just how I like 'em. And the sausage isn't too bad either." He looked round at Masters. "And thanks for putting it the way you did. Quite honestly, I've had a hell of a time, ever since that letter arrived."

"There's still a bit of meat left on the chicken, Bill. Let me carve again for you."

"Ta. I don't mind if I do. This is the first real meal I've had for days. I've been quite put off my food."

"I hadn't noticed," said Doris.

10

"Are you serious, William?" asked Wanda. "About being off your food, I mean?"

Masters put the replenished plate down in front of Green. "What actually have you done, other than think, Bill?"

"Quite a lot, actually. Or, rather, I think I've got somewhere—or could have."

"Care to tell me?"

"That's what I'm here for." He turned to Wanda. "I heard your question, love, and I didn't ignore it. The answer is I've been worried—just a bit more than I usually am, you know. So if the fact of what I've said about food is not actually true, the figure of speech describing it is."

"I'm sorry to hear it. But I feel sure you'll cope with it all eventually. Probably not in the best possible way, because circumstances won't allow you to do so."

"What actually have you done, Bill?" asked Masters.

"Two things. Tried to find out if we know anything of Drinkall and Slob; and where one could take a shot of the full moon about a week ago."

"Any success?"

"Yes."

"Yes? Congratulations. What did you do to get whatever it is you got?"

"Stairs and Kicks on the VDU."

Doris turned to Wanda. "What on earth are they talking about now?"

Wanda shook her head. "Don't ask me. I think I know what a VDU is. It's a visual display unit like a TV screen on which a computer can show printed answers to questions you ask it by pressing keys on a panel like a typewriter. But kicks and starts...no."

"Stairs and Kicks, poppet," said Masters.

"What are they?"

"Systems."

"I see."

"Do you, Wanda?" asked Doris. "It's more than I do."

"Of course I don't. Men! They're about as good at communicating as oysters. We might as well not be here when they're in this sort of mood. Monosyllabic grunts for answers, and..."

"Hey, hey, hey!" said Masters. "What's all this? Mutiny?"

"There will be if you don't tell Doris and me what Stairs and Kicks are."

Green winked at Masters and said: "By the way, George, have we got these two on either Stairs or Kicks? Vital statistics and whatnot?"

"It would make it interesting," agreed Masters with mock-solemnity. "Wanda the Cutpurse and Doris the Dip."

"This particular Cutpurse," said his wife, sweetly, "will be using a very sharp blade for some purpose other than detaching people from their money. She'll be using it to detach herself from a husband and an erstwhile friend who..."

"Stairs," said Masters, "simply stands for Storage and Information Retrieval System. Kicks, for Criminal Information Consolidated Control System."

"But Criminal doesn't begin with a K," said Doris.

"Okay," said her husband, "Start it with a C."

"I always suspected the Yard couldn't spell."

"Neither can it," said Green. "Only yesterday I asked it how to spell diarrhoea and you should have heard the answer it gave. Now you'd expect a modern building like that to be able to..."

"William," counselled Wanda, "we all know you've been worried. We're sorry about that and we're pleased you are now beginning to feel somewhat relieved in your mind. But if you, and George, are going to carry on acting the goat..."

"Sorry, love. I'll tell you what I know about... But I'm not very knowledgeable about computer systems, so don't expect anything but a simple explanation."

"That's what Doris and I have been praying for these last ten minutes."

"Right. You know Stairs is a storage and retrieval sys-

12

tem. What we use it for at the Yard is simply a sort of name and address list of known criminals. Nothing more than that."

"So you can see if they have ever been in police hands, you mean?"

"That's it love. Then, if they appear on that list, you go over to Kicks to ask what they've done and what is known about them."

"That's clear. And you've had some success? Drinkall and Slob appear there?"

"Not quite like that. The thing about Stairs is that if you don't know a name and address fully or correctly, you can ask the computer to search through the bits you do know. What I mean is, say I had an address but no name, the system would find the address and then tell me who lives there."

"If it had such information at all?"

"Right. But it is a lot more sophisticated than that. For instance, I asked the operator for Drinkall. No joy. No criminal of that name on the list. So I went to Drinkwell. Same result. So the operator asked for all names beginning with Drink. Only two came up. Drinkell and Drinkwater. I wasted a bit of time on those two though I reckoned Drinkwater was out, because it's a lot different from Drinkall."

"But Drinkell isn't, is it?"

"No. It's pretty close. So I did investigate him carefully. But for reasons I won't go into, I had finally to rule him out as well."

"That's the way it goes," murmured Masters, getting up to refill the wine glasses.

"So what did you do, William?"

"I consulted Stairs again. This time the operator just asked for names beginning with Drin."

"But you'd get the same ones again," said Doris.

"Of course. And lots of others, too. Dring, Drinter, and so on."

"And?"

"I asked for Kicks on each of them. There were several

possibles. But nothing definite. So I had to start on Stairs for Slob or Squab." Green turned to Masters. "It took a long time, George. No Slobs or Squobs or Stobs."

"But you persisted."

"Nearly drove the operator mad, actually. But after a great many hours, we got a lead."

"Ah!"

"A chap called Swabey."

"Swabey? Shortened to Swab?"

"We had no report on the fact that he shortened his name, but we did eventually find that this chap was thought to operate with a chap called Dringle..."

"And Dringle was one of your possibilities from the Drin group?"

Green nodded.

"Bingo, in fact."

"Well, they're both nasty pieces of work and both have been inside. Dringle for hijacking a long-distance consignment of Scotch—over a thousand cases—and Swabey for GBH. But it was the 'thought to be connected with' bits that were interesting. As far as I could see their names have been connected with nearly every type of devilry in the calendar."

"But not proven?"

"Apart from the two cases when they went inside, they've not even been arrested, except Swabey once, and he got off. It was old Fred Lane's case. I spoke to him about it, and he reckons they'd got Swabey dead to rights but Tinblatt appeared for him..."

"Tinblatt? He's good, but he's not notably a criminal's mouthpiece."

"Fred Lane said that the key witness for the Crown was a chap Tinblatt had once defended. He reckoned Tinblatt knew too much about him for the good of the case. Tore him to ribbons by innuendo."

"Easy enough to do I suppose, with some witnesses."

"Is it, darling?" asked Wanda. "Counsel can't mention a witness's record in court, can he?"

"No, sweetie. But if, say, the question before the court is one of raiding a bank. You are defending, and you know that one of the principal witnesses for the prosecution is a man whom you have defended either successfully or unsuccessfully on a charge of car ringing. That charge involves the theft of cars, respraying them and generally altering their appearance for resale. Bank raiders usually acquire 'wheels' for getting away from the scene of the crime. So you rise and ask the witness not if he has ever stolen a car—that would be improper—but if he is familiar with the mechanics of car theft. The theft of a car is a pertinent part of the prosecution's case, so nobody can object to the question. So the man in the box has to answer. What does he say?"

"Yes or no, I suppose."

"Exactly. If he says yes, the depth of his knowledge is enquired into. It shows him to be less than pure as the driven snow. In other words it discredits him. If he says no . . ."

"Knowing full well Counsel knows he is lying?"

"Quite."

"He would be well and truly rattled, I suppose."

"That is the best he would feel, and hardly the frame of mind in which to answer penetrating questions. But he is on oath in the box, remember. And perjury is a serious crime. Counsel who knows of it will approach the judge. Perhaps not in open court because such points are often made in chambers in the first instance."

"But, George," said Doris, "you said that Counsel may have previously been successful in getting the man off his car charge. So couldn't he say truthfully that he didn't know about the mechanics of car stealing?"

"No, love," said her husband, "because all that would have been gone into at his previous trial, so he would have to say he had heard a bit about it. And counsel would winkle it out of him, quite cleverly. It would be the character of the witness that the defence would be trying to demolish, with no thought for his evidence in the case. That would fall by the wayside if he were proved to be a villain in his own right. Not always, of course, but it does happen."

"And Mr Lane thinks that something like this happened when Slob or Swob was tried?"

Her husband nodded.

Wanda got to her feet. "Will everybody have fresh pineapple and ice cream?" She began to collect the dirty plates. She said, as she carried them into the kitchen, "Go on talking, William. I can hear you from here."

"Do we know the whereabouts of Dringle and Swabey, Bill?" asked Masters.

"No. That's the trouble. They appeared to drop out about four years ago and there's nothing about them since then."

"No trace whatsoever?"

"Not a sign. Their last known addresses are now occupied by other people. No connections there."

"In London, were they?"

"They operated in the east, south of the river."

"So for anything CRO knows, they could both be dead?"

"Right. Only they're not. I've checked that, too."

Wanda put the dishes in front of them. "So you have to assume they have resurfaced, William?"

"It looks like it, love. But we have no proof. Only the letter."

"I know that isn't proof, exactly, but don't you often act on information received in that way?"

"We do," said her husband. "But think of Bill's dilemma."

"He's sorting it out very nicely."

"Not as nicely as all that," confessed Green. "We don't know the location of this murder nor the identity of the victim. I told you I asked the boffins to tell me where a photographer could get a picture of the new moon that night. Their answer was a lemon."

"It had to be," said Masters. "It could be anywhere in the country where there was water. I suppose we all thought of the sea when we first read the letter. Fair

16

enough. But the moon comes up in the east or south-east, so anywhere on the south or east coasts would be suitable. But so would places in the Lake District or the north-west sides of places like the Bristol Channel or the Mersey. In other words, it could be anywhere in Britain."

"But the letter was posted in West One."

"I know, sweetheart. And that could argue that Mr T. A. Lamief is down this way somewhere. But I know if I were in his position and my life were in danger, I'd travel a long, long way to cover my tracks."

"So you discount the postmark?"

"Entirely. I don't know about Bill."

"I do, too. But I reckon if it had been posted in Newcastle I'd be inclined to look north."

"Maybe," agreed Masters. "What you mean is that although your pal doesn't live in London, it is the nearest town big enough to be anonymous or not to give anything away."

"That's my belief, George, unless he's pulling a real fast one and somehow I don't think he is. His letter shows he's a cautious man, but it strikes me that he is, by nature, a garrulous old boy, and he's had to work hard not to give anything away and to lay on his bit of cloak-and-dagger stuff about a reply in the personal column. What I'm trying to say, I suppose, is that he doesn't come across as somebody who would work out and put into operation a double bluff such as posting his letter in the area in which he lives because he reckons that will be the last place we will look for him."

"Simple serpents," counselled Masters.

"I know. The apparently guileless bloke is often as cunning as a fox. But this chap—you said yourself he was a flowery customer."

"A lot of con men are."

Green put down his spoon. "So what are we saying, George? Just that we don't know his location?"

"I think so, don't you?"

"You're not saying he's trying to hoax me?"

"I can't answer that either way, Bill, but I'd be inclined

17

very definitely to act as though I believed his story implicitly until I proved otherwise."

"You're sure of that?"

"That is my opinion and my advice."

"Thanks."

"For what, exactly?"

"For the chat."

"I see. I've got a nice bit of cheese you might like to taste, Bill. A friend brought it over from France..."

"No you don't," said Wanda. "I mean you can have your cheese and biscuits, but you are not going to leave Doris and me in mid-air concerning William's problem. It's all very well for you two. You can meet in your office tomorrow and thrash it out to your hearts' content. But we should like to know how you intend to proceed. You have whetted our appetites. Now you must satisfy them."

Green grinned at Wanda. "The trouble with you, love, is that you grow more like your old man every day. It comes from living with him, I suppose. You pick up bad habits without noticing you're doing it. And this is really good cheese. I once knew a chap who told me that cheese, in France, is a living thing. Ours over here is all dead. The sort that would be sold off cheap to..."

"William!"

"Yes?"

"What are you two proposing to do about that letter?"

Green shrugged. "I've shown it to my boss and discussed it with him. The direction of affairs is now out of my hands."

Masters said: "In all seriousness, my darling, we shall play it by the book. Tomorrow it will be shown to Anderson, together with what Bill has learned from the computer. The decision is then his. If I know him, he will take action of one sort or another. The most likely being to hand it over to Bill and myself. He will do this, I believe, for several reasons. One, it is alleged murder and he cannot ignore a report of murder, alleged or otherwise. Two, a police officer has been accused of complicity in the alleged crime. He cannot ignore that, either. Three, he

18

will want as few people as possible to know that a senior officer has been accused of being party to a crime—for obvious reasons. So, as Bill and I already know about it, and we have, from time to time, investigated a few murder cases, the likelihood is that the matter will be dumped on our laps."

"And what will you do if this happens?"

"First off, I think we shall have to compose a message for the personal column. Our informant has now waited five or six days for his reply, and we don't want him to get too impatient. After that? Who knows? We may get more helpful information from Mr T. A. Lamief, but that will take a day or two to reach us. In the meantime, Bill and I will have to try to start some line of enquiry. And before you ask what it will be, I'll tell you. It is to determine the identity of Bill's old acquaintance and then to track him down without recourse to the services of local police forces."

"You will keep faith with him then?"

"Did you suppose otherwise?"

"No, of course not but for you to operate outside the London area, without the knowledge and consent of the local force involved, is going to be very difficult, isn't it?"

"Fraught," said Green. "God knows how we'll manage to do it—if we ever get that far."

"T. A. Lamief may tell you where."

"Even so, love, we'll be faced with investigating a murder on the patch of a local force that doesn't know murder has been done."

"But if you find the body ... ?"

"We can't just say Dringle and Swab and an unknown copper did it, love. It would have to be proved, and properly proved. Don't forget that parts of that letter could be true and parts untrue. Say the murder took place as described, but our boy who witnessed it put in a few false names just to pay off old scores. What then?"

"One other very big difficulty," said Masters, "is the fact that if a body is found, it then becomes, officially, the business of the locals, who may say they don't want

19

or need our help. They will demand to know what we know and in spite of our protestations we should be obliged to tell them. Then the senior officer who is alleged to have been present will know all about Bill's correspondent."

"And that would put paid to him," said Green. "After all, the best way to deal with a hostile witness is to stop him testifying—permanently."

"It's all very worrying," said Wanda.

"Now you know how Bill's been feeling these last few days."

"Of course. He foresaw all this, and you, too."

"It would hit any cop worth his salt like a sledge-hammer on first reading that ... that missive. I confess I wish it had never reached Bill. As it is ... well, I've satisfied your curiosity as far as I can."

Wanda got to her feet. "We'll have coffee in the sitting room, shall we?"

— 2 —

Anderson, the A C (Crime), was quite definite about it. Masters, Green and their two detective sergeants, Reed and Berger, were to investigate. "Not the crime," said Anderson. "That may come later. The letter. Is it true? Is some of it true? Who wrote it and where? But I don't need to tell you, George."

"I think not, sir. My brief is to establish whether there is a crime—as described in the letter—to be investigated. The solution of the crime—should there be one—will be a separate operation."

"Quite. Just so long as we do not know for certain that a crime has been committed, or where it is said to have taken place, or who informed us, we are within our rights—in fact it is our duty to investigate. But should we ever establish that a crime was actually committed and that it took place outside our bailiwick, then it is equally our duty to stop there and hand it over to the force concerned. In this case that route may not be open to us and we should need to seek dispensation to work, uninvited, outside our own territory. To this end, the Police Liaison Officer at the Home Office must be informed, as must the Commissioner. Beyond that, nobody. I look to you, George, to see that as few people as possible outside your team know what you are about, and I shall personally see that the Home Office keeps its counsel. Things have a nasty habit of getting leaked to the press these days even from the innermost rings of bureaucracy. I don't want that to happen here. If it does..." Anderson shrugged. "Another man could die, two murderers escape and a rogue policeman go scot free. I look to you, George."

"Understood, sir."

"And Bill."

"Yes, sir?"

"I know you find this pretty distasteful. But remember that if there is any truth in all this, a man who knew you years ago is still trusting you. He has tried to do his bit as a citizen and in doing so could well have jeopardized his life. Yet he entrusts his safety to you. That is, in its way, a great compliment. You've done some excellent work so far—all that business with the computer—so don't let your worry and distaste cause you to let your old army colleague down."

Green grunted. There was no other reply he felt he could give. It was equivocal, but Anderson accepted it as the answer he expected. He got to his feet to usher Masters and Green out of the office.

"We shall need to brief the sergeants, Bill, and to have a council of war. Tell them to hand over anything they may be doing as this job could be full-time for several days."

"They should be ready. Without telling them anything I gave them the hint first thing this morning."

"Good. There's just one thing. What about the VDU operator who has been doing the search for you? How much does he know?"

"Nothing. I told him we'd had a whisper from a grass. That's all. He wouldn't find it remarkable. Pretty commonplace, in fact. It wouldn't rouse his interest."

"So there's no need to impress on him the need for extra security, then? Not that I'm suggesting he would talk outside, but he may chat to his pals inside the Yard."

"He'd have no reason to. I honestly think it would be better not to rouse his interest by making a thing of it."

"Fair enough." They stopped outside Masters' door. "Come along when you and the lads are ready, Bill. And get one of them to bring some coffee in. We could be in for a longish session."

22

Green nodded, but did not go. "George," he said after a moment or two. "I feel I've let you in for something that could be a bit tricky."

"Not your fault, Bill. And even if it does turn out to be tricky, it could be different. Ain't that something?"

"As long as you look at it that way."

"I do. What I suggest you do, too, Bill, is to disassociate yourself from it. The letter was addressed to you, I know, but we should be in exactly the same situation had it been sent to any other CID man. Regard it as having been sent to Anderson which, if the lines of management we're always hearing about are valid, it technically was."

Reed and Berger listened in silence to the story their senior colleagues had to tell them, then the discussion followed.

"Chief, before we start in earnest," said Reed, "could I just ask if the letter was checked for prints? Before too many other people handled it, that is? What I mean is, we—Berger and I—didn't do it, so..."

"I did it myself," grunted Green.

"You dusted it yourself?" asked Reed incredulously. "There were no signs of powder."

"I shoved it in that new fangled laser machine in the lab," replied Green. "The chap there didn't read it. He just switched on his beam and took the photographs. They could have been blank sheets of paper as far as he was concerned."

"You got some photographs, then?"

"Yes. Mostly my own. Some others, too. Not on record."

"Still, they could be a help, later."

Masters cut in: "Can we please discuss the message we are to insert in the *Daily Telegraph?* If it is to appear tomorrow morning the matter is urgent. We may even have to do some special pleading to get it in by then."

"What sort of thing you want to say, Chief?" asked Berger. "Ask his name and so on?"

"I have a feeling we shall have to play this customer like a pretty cagey fish, haven't you, Bill?"

23

Green nodded. "Come on too strong and he could shy away. I reckon we've got to give him a bit of confidence in us, George."

"Agreed. How would you propose to do it?"

"Something about believing him and being prepared to help. That sort of thing. No definite questions. To encourage him to write again."

"Exact words?" asked Masters drawing a pad towards him.

"Oh, I dunno. Start with..."

"Hang on, Chief. It's got to be addressed to somebody first."

"Of course. The name painted on your gun, Bill. What was it?"

"Julie," said Green.

"Julie? Not Doris?"

"I inherited the name when I took over the gun," grunted Green. "The lads in the sub wouldn't have liked it changed."

"Sub?"

"C Sub. Sub section, actually. Designation of the gun team. Used to come into action third from the right in the troop gun line."

"I see. So, Julie is the recipient. Now, how about, 'I trust and believe in you. You can count on my interest and full co-operation'?"

"And full co-operation of all my influential friends," amended Green. "Let him know it's not just me, but you and Anderson and so on."

"Good point. That really should be about enough, shouldn't it? We don't want to write an essay."

"Put in," suggested Green, "something about us longing to hear from her again at the same address with all her news and gossip."

"I like the gossip bit," said Berger. "It sort of invites indiscretion, and we could do with a bit of that from this chap. If he would be really indiscreet and let slip some vital clue it would help a lot."

"Signature, Bill?" asked Masters. "Haven't we to be a bit careful here? The name of your gunlayer at one particular time?"

"At Mareth. That's right. My proper gunlayer was wounded in the Tripoli battle. Ted Canning. He was taken back to hospital while we were pulled out of the line for a bit to rest and re-equip. I'd had to get a new layer, of course. Miller his name was. And he was with me as number three in the Mareth line. But just about the time we broke through there, Ted Canning was sent back up to us. His wound hadn't been all that serious, and six weeks or so had seen him right. Miller left us when Ted got back. He went back to a troop in another battery. I think he went as a number two—on promotion, like."

"I think I understand that, and I think I understand why T. A. Lamief specified this particular man as the person to sign the message. What do we put as the signature? Dusty Miller?"

"Funny thing was," replied Green, "we never called him Dusty. The only Miller I ever knew in the army who wasn't a Dusty."

"I thought so. As I said, nobody but you would know that and somebody impersonating you could have fallen into the trap of calling him Dusty."

"Stinky, we called him."

"Stinky?" asked Reed in amazement. "You mean he stank? Had B.O. or sweaty feet or something?"

"No. You won't remember, but there was a couple of American comedians who used to make zany films. One was short and fat . . ."

"Laurel and Hardy," suggested Reed.

"No. Two other characters. I can't remember their names. Anyhow, in one of their films made about that time, the screen went blank—on purpose, that was—and then a scrawled message was flashed on. 'Stinky Miller go home.' It was one of their jokes."

"And your chap became Stinky because of that? He must have been Dusty at one time," said Reed.

"Maybe," snarled Green. "But we called him Stinky."

"So how shall we sign the message?" asked Masters soothingly.

"Stinky Miller."

"Right. So that's that." He handed the top sheet of the pad across to Reed. "Have that typed up immediately, please, and then have it sent to the *Daily Telegraph* office by hand. See the messenger is carrying enough cash to pay for the insert and see that he understands that it must appear tomorrow."

"Right, Chief." Reed left the office. Masters turned to Green. "What next, Bill? Any ideas?"

"He knows me, but I don't know him," replied Green. "My memory's fairly good, but quite honestly, after all these years I'd find it very difficult to remember names and faces of men I wasn't intimately concerned with. What I mean is this. There were six men and a driver in each sub. We literally lived together, side by side, as near as I am to you the whole time. We manned the gun, we cooked our own food and ate it beside the gun pit, we shared slit trenches, we travelled hundreds of miles in the same Quad—that's the gun-towing vehicle—and we slept alongside each other on the sand. All of us closer together the whole time than any man and wife in their own home. You remember those men. You couldn't forget them if you tried. But others? Very few, really, because you were no more intimately connected with them than you were with somebody who lived six or eight doors away down the road. Some, of course, you did get to know. The troop officers, the sergeant majors and so on, because they came round the guns a dozen times a day for years. Only now and again, when you came out of action, did you mix, even with blokes in your own troop. You talked to them—got to know them on a temporary basis, if you like. But not enough to remember them after forty years.

"But I've been describing men in the gun teams. There were two hundred chaps in a battery. Drivers, fitters, signallers, specialists, command post and OP people. Q blokes and so on. Only forty-eight were actual gun numbers. The other hundred and fifty got about among themselves and the echelons. Any one of those could get to know me by sight or just to say hello to. Some, like the batters clerks or the pay wallah, would have quite a lot of information about me and everybody else, on our papers and in the orders of battle and so on."

"Orders of battle, Bill?"

"Not battle orders, George. An order of battle was a list of every man actively engaged in a fight. Equipment, too, of course. All that information had to be known, to keep track of who came out of the sausage machine at the other end. I mean you didn't want to post somebody as missing in action when he was on a course in the Canal Zone, for instance."

"Just a method of keeping tabs on everybody?"

"Highly necessary. Some strange things happened."

"I can imagine."

"So you see, George, the chap who wrote that letter could know me better than I knew him, if you get my meaning. And then again, he says he's heard about me in press reports from time to time. Saw me in a TV show, too. Those occasions would mean he had been actively reminded of me from time to time over the years. But I haven't had the same advantage. All of which leads me to giving you an answer to your question about what to do next."

"Which is?"

"We've got to find somebody else who would know both him and me at that time and see if they can help us to identify him."

"I get the drift. Even if they can't help directly to identify him, they could suggest another likely contact. And so on. Sort of policy of attrition or of crumbling away the opposition."

Green nodded. "It could be a long haul, but I can't think of a better way."

Masters filled his pipe slowly with rubbed Warlock Flake. "Any suggestions as to whom we should approach?"

"I've been thinking it over. In bed last night, actually."

Reed knocked and entered. "It's on its way to Fleet Street, Chief. If there's any difficulty, the DC who took it will ring here."

"Thank you. We've not got far, Reed, except to decide that we must approach some of the DCI's old army colleagues to ask for help in identifying Mr. T. A. Lamief."

"Good idea, Chief. But first we've got to locate them, haven't we?"

"The DCI was about to give us his thoughts on the matter."

"I think our first effort must be to see if the battery commander is still alive. He ought to be, barring accidents, because he's not much older than me. He was a young regular officer at the outbreak, and got shoved up rather quickly when the army had to expand so much. So he could be on some War Office list of retired officers. Failing that, he's likely to belong to the RA Association and I think we could get his address from the Woolwich Depot."

"He's the most likely to be able to help us?"

"I don't really know, but he should be. In theory he should have known something of every chap under his command. But there is another possibility. His second-in-command, the battery captain, to give him his official title, was a Territorial. He was a young solicitor from somewhere near London. The Law Society might provide us with his address."

"Excellent. Now, all these associations and societies can be a bit cagey about giving the addresses of members to strangers. Particularly to police. They usually ask enquirers to write in and then the letter is forwarded. That takes too much time. So, Bill, we'll have to take a few short cuts. If you'll give me the solicitor's name, I'll get Frank March to ask the Law Society if they have any details of him. Meanwhile, I suggest that you, Bill, try to track down the battery commander in a similar way. If you fail . . . well, the solicitor might be able to help us. These old army chaps have a habit of getting together once a year for dinner, don't they? They keep in tenuous touch."

"And us, Chief?" asked Reed.

"Ah, yes. I want a profile of T. A. Lamief. You two can do it between now and lunch. We'll meet here again at two."

"Er...profile, Chief?"

"Yes. Every possible fact you can glean from his letter. For instance, he's obviously well enough off to buy binoculars and camera with tripod. He specifies the *Daily Telegraph* for the notice—another pointer that he is probably not just a pensioner on supplementary benefit."

"Got it, Chief. Can we photocopy the letter."

"Do it discreetly."

The meeting broke up.

At two o'clock, Reed handed Masters a document.

T. A. LAMIEF

1. Male, 65 or 66 years old.
2. Presumably British. (Fought in British Army etc.)
3. Sound in wind and limb. (Can negotiate countryside after dark carrying photographic equipment etc.)
4. Retains eyesight. (Could see what went on in dark a few yards away. Could wear spectacles)
5. Good hearing. (Heard all that went on some yards away. Hearing aid?)
6. Knowledge of mathematics. (Essential in astronomy. Could work out moon tables, times of rising and angles etc.)
7. Knowledge of English. (Literate letter, somewhat fussy)
8. Well-read. (Academic interests, reference to Nelson etc., no spelling mistakes, uses words like stultifying and impedimenta)
9. Retentive memory. (Remembers morse-code signals etc., name on gun, name of gunlayer after 40 years)

10. Not on bread line. (Owns expensive equipment, used good-quality notepaper)
11. Reads good-quality newspaper.
12. Keen on law and order.
13. Probably votes Conservative. (See 11 and 12 above)
14. Probably lives in South and West of London. (Hedges on banks and double hedges common in South and South-West. Referred to in TV series on hedgerow birds and plants)
15. Knowledgeable about local affairs. (Not many people would recognize the senior police officers in their area when not in uniform)

Masters read the handwritten sheet and then passed it over to Green. He then turned to Reed and Berger. "Very good. Comprehensive and informative. I like the deduction about the South and South-West. Let's hope that before long we can add a few more points to it."

Green added his congratulations. "There's only one thing I can think of that you haven't added, and that is that he writes in a good hand. Fairly big and neat. He might be a good subject for one of those graphologists."

"But that isn't on, is it? Not if we've got to keep the business secret?"

"Definitely out," said Masters. "Now, our other investigations. Any joy with the battery commander, Bill?"

Green nodded. "I had a bit of luck. He retired as a lieutenant colonel. I didn't know that, of course, but I had an idea that he might belong to one of the clubs. So I rang the In and Out and asked if Major Penn-Northey happened to be there. They were a bit icy about it and said that Colonel Penn-Northey had come in. Anyway they got him to the phone."

"And?"

"I told him who I was. I think he remembered. At any rate he said he did. When I said that one of the lads from the old days could be in a bit of trouble and had appealed for help, he immediately said I could count on him. Anyhow, the upshot was he couldn't see me today, but we've got an invitation down to his house tomorrow morning at eleven. He said he preferred that to staying in town and, in any case, he has a few papers from the old days tucked away somewhere at home. We both agreed they might be useful."

"Excellent. Where does he live?"

"About twenty miles the other side of Reading. A place called Harehill Crucis, whatever that may mean."

"Crucis? In the form of a cross. I suspect in old times two tracks crossed there, close to some hill where hares abounded. We'll probably find very little there except perhaps a church, pub, bus stop and his house." Masters looked at the pad on his desk. "The captain you mentioned—now Mr Jason Burnett, Solicitor, Commissioner for Oaths, etcetera—is senior partner in the firm of Alickson, Burnett and Gray. They operate in Wimbledon, on the main street, between the station and the theatre."

"Frank got you the address?"

"Yes. He was a bit curious, but accepted quite placidly my refusal to tell him anything. Unfortunately Mr Jason Burnett is not available today, nor tomorrow. But should I care to ring the day after that I might, just might— according to the young woman who took my call—be able to see Mr Burnett."

"You accepted that, George?"

"Normally I wouldn't. But I thought it better not to press matters with Burnett until after we'd seen whether Penn-Northey was available to us and I didn't really want Burnett to get the idea that I am involved in really serious and urgent business. Best not to rouse his curiosity—and that of his staff—too much."

Masters turned to the sergeants. "It's a week or thereabouts since the alleged murder. Somebody should have noticed the absence of the victim by now. I want you two, this afternoon, to sort out all missing males from every district for the past ten days in order to leave a margin in case T. A. Lamief wasn't as quick off the mark as we think he was. If there are details and descriptions given, try to match them up with anything in the letter. You may get some points of resemblance."

"Right, Chief. And we go off to this Harehill place to-morrow?"

"At nine o'clock, please."

The sergeants left the office.

"What about us?" asked Green.

"Bill, could you ask some boffin or other the exact date of the full moon and the time of rising? We ought to know the time of death as exactly as possible. I propose we call it a quarter of an hour after moonrise that night."

"You know, George, I hadn't thought of that. Every time we investigate a death we drive doctors spare trying to establish the time of death, and here's the information practically handed to us on a plate, and I don't even consider it. I'm going barmy."

"It's the fact that the letter you received could lift the lid off a very nasty can of worms that's doing it, Bill. Temporary insanity. You'll recover."

"Let's hope so."

Colonel Penn-Northey lived in the sort of house that would charm most people. Masters and Green stood still to admire it. Not large. Not on an estate. Standing alone behind a relatively small front garden, it was separated from its neighbours on each side by no more than a dozen yards. But it was of rose-red brick, with great mullioned windows. It was the sort of house that nestled so correctly behind what would be, in high summer, a well-kept cottage garden, that one automatically assumed it had grown there, among its trees, expecting to be a well-loved home that would always do its owners proud no matter what the company that visited them.

The door was of well-oiled oak, the knocker wrought iron—made over a hundred years earlier according to Reed, who professed to know these things—in the shape of an open book, hinged at the top, so that the spine could fall on to the back plate.

The knock was answered by Penn-Northey himself. Had

he not met the man, but had been asked to describe what he expected, Masters would have got most details right. Cavalry twill trousers and well-buffed brown shoes; rough sports coat cut hacking-jacket style; healthy, well-scrubbed cheeks; and a head bald except for short cropped sides turning from brown to grey.

"Green, my dear fellow!"

"It's been a long time, Colonel," said Green, voice gruffened by emotion.

They shook hands for what seemed to be an interminable time.

"Come in, come in. Your friends...?"

Green made the introductions. They were then ushered into a sitting room, light and cheerful, where every chair seemed quietly inviting, every surface shone, and the wall pictures suggested that the English landscape had no equal in the world and knew it.

"My wife will be bringing us coffee. I realize from what Sergeant...er Mr Green said yesterday that she can't be party to our conversation, but I should like her to meet you, gentlemen. I have a surprise for later." He turned to Green. "Do you remember Pitkin?"

"Pitkin? Bombardier Pitkin?"

"He would be a bombardier perhaps when you knew him. He was a young regular and stayed on, of course, after the war. He was a battery sergeant major in Korea. Lost a leg there, poor chap, and invalided out. Hails originally from this part of the world and wanted to get back here after his service. Anyway, he's got a cottage not far away. He's the verger at the church. Not very onerous duties, you know, so he's become our local handyman. Manages to get up and down ladders, too, even with a game leg. He often drops in to see me. His boy's done very well. Went to Sandhurst and then into the regiment. He's adjutant of a self-propelled regiment in Germany at the moment."

"We'd like to see him," said Green. "In fact, he may be able to help us."

"Excellent. Ah! Here's Mary with the coffee." The colonel sprang agilely to his feet to help his wife bring the trolley through the door.

More introductions. For the most part, Masters and the two sergeants sat silent as coffee was dispensed and taken. The colonel and Green chatted animatedly. Mrs Penn-Northey trotted out and returned with two or three heavy photograph albums. The session looked like being a prolonged one, until Green, looking up and catching Masters' eye, said reluctantly: "Colonel, I don't like breaking this up, but we're on parade, you know, sir, and my boss has a big operation on hand."

"Of course. How thoughtless of me. Mr Masters must be a very busy man. I'll just give Mary a hand out with the dirties..."

As soon as they were settled, Masters said: "Colonel, we are on a delicate mission."

"Delicate? Meaning difficult or hush-hush?"

"Both, but I was referring specifically to secrecy. I know you will respect our confidences, but I feel obliged to mention that the operation is categorised."

"Understood. I should say, however, that if you are seeking my help to nobble one of my old chaps on some serious criminal charge, I shall do what I can, but I shan't be too happy about it."

"Let me clear the air, sir. We believe the life of one of your former soldiers could be in danger. We don't know his name, nor where he lives. Our job is to identify him and—so far as we know—protect him from the danger that threatens him."

The colonel frowned. "I don't pretend to understand what you have just said, but I shall do my very best to help you."

Masters turned to Reed. "Please show the colonel the photocopy of the letter." He then addressed the ex-soldier. "Please read this carefully, sir. It will go a long way towards explaining what I have said."

Penn-Northey took his time, turning back from time to time to re-read and check on some point. When he had

34

finished, he looked up. "God bless my soul," he said. Without a word, Masters handed him that day's copy of the *Daily Telegraph*, with the entry in the personal column outlined in red ink.

"You've said you believe and trust him."

"Can you give us any reason why we shouldn't do so?"

"None. I would have done exactly the same, purely out of sentiment. The police cannot afford such feelings usually."

"I assure you sir, that our decision was arrived at coolly and logically."

"I feel sure it was."

"Any ideas about him, Colonel?" asked Green. "Do you think you know who he is or where he's hanging out?"

"Nothing definite."

"Indefinite, then."

Penn-Northey handed the letter back to Reed. "I'm sure you gentlemen have gone over what he has said very carefully."

"The profile, Reed," said Masters.

The colonel read the points the sergeant had listed.

"This sounds all very true," he said. "Perhaps I can add to this... profile, did you call it?"

Masters nodded.

The colonel leaned forward. "The ordinary gunner, and by that I mean the total rank and file, was the salt of the earth, just as was every other fighting man. But very few of them were literate enough to put a letter like that on to paper. Don't get me wrong. They could all read and write well. They wouldn't have been gunners otherwise, because gunnery demands the use of calibrated instruments, a knowledge and appreciation of angles and so forth and I am sure in my own mind that the basic schooling in the three R's was superior in those days to what our children get now. But we had to censor their letters during the war. I can honestly say I have read hundreds of thousands of letters to wives, sweethearts, children and friends. Very, very few, if any, were of the standard of the one you showed me. My guess is that very few *young* men

35

in those days could have written it, but I suspect that maturity and experience could lead *older* men to write in such a way."

"Agreed," said Masters, slightly mystified.

"So I cannot recognize that letter as even likely to have come from any man who served under me."

"You are suggesting it is a fake, sir?"

"Not a bit of it. What I am trying to say is that the only picture we can gain from that letter is one of a mature man. These days, I am myself a chap who can sit down and write a decent letter, or so my friends are kind enough to tell me. But when I was a young man, serving abroad and missing Mary like hell, my letters to her were, to use her description, perfunctory. So, though I must admit the foundations of literacy were there at the time, they were not apparent in my case. They could equally well have not been apparent in the case of the author of that letter. So we must not necessarily cudgel our brains to try to recall a budding essayist. Am I making sense?"

"Please go on, sir. You said there could be several points you could raise for discussion."

"Our chap mentioned the Mareth line. So far, if I've understood you correctly, you think he mentioned that particular battle or situation because that was when Green had a temporary change of gunlayer."

"True, sir."

"What if that time was chosen because that was virtually the only time our correspondent was with the battery? Personnel came and went, you know, for a great variety of reasons. Death, wounds, sickness, courses and so on took our men away from us."

"Obviously not death in this case, sir."

"Quite. But our fellow is numerate and literate. He was probably the sort of chap who would apply for a commission. He could have been hauled off, right back to Cairo, for a selection board and then up into Palestine to the Gunner OCTU for training. And that could have happened, say, within a month of him being posted to us. So we must try to think of people who were with us for very short terms, centered on the time of Mareth."

"Which was when, sir?"

"Ah! Now Rommel made his last attack on the Eighth Army on March the sixth, 'forty-three. But we weren't up there then. Pity that. We were out of the line, re-equipping." He turned to Green. "Did you know the first Tiger tank ever knocked out was knocked out that morning by the Guards, using a two-pounder?"

"No?" said Green. "A two-pounder? Impossible."

"So one might think. Even a six-pounder would have been surprising. And you mustn't forget the first seventeen-pounders were coming into use then."

"They'd have knocked out practically anything."

"Oh, they would. Do you know, Green, the first seventeen-pounder I ever saw—just before Mareth—had been made in Birmingham by Avery—you know, the people who make scales and weighing machines."

Masters coughed loudly.

Penn-Northey apologized. "I'm terribly sorry, Mr Masters. I do tend to run on."

"You were about to give us the date when your battery went into the Mareth line, sir."

"Ah, yes. Well, as I think I said, Rommel had his last fling on March the sixth. Saturday, I believe that was." He turned to Green. "We were actually on the way up there then, weren't we?"

"We were, Colonel. If you remember there was a large area of marsh between Tripoli and Mareth, and the coast road was simply a causeway that led over it. We were stopped to the east of the causeway and had to put the guns into action to cover the road at that point—just in case of a breakthrough by Jerry."

"By jove, yes. I remember that. And I saw my first flamingos there, on the marsh. Several dozen of them. I went forward in my jeep, you know, and thought I'd recce the area between the road and the sea, and there they were, large as life. I'd never seen one, even in a zoo, and..."

"Colonel!" prompted Masters.

"Sorry. I think we actually surveyed the positions on the following Tuesday, and took the guns in on the Wednesday. After that, Mr Masters, I think we were there for at least three weeks, probably a month before we got through their line."

"No more than three weeks," said Green.

"Right," said Masters briskly. "A lad who was with you during those weeks of March, at least, with, I think some time before that, too, otherwise he would not have known of your regular gunlayer, the fact that he had been wounded, and that you had a replacement."

"Good thinking," said Penn-Northey. "Now, I was going to say something else which really is part of what I was saying before about chaps who were above-average literate and numerate. In the gunners we had a lot of good people, but usually those with the highest educational standards became Specialists. That was the proper name for them as a group. Specialists. They were immediate assistants to officers, and so were known as Acks. Thus the GPO—gun position officer—had a GPO Ack. The Ack's job was clerical. For instance, officers used theodolites, called Directors, for pointing the guns in the right direction. As the officer manipulated the thing, he had to read off angles. His Ack would take them down and then check the maths involving them."

"I think I've got that quite plain, Colonel."

"Observing officers also had Acks. Now these had somewhat different functions from those of GPO Acks and command post Acks. All the Specialists at the gun end were required to do maths in survey work, the working out of barrages and so forth. At the sharp end there were very few mathematical jobs, but there were observing skills, knowledge of different types of shoots and so on. The OP Ack was there to take over and continue the shooting should the observing officer become a casualty, because one could never leave infantry without gun support."

"So they were bright lads?"

"Just so. Being bright lads, they could do a bit of every-

38

body's job in the OP. And the OP party had a signaller with a wireless set..."

"Ah," breathed Masters. "A signaller who might use either voice or morse code?"

"I think you've got the point I am trying to make, Mr Masters. Bright lads can learn the morse code as well as how to work a set. One of the commonest laid-down phrases in voice procedures is, 'I say again', which is, when using key, 'Ink Monkey Ink', a phrase or form which none but a signaller or officer would normally know."

"So, sir," asked Reed, "why couldn't our man be a signaller? They must have been fairly bright lads, too."

"They were indeed. But obvious literacy and numeracy suggest a Specialist. OP Specialists could normally work wireless sets. And then, our man knew TALAMIEF, which a member of an OP party had to know when passing orders down to the guns. He also made a point of mentioning an observation post. Could that have been an intentional hint? He had obviously been in OP's, because he could liken the experience he expected when he went out to take pictures that night to being in an OP, and a quite accurate picture it was, too."

Green got up to offer cigarettes around. "Colonel," he said, "you're making a good job of adding to our man's profile."

Penn-Northey smiled. "Nice of you to say so, Green. I thought myself that I wasn't doing too badly."

"I'm going to become a bit fanciful myself, in support of one of your points. You said he spelt out in full the two words 'observation post'. Now no gunner ever referred to an observation post. It was always, always, always an OP—at least in our regiment. Wouldn't you agree, Colonel?"

"Most emphatically. Some lesser regiments did, I believe, try to introduce all that FOO nonsense. Forward Observation Officer. Load of rubbish, that was. Where did they expect the observer to be? Behind the guns? One spoke about the OP, the OP officer, the OP Ack, and OP signaller, not FOP, FOO, FOOACK, FOOSIG and such ungainly titles. No, Green, you're right. Everybody called it the OP."

"In that case, Colonel, why should a man who was accustomed to referring to the OP spell out the two words in full if he did not intend it as some sort of hint to us?"

"By jove, Green, I think you may have something there."

"But, sir..." began Reed.

"Objections?" asked the colonel.

"Yes. If he wanted to give you so broad a hint as to his identity, why not go the whole hog and sign the letter?"

"Because," said Masters, quietly, "had our correspondent done as you suggest, Sergeant, anybody who opened the letter would immediately know his identity. I think it fair to assume that only people well acquainted with wartime gunnery in the desert, like the colonel and the DCI, could possibly have picked up that hint. And read between the lines, too, as you have heard them do." He turned to Penn-Northey and Green. "Does anything else strike you, gentlemen?"

"Yes," replied Green. "Maybe not as strong a pointer as the last one. But the OP Ack had one duty the colonel hasn't mentioned so far. That was the drawing of panoramas."

"Like... like artists, you mean?"

"In a stylized way," replied the colonel. "Yes. Just like an artist. Panoramas of the zone to be observed and covered. All things like churches, woods, isolated houses and so on would be placed very accurately by taking compass bearings. But it would take too long to explain fully their use..."

"The point is," said Green, cutting in, "you've heard what the qualifications for a Specialist were. But the colonel did not mention the need to be able to draw in a lad who was to become an OP Ack. Don't get me wrong. He didn't have to be a Royal Academician to get the job, but if he couldn't draw a recognizable panorama he was not for the OP. Right, Colonel?"

"Absolutely right."

"So," continued Green, "I reckon we must credit our man with a modicum of artistic ability—just about the amount which may cause a man to take up, late in life, the sort of photography that includes shots of the moon shining on water. What do you think, George?"

"I think it could strengthen the case for believing that our man was an OP Ack or ..."

"Or?"

"Or an observing officer himself." He turned to the colonel. "Everything you have said, sir, could apply equally well to an officer as to a non-commissioned rank. Am I right?"

"Perfectly."

"Officers had to draw panoramas and learn morse and so on, did they not?"

"Yes. Yes, of course they did. *I* made sure of that."

Green said: "Do you know, George, I never thought of the possibility of it being one of the officers."

"Understandable, Bill. You've been cudgelling your brains trying to think of which of your old mates could have approached you. The letter looked that way. Was probably meant to look that way. So why should you, before we were made free of the colonel's thoughts on the matter, have even considered anybody other than one of lads with whom you served—as opposed to one of the battery officers, I mean?"

Green shrugged. "All possibilities should have occurred to me. I've had four or five days to think about it."

"Tricky business, Green," said the colonel, shaking his head to lend gravity to the thought. "And the possibility of it being an officer widens the field vastly."

"Would you explain, Colonel?" asked Masters.

"Certainly. There were three OP Acks in the battery. Battery commander and two troop commanders had one apiece. But all officers took a turn from time to time in the OP. What I mean is, one kept an officer, awake, all the time an OP was manned. The OP Ack, however, could, if events allowed, be given the chance to get a few hours' sleep. But observation was the job of an officer and that

41

was constant. Lying out there for hours on end was very tiring in the desert sun, and even more tiring to the eyes, using powerful binoculars in hot sunlight, for long stretches at a time. So, where we had to consider only three OP Acks in a battery, we now have to add nine officers to the list."

"I see. Still..."

Masters was interrupted by a tap on the door and Mrs Penn-Northey entered. "Lewis is here, darling. Shall I bring him in?"

The colonel looked across at Masters. "Sergeant Major Pitkin, whom I mentioned to you earlier, has arrived. Would you like to see him now, straightaway? Or is there something more to discuss before he joins us?"

"There's no need to keep him waiting, Colonel, particularly as he is doing us a kindness in coming."

"Lewis won't mind," said Mrs Penn-Northey. "He can sit and chat to me in the kitchen, if you like."

"We'll have him in, my dear, please. And the drinks tray, if you don't mind."

Green and Pitkin, as was to be expected, greeted each other with the sort of gruff emotion that hard-bitten old softies usually produce on such occasions. At Penn-Northey's request, Berger served the drinks and then stood by Reed and Masters, silent listeners to the three old comrades-in-arms.

"How long's this going on for, Chief?" asked Reed in a whisper.

"For ever, probably. But I honestly don't know whether it is wise to interrupt. They've got their minds into gear for remembering forty years ago. The more they talk the more they'll remember. If I interrupt I could bring them back to the present day just before one of their memories dredges up something useful to us."

"Understood, Chief, but are you very hopeful?"

"What of?"

"That they'll identify the writer of that letter?"

"No. Not precisely. But between them they've added several points to your profile. The more points we get, the nearer we are to identifying him."

"That sounds reasonable. But after getting a name, we've got to locate the chap. That could be harder."

"It could. How would you go about it, Reed?"

"Ask every force to look at voters' lists and telephone books in their areas, I suppose. Unless he turns out to be a Smith or a Williams or some very common name. I mean, if his monniker is RU Smelly, to discover him and check up very quietly to see if he's over sixty-five should be very easy, and it wouldn't be giving anything away to put his life in danger—if we didn't say why we wanted to trace him."

Masters nodded. "We could apply to people other than local forces, of course. He'll be a pensioner, so the Newcastle office ought to know of him. Tax office, perhaps. Car computer people in Swansea. And so on."

"Why not try them all, Chief?" asked Berger.

"Why not? If we get a name it would be a nice little job for you and Reed."

"If we get a name—and initials."

Masters shrugged. He was watching the trio of old soldiers. They were showing signs of coming back to present day.

"George," said Green. "Sar'Major Pitkin has remembered something that may help a bit."

"You've told Mr Pitkin something of our problem?"

"Briefly."

"In that case, Mr Pitkin, could I hear what you have to say?"

"It's like this, Mr Masters. As I understand it, you've been considering somebody who was with us just a fairly short time round about Mareth. That's all right as far as it goes, but I reckon the short-stay merchant we should concentrate on is Stinky Miller. I remember him pretty well because we were both regulars and both gunlayers and we chatted a bit. He came over from another battery for a few weeks, as you've heard. But I know he had a pal in our battery. Natural, when you come to think of it. I mean he would have left his own pals in his own

43

battery and he'd want somebody to talk to in ours."

"Please go on, Mr Pitkin. You're opening up new avenues."

"I reckon so, because I remember Miller showing me a drawing that his pal had done. Just a pencil sketch, you know, of Stukas, dive bombing. I've always remembered it, because we got a bit of a pasting from Stukas on the Wadi Zem Zem. They came in as regular as clockwork, sixteen or so at a time. That was when the drawing was done, and it said underneath it, 'Wi' a hundred Stukas an hour, an hour.' We didn't get much to laugh at, and I've always remembered it."

"So what are you saying, Mr Pitkin?"

"That the man who did the drawing, as a close friend of Stinky Miller's, would know Miller had come across to us for a week or two at Mareth."

"I take that point. Did you ever meet the artist?"

"I don't know who he was, so I can't say. But Miller would know who he was, and we can get hold of Miller. The War House will still have his details, seeing he was a regular and consequently will be an army pensioner now."

"If he's alive."

Pitkin grinned. "Old soldiers never die. I've run across him since the war and he was still alive and kicking."

"Let me get it straight, Mr Pitkin. You are putting forward a suggestion that the man who joined Mr Green's gun in the Mareth Line was mentioned in the letter because the writer was a personal friend of his. That we should forget, therefore, that the writer might have stayed only a short time with the regiment but should continue to believe in his artistic prowess."

"That's about it."

"Do you subscribe to the view that this man would be a Specialist in your own battery? That he was, in fact, an OP Ack?"

"He had to be, sir, in my opinion. Why I say that is this. We hadn't got all that much Specialist talent to spare. There were a lot of gaps for bright boys, and the Gunners had to compete with everybody from the Intelligence Corps to Signals, Engineers and OCTUs for their services. When we were lucky enough to get one, the regiment made use of him. And I don't mean as a sanitary orderly or ammunition number. My bet is, sir, that Stinky's pal was an OP Ack."

"We can soon put your theory to the test if, as you say, he is still alive and drawing an army pension. What were his initials, please?"

"Initials?" Pitkin glanced at Green. "Blowed if I know. I always just knew him as Stinky."

Green shook his head. "I didn't know his Christian name, either, George. Sorry."

"I wonder how many Millers there were in the wartime army?" said Reed.

"Not too many, S'arnt," said Pitkin, military-style. "In the Gunners—no other mob. Sixty-fivish. There won't be many sixty-five-year-olds called Miller on the RA list. He wouldn't be seventy or anything like, so you've a precisely registered bracket for going to fire for effect."

Green translated. "Mr Pitkin means you're to ask about men called Miller and aged between sixty-three and sixty-seven, and confined to the RA list. Don't step outside your brief." He turned to Pitkin. "We're missing something. He must have got a bit of rank by the time he retired. He was a lance-jack in 'forty-three."

"You're right," agreed Pitkin. "Do you know, I seem to think he was a BQMS ... yes, he was. I remember asking him the old joke about Q blokes. You know, the one about whether he'd fiddled enough from the stores to buy his first row of houses."

"The bracket is narrowing," said Green to Masters. "He was at least a senior NCO, probably a Warrant Officer by the time he got his ticket."

"Leave it to me," said Penn-Northey. "The enquiries about him, I mean. Like all regular officers who reach my rank I had to do a tour on the Staff. I did mine at the War House, in AG Six. That's the section that dealt with officers' appointments. I still have a few contacts there.

45

The chap who was my senior clerk is still there. He can get what we want from other departments."

"Old-boy basis?" asked Masters, smiling.

"Why not? Don't tell me that such a network doesn't exist between you and Green and your other colleagues and that you don't make use of it."

"I confess to making use of every source of information I can."

"Give me ten minutes. Help yourself to another drink, and we'll have a bite to eat when I rejoin you."

In the event, nearly half an hour passed before the colonel came back. After apologizing for his long absence, he said: "I'm afraid we're out of luck, Mr Masters. Miller is dead."

"Dead?" asked Green quietly. "Dead? You said that, Colonel, as though he didn't die in his bed."

"He didn't. Or at least I gathered he didn't. Records, of course, know none of the details, except that his pension is stopped, but the last entry as far as I can find out is just a note that he was found dead."

"When?" asked Masters.

"I didn't get the date, but it must have been fairly recently for his papers to be still extant. Lots of stuff is micro-filmed these days, but I can't believe that the army authorities hang on to such information for long. They destroy unwanted stuff at quite regular intervals."

"We can get information on Miller if there was anything out of the ordinary about his death," said Masters. "It will be somewhere on police files, but that won't help us with our present problem as we should need information from him in order to proceed along our present course of enquiry."

"All may not be lost," said Penn-Northey. "He was a married man. His widow will still be in receipt of a pension. Oh, and by the way, his names were Eric Alfred. I have asked my colleagues to find her address for us. They hope to ring me back after lunch. Talking of which, come along through to the dining room. Mary has prepared sandwiches for us. Bring your glasses with you."

Sandwiches, slices of cold chicken, whole small tomatoes, several sorts of cheeses...it was a delightful repast. As Green said to Berger, he wouldn't mind if he got the same every day. As he spoke he sprinkled a tomato with salt and popped it whole, into his mouth. It was at this moment that Penn-Northey asked him: "Remember the bridge at Scafati, Green?"

Berger said to the colonel: "An inconvenient moment to ask questions, sir. The DCI is otherwise engaged."

"What? Oh, yes. See what you mean." The colonel turned to speak to another of his guests.

"What happened at the bridge of Scafati?" asked Berger when Green's mouth was empty.

"Good job I couldn't answer," said Green.

"Something nasty?"

"Yes, I nearly killed him."

"And you're still mates?"

"Things happen in war, lad. It was only a little humped-back village bridge and he'd outrun the people who were with him. He'd got on to the bridge and the enemy was just on the other side, preparing a counter-attack to retake it. He wanted to break up the attack, so he asked for a ranging shot. He gave the map reference of the bridge as the target, knowing we wouldn't hit it first shot. He could then correct the range on to the Germans. Trouble was it was the exception that proved the rule. It was my gun that fired the ranging shot and we hit the bloody bridge. As I said, it was a small bridge."

"He escaped though, obviously."

"God knows how, and it's an incident I prefer to forget."

"I can see why."

The phone bell rang in the hall. Penn-Northey went to answer it. He returned after a brief conversation. "Mrs Miller lives in a village called Caldenham."

"That's on the coast," said Pitkin. "Due south of here, in fact. About thirty miles away."

47

— 3 —

"You're not saying much, George," said Green as the Yard Rover sped back towards London in the early afternoon.

"Sorry, Bill. I was thinking things over."

"And?"

"Specifically? I was wondering whether we would be wise to follow the lead Pitkin gave us to the exclusion of everything else."

"We don't have to. We can try everything."

"True. But I am not all that satisfied in my own mind that your correspondent was clever enough—as has been suggested—to plant hidden clues in his letter in the expectation that we would be able to spot them and then interpret them correctly."

"He wasn't," said Green emphatically.

"You sound very sure about it."

"How many people are that clever? Before that letter arrived I'd have said that none of the swaddies I served with had that sort of mind. Don't get me wrong. They were a cross-section of blokes. They included cunning, devious, mean, idle and criminal elements among, for the most part, decent everyday chaps. But none stood out as ...how shall I put it? A sort of academic puzzle writer? My opinion is that when somebody sends a letter like that, he puts so much of himself in it that when people like us shove it under the microscope, we learn a lot. But he's not given anything away on purpose. He's done it unwittingly."

"I'll accept that, Bill. Indeed, I've got to accept most of the things you, the colonel and Mr Pitkin have said, because you three know the background. You're the experts in a field I know nothing about. But having said that, as the onlooker, I think I must try to act as a filter."

"Panning for gold," said Berger from the front passenger seat. "Wash away all the dross and try to rescue a few bright grains in the bottom of the dish."

"Dross, did you say?" demanded Green.

"I did. The worthless muck."

To everyone's surprise, Green said mildly: "I suppose it did seem like that to you people. Actually, I enjoyed myself."

"We noticed. Your jaws were going the whole time, either talking or eating."

"Drinking, too," said Reed. "He coughed back quite a lot of the colonel's ale."

"My ears were flapping, too," replied Green. "I got quite a lot of useful stuff there."

"Such as?"

"You mean you didn't hear anything useful?"

"Bits and pieces."

"And you, George?" asked Green.

"It was a useful visit. And by that I mean that your friends have helped. Quite how much will only become apparent if and when we find Mr T. A. Lamief."

"Thanks. I'm glad somebody appreciates what we've managed to do." Green slumped back in his corner seat. "And now, after all the food and drink I've had and the talking I've done, I think I'll have a little kip. Somebody wake me when we get home."

"When do you think we shall hear from T. A. Lamief again, Chief?" asked Berger.

"As a result of the personal column message?"

"Yes."

"If I were he, another letter would be in the post by now. He will have read the message in this morning's newspaper and the reply should take him no time at all to concoct. In fact, if he is an anxious man, and I would suggest any man who is in jeopardy, no matter how slight the danger, would be an anxious man, the reply would

49

already be prepared—in his mind if not actually on paper."

"You reckon he's written it by now and travelled up to the Smoke to post it?"

"That would be my guess."

"And what's he going to say, Chief?"

"I haven't got my crystall ball with me."

"So you don't reckon we'll get his name and address?"

"I can't really answer that, but this chap is a gamester..."

"You think he's pulling our legs?"

"No. I was referring to his character. He's cagey and he's scared and he's indirect. I think he will be somewhat reassured by this morning's message, but the odd doubt could remain. It would not surprise me in the slightest were Mr Green to receive another cryptic clue tomorrow. One much nearer an identification but not an out-and-out direct message saying 'my name is Joe Bloggs and I live in Southport'. In fact, I doubt very much whether we shall ever get that."

"Why not?"

"Our man is too frightened or too indirect to give us such information. If he hadn't been, he would have either called at the Yard or phoned and asked for the DCI."

"I hadn't thought of that. I suppose his state of mind is something for a psychologist to explain."

"I believe so. But we shall know tomorrow, I hope."

"If we don't," said Green still with his eyes closed, "the next day's paper will have to be printed on asbestos. The message it carries will be...er...fiery."

"They won't accept anything too hot," retorted Reed.

"Icily cold, then."

"That could be different."

"I'll work on it."

"Sleep on it, you mean."

Green still kept his eyes closed. Then he murmured: "Tell All, Lad, About Message or Investigation Ends Friday."

"Very good," said Masters. "I think the tenor of your

message, if not the actual words, would be the best line to take if you were to supplant Friday with Forthwith."

Green sat up. "Are you serious, George?"

"Entirely, if the need arises. It leaves him in no doubt as to our feelings on the matter, and you've said it in a way that will suit his particular mind. In fact, at the end of the letter he asked for your reply to be such as he would understand. Probably that was a plea for a hidden message."

Green grunted and closed his eyes again. The car neared London. Very little more was said before it reached the Yard.

There was a message on Masters' desk. A Mr Jason Burnett, solicitor, had phoned as he understood the DCS had been trying to contact him. Would Masters please ring back at the number given.

"Jason Burnett."

"Mr Burnett, Detective Chief Superintendent Masters here."

"Ah, yes. My girl told me you wanted to see me. I'm curious. I can think of no reason why the big guns of the Yard should..."

"It is a matter which probably concerns neither you nor your clients directly, Mr Burnett. Something rather strange has come up concerning a soldier in the battery in which you were a wartime officer. I would like to ask a few questions of some of the people who served with him."

"I see, or at least I think I do. What's the chap's name?"

"That is one of the things that are strange, Mr Burnett. We don't know his name. I wondered if we could have a chat in the hope that something we do know about him may help you to suggest what his name might be."

"It's a hell of a long time ago..."

"That is the great difficulty," conceded Masters. "One of my colleagues, DCI Green, who was a sergeant in your battery—C sub Number One at the time—is concerned in this business, and we have already spoken to Colonel Penn-Northey and a Bombardier Pitkin. They have helped us to narrow the field a little. I am hoping you will do the same."

"Why not?"

"I am grateful, Mr Burnett."

"Is this chap dead? In trouble?"

"He is not dead, but we believe him to be in some danger."

"So the sooner the better?"

"If you please."

"Look, Chief Super, I would say come out here now, but I think tomorrow morning would be better. I'll tell you why. You know how we chaps like hoarding documents? Well, I kept quite a number from the old days. Scraps of paper, photographs and the like. The last time I saw them was about fifteen years ago, stashed away in my old uniform trunk in the loft. If they're still there I could unearth them this evening. You never know. Something among them could be useful."

"Excellent. What time tomorrow morning?"

"Make it ten o'clock, would you? So's I can get rid of my mail before you come."

Masters arrived early at the Yard the next morning. Even so, Green was there before him, waiting for the post. The sorting-room staff had been told what to look for. The letter, should it arrive, was not to go on one of the routine delivery trolleys. A special messenger was standing by to carry it up to Green without delay.

"Came by the eight o'clock delivery," said Green as he entered Masters' office, bearing the white envelope.

"What does it say, Bill?"

"I haven't opened it yet."

"I must say I admire your restraint. What are you waiting for?"

"The sergeants. I told them to come along."

"Fair enough. Have a pew."

As Masters offered his subordinate the seat, there was a knock on the door and Reed and Berger entered.

"It's come then, Chief?"

"The DCI is about to open it up." As Masters passed over the letter knife he asked: "Same postmark, Bill?"

"Yes. West One." He slit the top of the envelope neatly. With a pair of tweezers taken from his breast pocket, he removed from it a single sheet of paper, folded in half lengthwise.

"It's a drawing," said Berger.

Green said nothing. He laid the paper on the desk and opened it out, using the tweezers and a ruler that was lying on the writing pad to help him do so.

Green stared silently at the scene depicted. A hump-backed bridge, a shell-burst cartoon fashion—and a tank. The caption read: 'A hit, a very palpable hit.'

Masters gazed at it, too. "Does this mean anything to you, Bill?"

Green nodded but said nothing. It was left to Berger to say: "That's the bridge at Scafati, isn't it?"

Masters and Reed, who had not heard the conversation at lunch about the incident on the bridge, both turned to Berger.

"Scafati?" questioned Masters. "You mean you know something about this picture?"

"It was something the DCI said, Chief. Earlier. One of his experiences in Italy."

"Bill?"

Green again told the story. All listened in silence. When he came to the end, Masters said: "I know the answer before I ask the question, but do you think the artist who drew this is the same person as drew the picture Pitkin mentioned?"

Green nodded. "I don't think I ever saw that one, but the captions...well, they seem to be by the same character, wouldn't you say?"

"They certainly seem so to me. 'Wi' a hundred Stukas an hour, an hour' is a play on the title of a Scottish song so well known that it is the sort of thing that could spring into anybody's mind. But the Shakespeare quotation— 'A hit, a very palpable hit'—is not only apposite, but correct. And that argues a degree of knowledge not normally found in the average young man in the army in a world war when far away from any reference books or libraries. So it would seem that Sergeant Major Pitkin was right, and that our man was the friend of your temporary gunlayer, Stinky Miller. Agreed?"

"Agreed," said Green. "And it tells us that he was with the regiment for longer than was suggested at one time— by the colonel—because Scafati is in Italy, and that little episode took place at the end of the following September, if not early October."

"Good. Now, why do we think he has sent us this drawing?"

"Act of faith," said Green. "To prove himself."

Reed said: "Have you realized that he was close enough to you to know you were implicated in that incident?"

"Not necessarily," said Berger. "There were two ends to that show. The DCI's gun end, and the colonel's bridge end. He could only have been at the bridge end if he saw what happened." He turned to Green. "Right?"

"There would be six or eight thousand yards between the two," replied Green.

Berger pressed on. "And how soon would the people on the bridge know which gun fired the shot that nearly killed them?"

"Probably never."

Masters said, "How's that, Bill?"

"Because people from the OP wouldn't have time to ask who fired the shot. They'd be too busy correcting it on to the enemy and then chasing him away so that our tanks and infantry could get across the bridge. Then we were on the move, and it could have been days before they got back to visit the guns again. By that time everybody would have forgotten the incident."

"But you didn't, Bill."

"No," said Green quietly.

"For any particular reason?"

"Any man would remember being pleased at not having killed some of his mates."

"I understand that bit. Please tell me how and when

54

you got to know where the shell landed if, as you said just now, the thing would be forgotten in the melee of war?"

"Immediately," said Green. "Penn-Northey on the blower to our gun position officer. 'Christ, do you know what you've done? You've hit the bridge.'"

"Hitting a target like that was a cause for such comment?"

"It was bow-and-arrow gunnery, George. What we called a quick action. We were travelling along the road when the call came. Off the road we went, into the first field. The spout of my gun pointed in the general direction and laid on by compass. The angle measured off the map by protractor. The range measured by ruler from a quick map spot of the gun to the site of the bridge. We shouldn't have hit it, George. Not even if we'd used accurate instruments. Not first shot. We couldn't have hit it in a thousand years even if we'd really tried. And we hadn't tried. We'd just wanted to put a round in the area so that Penn-Northey could see it and correct it."

"A million to one chance then?"

"I'd have said the odds were at least that, George. And that's why I remember it. A wildly improbable event and yet it happened with near-dire consequences."

"You are not, I hope, blaming yourself, Bill?"

Green shrugged. "Nobody could be blamed with odds that long."

"So why?"

Green looked up. "We were chasing the Germans, George. They were withdrawing away from the Salerno bridgehead. The ones at Scafati were the remnants of their rearguard."

"Go on."

"We passed through the village half an hour later. The shooting had moved on. The villagers had started to come out of their houses."

"And?"

"Some of them had come to look for a toddler."

They waited in silence for Green to continue.

"They had just found the child," he said at last. "Dead. Killed on Scafati bridge by a shell splinter. The mother was there..."

Masters got up and moved across to him. "Bill, it was not your fault. A small child toddling loose between the British Army and the German Army in the middle of a battle...Christ, man! The mother...she must have let him go, taken her eyes off him."

Green looked up. "There are some bloody awful moments in war, George."

Masters nodded.

After a moment or two, Green had recovered enough to say: "This isn't getting us anywhere."

"It is," said Berger. "Who among your crowd didn't like you?"

Green looked surprised. "Are you trying to say that drawing was sent out of malice? To remind me...?"

"A possibility."

"No," said Green, shaking his head. "I had to roast one or two of the lads from time to time as any NCO has to. But they didn't take lasting offence."

"We'll accept that," said Masters diplomatically. "Now the big question is, did Mr T. A. Lamief draw that picture himself, or was he given it by the artist, just as Stinky Miller was given the Stuka drawing?"

"Chief," insisted Berger, "whoever sent that drawing to the DCI knew it would be of significance to him. But to how many others would it mean anything? Damn it all, even the colonel was not told it was the DCI's gun that fired that round."

"I appreciate that, Sergeant. And the point that if Penn-Northey didn't know, none of his OP crew would know."

"So that means it was somebody from the gun end of the battery who would know it was the DCI who fired the fatal shot and would, therefore, know that this drawing would be significant to him. If not, why send it? It could be a drawing of anywhere at any time to anybody else. But the DCI knows different and the caption proves him right. Unless that had been a hit in a million, the

56

joker who drew it wouldn't have used that particular quote from Shakespeare."

"Hamlet," mused Masters. "Any mileage in that, Bill?"

Green shrugged silently.

Masters got to his feet. "We'll continue this in the car. It's time we were on our way to Wimbledon."

Jason Burnett greeted Green with as much emotion as had Penn-Northey and Pitkin. It was a fair indication to Masters that his colleague had been either a very able soldier or a very popular man. He inclined towards the former viewpoint. Green would always earn respect for his professionalism, but he would never be highly popular except among those who had served very closely with him for a very long time. From his own experience Masters knew this to be true. The idea had always pleased him. It had meant that Green was more reliable: was never likely to say the thing one wanted to hear in the interests of his own popularity.

Jason Burnett, despite all his secretary had said about his time being fully taken up with business, had obviously cleared the decks ready for the Yard men's visit. He listened carefully as Masters outlined the problem for him.

Burnett was a tall man. Though well into his sixties there was no stoop to his shoulders, no spectacles, no baldness. He was lean, and his face was heavily lined from the corners of a big nose down to a determined chin. An attractive ugliness was how Masters supposed a woman would describe the solicitor's looks. He, too, looked reliable, and he had the gift of listening. He had his hands together above the desk. The only movement he made was to finger the ring on his left hand.

Masters stopped before mentioning the drawing that had been received that morning. Burnett promptly asked if there had been a reply from the unknown correspondent.

"An artistic effort only."

"Am I to be allowed to see the exhibits?"

The letter and drawing were handed over to him. Unhurriedly he read the one and examined the other.

"The drawing means nothing to me," he said. "Does it convey anything to you, Mr Green?"

Green explained briefly.

"And Peter Penn-Northey suggested it was an OP Ack who drew this?"

"Yes."

"A reasonable deduction, I would have said, but for one thing."

They waited in silence for him to marshall his thoughts. Then—

"I would never have recognized that drawing as depicting the bridge at Scafati. Now you have mentioned it, I recall something of the story. I imagine Penn-Northey mentioned it to me later, but I doubt very much whether many people were so concerned about it as Mr Green. The time, you see, was not one for indelible memories of anything but one's own personal experiences to impress themselves on the mind."

"I haven't grasped that point, Mr Burnett," said Masters.

"I was being obscure, perhaps. Let me explain the position that day and you will understand my remark. The Allied Fifth Army had landed at Salerno and the fight to establish the bridgehead had been a fierce one. It had taken us, I suppose, a fortnight to enlarge the area to a size big enough to mount the break-out attack. We were to go northwards, past Vesuvius, towards the River Volturno. This attack was due to go in at six o'clock that morning.

"I say was to have gone in, because it never happened. By half-past five that morning our forward infantry had established that the Germans had withdrawn during the night. Had the attack gone in, it would have hit empty air. This is probably what the Germans wanted to happen. They would have liked us to waste all our shells on firing a useless barrage and—even more important—in wasting time in actually going through the motions of an infantry attack. It would have taken hours of time precious to a fleeing enemy anxious to get his troops back to their selected positions.

"Obviously they had guessed our intention to attack. Not a very hard thing to do when all our preparations had to be done in so circumscribed an area, when we had had so little space and time for camouflage and the like to disguise what we were about.

"That, however, is by the way. The point is, Mr Masters, that when an army is literally at the point of attack, it is off balance temporarily for any other sort of operation. When it was firmly established that the enemy had disengaged, we had immediately to leap from a set-piece attack to a mobile chase."

Masters nodded his understanding.

"We had orders to concoct a mobile column to move out immediately. The vanguard had to go at a minute's notice—literally. It comprised a squadron of Shermans, with whom Penn-Northey travelled because he was there, while his two formal OP officers, the troop commanders, were deployed elsewhere, away from the road. Next went a company of motorized infantry who had been waiting, ready in their vehicles, to exploit the breakthrough hoped for from the attack. And finally there went one troop of four guns—the troop in which Mr Green was a sergeant. That was the vanguard of the chasing column and it had orders to go at speed to regain contact with the enemy. The main body of the column was to get on to the road and follow along as soon as orders could be issued and it could be assembled in the right order. This last was vital, as you will recognize later.

"Now for my point—the one you didn't grasp. To fire the barrage, four hundred rounds of ammunition per gun had been dumped beside the pieces. The battery command post had been set up with phones, artillery boards and all the impedimenta. Such things cannot be left behind. As battery captain, it was my job to see they weren't. Furthermore, I had to get them forward as fast as possible for when the fighting began again in earnest. I don't suppose you can imagine what a business it is to pick up and load three thousand two hundred twenty-five pounder shells and a like number of cartridges from the middle of fields. To say nothing of all the rest. My point is that everybody was working flat out at the double. Nobody had time to notice anything that didn't happen to him personally. Green's shot at the bridge was important to him and his crew, to Penn-Northey and his crew, to the gun position officer and his crew, perhaps. But not to anybody else. There was no time for it to become so. After that round landed on the bridge, Penn-Northey corrected the range to plaster the enemy rearguard. That rearguard fell back. The battle moved on. We had one narrow Italian road along which to move everything. The fighting troops, ammunition, food and all the rest going up. Ambulances coming back. Signallers laying telephone lines in the hedgerows. It was hell let loose, with vehicles nose to tail like a present-day traffic tail-back at West Country resorts in the summer. A prime target for enemy aircraft, too. But it was organized chaos. We were seasoned troops and we knew our business. That is my point. We were very, very busy."

"I understand now," said Masters. "Perhaps you would continue at the point where I asked for an explanation."

"Of course. I said that Peter Penn-Northey's suggestion that our artist friend was an OP Ack was a reasonable one except for the point I have just made. It is this, in essence. The only OP Ack who would have known about that round hitting Scafati bridge would have been his own. For the reasons I've given you, I don't think any others would know a thing about it. With me so far?"

"Yes."

"Now, Mr Green. Can you remember who the BC's OP Ack was in the desert and Italy?"

Green thought for a moment or two, and then looked up. "He was a good-looking young chap who gave the impression of being about fifteen years old. The lads called him by a girl's name. Now what was it?"

"Maisie," supplied Burnett. "Maisie Mason. In fact he was our age but no one would have guessed it, and he was a mean man. One hears of baby-looking gangsters in the States, and Greene wrote about that young villain in *Brighton Rock*, but Mason, he was a hard case."

"Are you sure? I mean, I never heard of Maisie getting tough. The lads used to twit him about his name and his looks and he seemed to accept it without getting nasty."

"I'll tell you something I've never told anyone else, Mr Green. As you know, I used to relieve Penn-Northey at the sharp end from time to time. After all, I was his second-in-command, and the right person to relieve him should it be necessary. But I had no OP party of my own, so on those occasions when I deputised for him, I had to borrow his crew. One such occasion occurred shortly after we passed through Scafati. About two days later, I seem to remember. Penn-Northey had been hit. Not seriously, and not by shrapnel. An enemy shell had landed a few yards away from his tank as he was going through a village. It had hit the paving stones and a sliver of concrete had been thrown up. It got him on the back of the right hand. It had gashed him, but he had put a field dressing on it and carried on. What he hadn't done was cleanse it, and the concrete had been mucky. So before he knew where he was he'd got a blood-poisoned arm and he had to come back to let the MO attend to it. That's why I was up front at the time.

"We got to another small village where the Germans had left a small rearguard to hold us up. It had a small square with a big church on one side. You remember the type of building, I expect. The main doors opened directly on to the street. Anyhow, we had a bit of a battle there. Nothing terribly serious and the resistance broke very quickly. The armour had actually gone ahead, and we were left, more or less hidden, down a little side street off the square. It was then that a German infanteer broke cover and ran for the church. He'd actually reached the door and, I believe, expected to find it unlocked. But somebody had bolted it from the inside. The chap had hold of the latch and was battering on the door with the other hand. Rightly or wrongly, I made no move to shoot.

At the back of my mind, I suppose, were the old rules concerning sanctuary. Young Maisie Mason, however, had other ideas. He used the machine gun. He literally pinned that chap to the church door with bullets. And he enjoyed doing it. I knew I was on sticky ground when I roasted him. In battle the object is to kill the enemy. I hadn't a leg to stand on, and Mason knew it. He had his answers ready. The chap had not put his hands up. He still had a rifle slung over his shoulder and potato mashers hanging on his belt. And, as Mason pointed out, if he could have got into the church he would have climbed into the tower and shot at us with every chance of killing either him or me. Mason was right, of course, but boyish looks or not, the light in that lad's eyes left me in no doubt that he was a killer and had enjoyed doing what he did."

"It happened," agreed Green. "The opportunity for revenge after having been shot at for months on end made some lads go over the top. Not often, thank God, but a lad like Maisie, always treated by his own mates as a bit of a cissie, would want to show people what he could do once he had the upper-hand."

"There may be something in what you say," agreed Burnett. "However, all that is by way of illustrating that I don't think Mason was our artist with the knack of writing apposite slug-lines even though he was the only OP Ack who would know of the Scafati bridge incident."

"That doesn't follow, sir," objected Berger. "You can't just say that because a man kills an enemy soldier he can't draw pictures. Particularly as drawing panoramas was supposed to be one of his military skills."

Burnett nodded. "I would argue that way myself in court, Sergeant. What I have said is not proof, merely my impression. But something I found last evening, before ever I knew anything of this business, is proof to support my belief—in my opinion."

"What did you find?" asked Green.

Burnett picked up his briefcase from the floor beside his chair, opened it and took out a cheap and obviously old envelope. "This," he said. "I thought it might be useful." He opened the envelope. "You will remember it, Mr Green. Our Christmas card for nineteen forty-three?"

Green accepted the proffered card with a look of pleased recognition. It was a simple affair about four inches by four, concertina-folded to open out to sixteen inches long. On the front was the regimental badge and a simple Christmas greeting. Inside, across the length of the folds and again across their backs, the artist had drawn a series of thumbnail sketches linked by a road. It started at Alamein with a number of guns firing; Daba shells landing; Fuka raining; the Green Belt brewing up; El Agheila deep sand; Zem Zem Stukas; Tripoli buildings; and so on. Then the coast and a landing craft off-loading at Salerno. The land route continued, past a gently smoking Vesuvius, through a rainy and muddy scene to the River Volturno where minute guns were seen crossing a floating bridge and on to another river, the Garigliano, where little men were depicted shooting Very lights into the air.

"It was bonfire night when we were pulled out of the line and told we were coming home to Blighty," explained Green. "On the Garigliano, that was. The lads had a bit of fun with the Very pistols that night." He looked across at Burnett. "Good job we did come out then. It isn't shown here, because it hadn't become significant then, but just beyond the Garigliano was Monte Cassino, and we were well out of that."

"But you were only brought home to land in France on D-Day," said Reed. "It was only exchanging one big party for another."

"Maybe, lad. But I reckon we got the best deal."

"I think so, too," said Burnett. "We got a few months in England and missed the winter fighting at Cassino. However, the point is, I was responsible for having those cards printed. We came out of the line and waited in billets around Sorrento for the ships to come and pick us up from Naples. They came just a day or two before Christmas and we got back to the Clyde on the second of January. But while we were waiting, somebody had the bright idea about having some cards printed. There were none for us to buy, and we'd not thought about them at previous Christmas times—being otherwise engaged, as it were. But being idle and thinking of coming home ... anyhow, that format was suggested and drawn and I, as battery captain, had them run off at a little printing house in Salerno. As you can see, the paper, envelopes and reproduction are all of the poorest quality, because decent materials were not available in Italy in wartime."

Masters waited patiently for the meat of the matter. He had long ago realized that when old comrades in arms get together and talk they tend to ramble on as memory takes them. Even solicitors like Burnett were no exception. At last Burnett reached the point. "Does your drawing compare in any way with this Christmas card?"

The two were placed side by side on Burnett's desk. As they all craned over them, Masters said: "I can see distinct similarities. Please concentrate on details. The strokes denoting the blast of the shell on the bridge are exactly the same as those landing on the shore as the troops disembark at Salerno."

Green grunted his agreement.

"Cloud formations," went on Masters. "Do you see this little line with three dots above it leading into that huge cumulus balloon in the drawing? It's duplicated almost exactly above the sketch of Tunis."

"There's something here," said Burnett, pointing with the tip of a pencil. "Quite small. You'd only notice it if you were doing one of those 'spot-the-difference' competitions. The river. He's put bulrushes in the stream near the bridge and in the Volturno and Garigliano—a clump of three in each. A sort of cartoonist's standard river plant kit, just like our fighting maps where we had symbols for marshland, deciduous trees and evergreens." He looked up at Masters. "I suppose you'll want some expert to compare these to make sure we are not just imagining things?"

"I think that would be best."

Burnett sat down. "I am sure the artist is the same in both cases. Not only because of the similarities we claim to have spotted, but because I should find it difficult to believe that one battery of two hundred men or even a regiment, would have in their ranks two such capable artists so similar in style and outlook. We had scores of chaps who could paint signs for vehicles, of course. Square plates painted half red and half blue, with white numbers or letters superimposed. But that is a different business from sketching."

"I did some of that myself," said Green. "We used stencils the fitters cut out for us."

"Right. Now, Mr Masters, you would like to know who drew that Christmas card, I suppose?"

"If you can tell us, yes, please."

"It was one of the command post surveyors. Also an Ack or Specialist in our jargon, but not one that went to the OP's or worked on the guns. His name was Frampton. David Frampton, according to an old list in my trunk."

"Surveyor? Would he be a draughtsman?"

"Not in civil life, otherwise he'd have been with the Engineers. Just a chap who could use a pencil and instruments and to whom we could teach enough to help to tie us in to the regimental grid and to use a plane table efficiently."

Masters said: "I must admit I hadn't realized all the skills necessary in gunnery. But now we have a name. David Frampton. Can you tell us anything more about him?"

Burnett shook his head. "Sorry. Over the period of time that has elapsed since then ..." He shrugged his shoulders. "Many of the faces and names have blurred. Only those with whom one was very close retain any image."

"Bill?" asked Masters. "Do you remember Frampton?"

"No. The only command post Ack I can remember was a librarian who was pretty hot on accounts. Our pay got into a hell of a muddle in those days. Nobody bothered to draw any for months on end in the desert. People had no idea how much they were in credit and the weekly pay sheets were always going missing—mislaid, blown up or what-have-you, and without them as evidence to the contrary, the pay office always assumed you'd drawn the lot. That librarian helped a good many of us to keep track of what we were owed."

"They were my responsibility," said Burnett. "I sent them off religiously every week. But the trucks carrying that sort of thing back to Cairo were always coming to grief. And even if they reached Cairo, they then had to be sent back to the pay office in England. By any old means. Some were flown back, some came by sea. The latter took so long that June's accounts arrived after December's. You can imagine the muddle. When we got back home from Italy and the men were to go off on leave, they wanted their back pay, naturally. But we weren't allowed to give it to them. Some were owed hundreds of pounds, which was a lot of money in those days. I honestly don't believe the business was ever properly sorted out though a few weeks later some sort of balance was struck and we were authorized to pay out."

"Frampton," said Masters, bringing the conversation back to the matter in hand.

"No go, George," said Green.

"Right. Please tell me then whether you think it could be Frampton who has appealed to us for help, or was that drawing given to one of his friends who has now used it to authenticate himself?"

Green shrugged. Burnett said: "Anybody's guess, I'm afraid, Mr Masters."

"In that case, there are two courses open to us. The first is to insert your message in the personal column tomorrow to tell our friend that if he doesn't identify himself, the investigation will come to an end."

"Just like that?" asked Burnett.

"No. That is just a frightener. We can't give in so easily after a mere forty-eight hours, but the DCI's correspondent isn't to know that, or at any rate he can't be sure we don't mean it. Meanwhile, the second course is to locate someone who did know Frampton and to try to trace him by that route."

"Anything I can do..." offered Burnett.

"Thank you. Presumably Frampton reported to an officer who would be known to you, Mr Burnett?"

"Two, actually. The command post officer and the assistant command post officer who was, actually, responsible for survey and so would be in the closest touch with Frampton."

"Can you remember who they were?"

"At what stage in the game? The CPO was usually the senior subaltern in the battery, and they tended to be promoted from time to time, being next in line to fill the casualty gaps up front."

Green said: "I think we should go for the one who held the job in Italy. We were only there for about three months, so it's a nice, clean-cut period, and both the Scafati drawing and the Christmas card were done at that time."

"Agreed," said Burnett. He took an old pocket note-book from his briefcase and turned the stained pages. "CPO at that time," he said, "was Lieutenant G.A. Glencross. His Assistant CPO was Second Lieutenant P.O. Wadham. Wadham was a very new boy. He joined us only a few weeks before we sailed for Salerno."

"Have you any way of getting in touch with either of those gentlemen?" asked Masters. "Would Colonel Penn-Northey know where they are, for instance?"

"Not Peter," said the solicitor. "He was a regular and has served in quite a lot of units in his time, so he obviously doesn't keep in close touch with all his hostilities—only colleagues. But we wartime chaps have met for dinner once or twice over the years. The character who had always arranged the meetings is Herbert Gordon, who was commander of B Troop—not Mr Green's half of the battery."

"I remember him," said Green. "Big moustache. He was about thirty then—we regarded him as pretty old. Smoked a lot. The story is..."

"Please," said Masters.

"Sorry, George."

Burnett spoke on his inter-office phone to his secretary. "Cicely, would you bring my personal file, please, and lay on coffee for five."

The file arrived quickly enough to testify to the efficiency of the office's system. Burnett turned a few pages and then, with an exclamation of satisfaction, started to murmur: "Time we had another get together...soon all be too decrepit...hold it in November...let me know...temporarily booked for fourteen..." He looked up. "Gordon says he is in touch with a number of people. He lists them, and both Glencross and Wadham are there. Gordon's phone number is at the top of his letter, so if you'd like me to try and get in touch with him now, I will do so."

"I'd be most grateful," said Masters. "Phone numbers and addresses, if possible, please."

The coffee arrived while Burnett was dialing. He asked the four Yard men to help themselves and, almost immediately, was engaged in the sort of conversation that Masters had come to expect from the old and bold. But eventually the drift was towards getting the information needed. Burnett appeared to parry the question as to why it was wanted by saying he was acting in a professional capacity and so could not properly divulge his reasons, but added they were of little consequence, involving merely the disposal of a few wartime photographs. When the conversation ended he had a few scribbled notes on his pad.

"Poor old Gordon," he said, helping himself to coffee. "Crippled with arthritis, he tells me. Retired, of course, but not able to do much except sit about and read. Of course, as Mr Green said, he's a deal older than most of us, so he'll be well into his seventies."

"The other two?" asked Masters.

"Ah, yes. Glencross is something in the booze world and lives in Burton-on-Trent. Wadham had a heart attack last year, apparently, but is still working as the personnel director of some electronics firm in East Anglia. He lives

68

at Clacton-on-Sea." He handed Masters the sheet of paper. "Can you read my scrawl? Full address and phone numbers there."

"Thank you. Yes, I can decipher it all."

Burnett sat back. "Anything else, gentlemen?"

"Nothing that springs immediately to mind, but I hope I may call you if anything you might help us with does come up."

"Of course. I'm intrigued. In fact I'm hoping you will need to get in touch again. A problem such as this is a change."

"You've had to locate people yourself before now, haven't you, sir?" asked Reed.

"Once or twice. But the difference is I knew the names of the people I was looking for. That means I could advertise quite openly or at least give an agent some reasonable lead with which to start a search. This is much more intriguing." He turned to Green. "And I've had the pleasure of meeting you again, Mr Green. Funny how things turn out. We neither of us could have imagined, forty years ago, that we would next see each other in these circumstances."

"If we could have done," replied Green, "we'd both have paid a lot more attention to certain members of the battery. It would have saved us a bit of trouble now."

Masters got to his feet, and the others followed suit. After thanking Burnett and saying their farewells, they left the solicitor's office.

— 4 —

"Now what?" demanded Green as Reed drove them back towards London.

"Well, at least we're not up against a brick wall," replied Masters. "And that's a relief, because when we took on this job, I had visions of us not knowing which way to go. But your wartime colleagues, Bill, are a very helpful lot."

"I'm glad you think so. I mean that, because so far they haven't come up with any stone-bonker answers or facts."

"And you feel responsible for their contribution?"

"I can't help it. I'm parading them for your inspection."

"You can stop worrying. They are acting as a very good route map. Pointing the way to go and providing us with a continuation of progress. Almost the same as we need in a normal investigation. We have to have continuation of evidence and proof when a case comes up in court. One fact must lead on logically to the next, leaving no gap into which defence counsel can drive a wedge."

"And you can smell success?"

"I didn't actually say that, Bill, but I have a certain amount of confidence in our combined ability to follow a trail given enough signs to work on. And, for the moment, at least, we have a few finger-posts to help us."

"Glencross and Wadham?"

"Obviously, those two. But other things as well. For instance there's Stinky Miller, who was found dead. I think we ought to know something of the circumstances of his death. The chances are that they have nothing to do with our search, but just in case they have, we must get that information. I've been wondering exactly how to get it without applying directly to the local force concerned, and thereby running the risk of rousing unwanted interest in our activities."

"Have you reached a decision, Chief?" asked Berger.

"The only one I can think of is for the DCI to visit Miller's widow privately. Not as a police officer. I don't think that fact need even come to light. I felt that he should go, rather, as an old comrade who has just got to hear of Miller's death—through meeting other old chums who have given him the news and told him where Mrs Miller is living. Being in the area and so forth, he's just called in to say how sorry he is and to have a word about how Stinky..."

"Eric Alfred to his missus," interposed Green.

"...of course, Eric Alfred...how he stepped in and filled the gap at Mareth etcetera etcetera. Tongues loosened by the presentation of a bunch of flowers and a cup of tea. How did he come to die? None of the old pals seem to know. When? Where? How?" Masters turned to Green. "But I don't have to tell you, of all people, Bill. So what do you think?"

"Where does she live? Caldenham? I'd have to ask around for the address there...still, that would make it look authentic, I suppose. Cops reckon to know the houses they want to visit. Yes, George, it could work, though I don't like fooling a widow-woman."

"Would you be fooling her?"

"Doing good by stealth," said Berger.

"You mind your own barrer, and if you can't push it, shove it," retorted Green to the sergeant. "I know my own feelings in this matter and I don't want dowsing with bromides about being cruel to be kind or acting for the common good and all that sort of hogwash."

"Still..."

"Still nothing. It'll be false pretences, however much you dress it up."

"You'd rather not do it, Bill?"

"Oh, I'll do it."

71

"Thanks."

"When?"

"I think Berger should take you down there this afternoon. Straight after lunch. He can set you down inconspicuously and wait. Use a civvy car."

Green nodded his agreement.

"Another thing, Bill."

"What now?"

"Mr T. A. Lamief referred to a place called Jerabub."

"Oasis," said Green. "Way down south of the fighting area."

"That's what I thought. I looked it up last night. There are a number of such places. One I remember was Siwa."

"That's right."

"Did you ever visit any of them."

"No. I told you, they were too far south. I think the Long Range Desert Group and Popski's Private Army used to use them as staging points."

"Then why should Mr Lamief choose to mention one of them specifically? Jerabub?"

"I haven't a clue."

"As I said, I looked it up. There are lots of spellings in different gazeteers and atlases. Jaghbub was one. Girarabub another." Masters spelt them out. "But nowhere could I find Jerabub spelt as your correspondent spelt it."

"Go on."

"Nowhere else in the whole of that long letter was there a spelling mistake. Am I right, Reed?"

"Quite right, Chief. We checked all words we weren't sure about."

"So?" demanded Green.

"His words were: 'and the tree probably the outpost of the palm grove at Jerabub'. A definite statement, Bill. Definite enough, at least, for me to suppose he had seen that palm grove. That he had seen, noticed and remembered after forty years that there was a lone tree, growing apart from its neighbours. That, to me, means that he went there, and he still uses what I can only suggest is our anglicized way of spelling the place name. The soldiers' way, if you like. The way of men who hear a place name and use it without every having seen it written down. Something similar happened in the First War, I believe. Ypres became Wipers. But if, as you say, Jerabub was south of the battle zone, why should T. A. Lamief remember it if he wasn't familiar with it? He certainly didn't look it up in an atlas, otherwise the spelling would have been correct."

There was silence for a moment or two before Green replied.

"You've got me, George. I never went to Jerabub, of that I'm sure. But there were all sorts of little expeditions and side-shows at times. For instance, my troop of guns went with a light-armoured recce column to the Pink Hills, just to determine how far the enemy's El Agheila line stretched into the desert. It took about four or five days and I'm doubtful whether a lot of people on that particular swan would remember it, let alone those who weren't. And there were Jock Columns—small forces of all arms that went careering off in all directions. Our man could have been on one of those at some time."

"Say he had done that, would it help us to identify him?"

"I'd think so. There can't have been many gunners who did."

"Something to remember when the time comes," said Masters. "Now me. While you are seeing Mrs Miller this afternoon, Bill, Reed and I will go to Clacton. We'll be there, I hope, by the time Mr P. O. Wadham returns from his office. That will leave us free tomorrow to consider Mr Glencross at Burton-on-Trent."

"And the message in tomorrow's personal column, Chief?" asked Berger.

Masters turned to Green. "What do you think, Bill? Shall we scrub round that for the time being?"

"I think so. For one day, because we could have some positive point by tomorrow."

"Such as?" asked Reed.

"Well, instead of what we suggested might go in to-morrow, we could have said something like: 'So your name is Frampton. The sketch told us.' Not those words exactly perhaps."

"But we don't think his name is Frampton."

"He wouldn't know that. He'd think we'd failed and would have to cough up some genuine information to get us on the right track. But as I said, if we give it a day we may have something even better to beat him with."

"Understood," said Berger. "Though I think it would sting him into more energetic action if we were to say the drawing was not recognized. One of his barmy clues falling on stony ground would faze him a bit, I reckon."

Green grunted equivocally. Reed said: "We shall make the Yard soon after twelve, Chief. Do we set out for Clacton immediately? Two hours' travelling time to get there."

"Half-past three should do us. Bill, you and Berger get off as and when you like."

"Half-one," said Green. "I want a drink and a sandwich before I go."

Green had found the house by enquiring at the news-agent's shop. It sold vegetables, tinned food, wrapped cakes, bread and household bits and pieces. He reckoned everybody who lived in the village would have to use it at some time, so that is where he asked for information.

"Mrs Miller? Ah, yes. Now! Do you know the village at all?"

Green confessed his ignorance.

There followed a complicated set of instructions, made so by the fact that Caldenham was not a close-knit village, but one which had apparently been built in dollops. A few houses round the church. A few near the old farm. More at the little crossroads. Some at the end of the lane near the shore. And so on. These had then been connected by a sort of intermittent ribbon development, leaving old tracks and footpaths to be turned into private roads guarded by barriers. Fortunately for Green, ways had been left for pedestrians round the barriers. He followed his instructions and found himself in a road of new bungalows with well-kept gardens and equally well-kept and planted areas on the pavements.

"Mrs Miller?"

He had the idea that she had lived all her adult life in military quarters. It could have been the fact that the rocks that edged the path to the front door were regimented as to rank and size and had been whitewashed and so had gently plucked some chord of memory that recalled military life. He didn't know, but he had the impression, and it was a strong one.

"Yes."

"My name is Bill Green. I was a sergeant in the gunners in the war. I think your husband was my gunlayer for a time, Mrs Miller."

"My husband is dead."

"Yes. I'm sorry to hear it. I only got to know yesterday. Sar' Major Pitkin told me..."

"Lewis Pitkin, would that be?"

"Yes. He used to be in the old battery, too. Course, he was only a bombardier then."

She opened the door wider. "You'd better come in, Mr Green. You're the only one who has...called to see me since Eric went. I...come in, do, and have a cup of tea."

Green remembered the flowers he was carrying.

"These...these are for you." He held them out. "They seem to be able to say all the things I ought to be saying. How old Sti...er, Eric was..."

"You were going to call him Stinky, weren't you? Everybody did. I did myself, very often. He never minded." She took the flowers. "They're beautiful," she said. "Just beautiful. Go into the room, Mr Green, and make yourself at home. I must put these in water."

It was as if he had sensed this room while still outside the front door. It was, to his mind, laid out for inspection. Not that it appeared either uncomfortable or unlived in, but he got the impression that had the owner been able to do away with the window and door, one half of the room would have been the mirror-image of the other.

Everything seemed to have been bought in pairs and measured into exactly corresponding positions. Two exactly similar vases on the mantelpiece, two exactly similar sawn-off cartridge cases in the hearth, two exactly similar armchairs set at exactly similar angles to the fireside, each neighboured by exactly similar standard ashtrays and small pie-crust tables. A wall bookcase in each alcove with the contents tightly ranked by size. The regimental plaques on the wall corresponded to the millimetre, the two picture frames matched each other, the stereo loudspeakers were as exactly twinned as a car's headlights and the pot plants on the broad window ledge were correctly aligned with the side panes.

She returned with two exactly similar glass vases, each bearing half the bouquet he had brought. As he knew they would be, they were placed, one on the top of each bookcase, exactly central, fidgeted into a position that corresponded precisely to the pattern of the wallpaper behind them.

"There. They look nice, don't they?" she said, standing back as if to make doubly sure the symmetry was correct.

"Very nice indeed."

"I've mashed the tea. It should be well-brewed by now." She left him again. He counted the books in the bookcases and was disappointed to discover that the numbers were not the same on both sides.

As they settled down to the large cups of good strong tea, Green said: "I heard Stinky got a bit of promotion before he finished. Lewis Pitkin said he was a BQ the last time he met him."

She set her cup down. "He made RQ in the end."

"Didn't make lieutenant Q, then?"

"No. That's what he wanted, of course, but things were against him."

"Things? People?"

"Reorganization of the regiments was what did it."

"Cut-backs?"

"Not really. When you were in the army there used to be two troops of four guns in a battery."

Green nodded.

"That meant three WO's and a BQ. Stinky was a BQ and expecting to go up to troop sergeant major when they reorganized. Instead of two troops of four twenty-five pounders, a battery suddenly became just a single unit of six of the bigger one-oh-five guns. That meant there were two redundant troop sergeant majors in every battery. Stinky's expectations of promotion went for a burton."

"Just like that?"

"Not quite. They wanted Stinky to take an AIG's course at Larkhill. They spelt it all out for him. The AIG's had been given a new promotion route."

"To IG?"

"No. To a new commissioned appointment called TIG."

"What's the T stand for?"

"Technical. Technical Instructor Gunnery. The TIG's were to be sent out as instructors to TA units, leaving the IG's for the regular army."

"Sounds a reasonable arrangement to me."

"It wasn't for Stinky. He'd done a spell with a TA unit. You know how regular NCO's are seconded to them? He'd hated it. Sitting in a drill hall all day with no proper job to do until the TA men came in for an evening's training once a week or a weekend exercise now and again. Don't get me wrong. He liked the people, not the job. He wanted life in a regular service unit. Full-time soldiering was what he'd joined up for, he said."

"I can imagine. So he turned down the Larkhill course?"

"He preferred to stay where he was. It was his life, you see, and he was happier that way. But he had to wait for his promotion as there were so many in the pipeline. He became BSM and then, after three years he made RQ. But that was his last tour. His time was up when he'd completed it. He was too old for them to commission him."

"Pity."

"It was, really, because the new rules these days let non-commissioned service count towards automatic pro-

77

motion as an officer. He'd have probably been a major quartermaster had he made it."

"Was he a bit embittered by it all?"

"Not much. We'd had a good life together and he'd enjoyed his work."

"I'm pleased to hear it. He was a good bloke. But I don't suppose you even knew him when he was on my gun."

"Not when you were in the desert. I met him when he came home from Italy."

"Did you now?" asked Green, interested. "Would that have been up in Norfolk by any chance?"

She smiled. "In Downham Market actually."

"I know it," said Green. "My battery was billeted in Fakenham. So you're a Norfolk lass?"

"Oh, no. I was stationed there, too, in the ATS."

"I thought you were very familiar with all the army jargon. So Stinky met you there."

"Actually I was in the Catering Corps. It hadn't been formed long at that time. If you remember, every formation had its own unit cooks before then."

"We certainly did."

"When your Division came home, there was a lot of preparation made for it. The billets were ready, the messes, offices and kitchens."

"We came home with just our personal kit. All the stores and equipment had been handed over to the blokes who relieved us in Italy. It saved shipping, I suppose."

"That's right. And there was a big welcoming meal laid on. Something you hadn't had for years. Roast beef and Yorkshire with roast spuds and sprouts with Christmas pud and custard to follow. The trouble was, Stinky's battery train arrived in Downham Market at two in the morning."

"Ours at Fakenham was about that time, too, I remember. And they'd put a dirty great barrel of beer in the men's dining room. On the army! I think that was the biggest surprise. A packet of fags a man, too."

Mrs Miller smiled. "I was one of the people who helped

to prepare that meal. It was difficult, because we didn't know when the battery would be arriving, not to an hour or two at any rate. Then the sergeant cook put me on to minding that beer barrel. One of those big white army pint pots per man. They had to drink the beer and then use the mugs for the tea that came up after the meal.

"That's when and where I first met Stinky. All the lads were saying things..."

"I'll bet."

"Stinky said something different." She blushed slightly. "He said, 'Blighty, beer and beauty. I've got the first two, love. I'm going to have the third an' all, and you're it.' When the crowd had gone and I was alone at the barrel, he came up and asked me to meet him next day. He said he wouldn't be on parade, except to draw his pay and kit and he'd get away to see me. I reckoned he'd just gone a bit silly because I was the first English girl he'd seen and spoken to for years."

"But you turned up for the date?"

"Yes. I didn't think he'd come, but he did, and we went to the pictures. The next day he went off on leave. I thought that would be the end of it, but it wasn't. He wrote to me every day he was away."

"Did he now! I wouldn't have said old Stinky was that good a correspondent. A great letter writer, was he?"

"Not him. I suppose his letters were awful, really, but I liked getting them. I met him at the station when he came back off leave. In March, he got another week and he took me home with him to meet his mother."

"Then he went to France on D-Day."

"That's right. He wrote when he could. He asked me to marry him in one letter. Then he got that first leave from Europe, after Nimegen it was, when everything out there had sort of settled down for the winter. We got married then."

"And lived happily ever after?"

"Something like that. We had two children. I'm a grandmother now."

"And a widow," said Green quietly.

"Yes," she replied. "And I'll tell you what, Mr. Green, I miss him like hell."

She was near to tears. Green gave her a moment or two to regain her composure and then got to his feet to pour her a second cup of tea.

"Lewis Pitkin couldn't tell me how Stinky died," he said, handing her the cup. "What was it? A heart attack?"

She shook her head, pursing her lips in her efforts to keep the tears back. "Accident, they said."

"They? The police?"

She nodded, still struggling against the tears.

"But you didn't believe them. Is that it?"

She nodded again and bit her lip.

"Have a drop of tea, love, and then tell me about it. It will do you good to talk it over."

She did as he had suggested.

"It was only about two months ago," she began. "In March. Stinky was a very practical man, you know. Did everything himself." She took another sip of tea. "He'd grown fond of gardening, too. Never idle. He'd decided he'd like a little greenhouse. Just somewhere to bring on a few seeds and tomatoes. We haven't got that much room, so he bought one of those little lean-to greenhouses, the sort you put up against a wall."

Green nodded to show he was following her story.

"He decided he'd put it up against the garage wall. It's concrete, you know, and Stinky knew he'd get the full benefit of the sun there. So the afternoon it was delivered he sorted all the bits out, did the measuring for the holes he had to drill in the concrete, then he got out his hammer drill and he made the holes. He actually finished the drilling before he packed up. He told me so."

"I went out the next morning. To do a bit of shopping and have a cup of coffee with Mrs Tyson. Wednesday it was, because I always did call on Florrie Tyson on Wednesday. She came to me Fridays. I left Stinky putting up the framework. Happy as Larry, he was and not looking a day over fifty. I was out for the best part of an hour and a half, and when I got back I found him dead in the garage with the doors pulled to."

Green said nothing. He waited for her to go on in her own good time.

"He'd had a hit on the head. On the top. He was lying there with a bit of blood about and a stone on the floor near him. It had blood on it, too. Just a patch."

Green didn't know whether to urge her to carry on or to keep silent until she proceeded of her own free will. Had he declared himself as a policeman when he first arrived, he knew he would have questioned her closely, but as it was, he wasn't sure how such a revelation might be taken. But he needn't have worried. She got to her feet, put her cup down and left the room, only to return a moment or two later.

"This is the sort of stone," she said, handing him a grey, smooth oval of rock, about four inches by three and an inch or so thick. It was chamfered and rounded by the action of the sea, and on one face, in the brightest of colours, was a painted drawing of a yellow dingy, with red sails, floating on blue waves, with a few puffs of white cloud about it.

As she sat down, she said: "Stone? It's little more than a pebble."

Green was weighing it in the palm of his hand. "Still..." he said, "...it must weigh a pound or more."

"It's not heavy enough to have killed Stinky when it fell on him from less than a foot."

"This isn't the same stone, is it?"

"No. The police took that. But they're all more or less alike."

"You've got a lot of them?"

"If you go down to the shore here, you'll find millions, just like that. And I mean millions. In great shingle banks six feet high and twenty feet across. Stinky gathered some. The best he could find. About a dozen or so."

"To paint on?"

"Oh, that! No. Stinky couldn't paint like that. But lots of people do. Women mostly. You know the sort. The arty-

81

crafty ones. Then they sell them to gift shops. People who come on holiday buy them."

"But he collected a dozen stones."

"For a friend of his who is a real artist."

"A soldier friend?"

"That's right." She paused. "Wait a moment. You might know him."

"David Frampton?" asked Green quietly.

"That's right. Fancy you knowing Dave."

"I don't—not all that well, I mean. He was a CPO Ack in the old days. A surveyor in battery HQ. I didn't see a lot of the BHQ people."

"But you knew he was an artist."

"He drew our Christmas card one year and he used to do sketches in his spare time. He gave them to the lads who wanted them. I saw a few at one time."

"Dave was going to paint some military scenes for Stinky. What Stinky wanted them for, I don't really know, but he collected bits and pieces." She nodded to the two highly polished, sawn-off shot cases. "That sort of thing, badges, unit signs and such like. It's all laid out in the spare bedroom."

Green nodded. "Is that where he kept his stones?"

"He had them on a shelf in the garage."

"And one fell off and hit him on the head?"

Mrs Miller sniffed. "As if it would."

"Would what, love? Fall off the shelf or kill him?"

"Both. The police were round here for long enough. Then they said what had happened. They said that when Stinky had been using his hammer drill on the outside of the garage wall the vibration had juggled the stones until they were nearly falling off. That was the afternoon before he died. Then the following morning, they said, Stinky had gone into the garage to hammer the bolts through the holes or something like that and the shaking he'd caused had brought one of these down on his head and brained him."

"Only you don't think so. Is that it?"

"I'm sure so. For one thing, when I found Stinky the

82

garage doors were almost closed and the light wasn't on. Stinky would never be working in the dark. Nobody would."

Green nodded his support for this view.

"And there was no sign of a hammer or any other tool anywhere near him. They were all on the bench, six feet away from where he was, across the back of the garage. And like I said earlier, that shelf was not much more than head high for Stinky. If a stone like that plopped off and hit him it wouldn't have done him much harm I'm telling you. Hard-headed in every way was Stinky."

"He could have been stooping down, love. Then it would have had further to fall."

"Maybe. But it couldn't have hit him full on top of his head if..."

"It could, love. If he'd been down on his hunkers, with his head up looking for something."

"I don't believe that. Why would Stinky have been crouching near the garage wall with no tools in his hands, just looking for something?"

"Judging alignment or distances or something like that, perhaps?"

She shook her head. "I can't see it that way at all."

Green looked at her shrewdly. "What way do you see it, then?"

"You'll think I'm fancying things, but I reckon somebody hit him over the head with something and then, after he'd fallen, grabbed one of those stones off the shelf and hit him again in the same place. That's why the stone got blood on it."

"I don't think you are fancying things," said Green, to her great surprise. "If the stone had hit him and bounced off immediately, there wouldn't have been time for it to get bloody."

She stared at him. "I'd never thought of that. You mean it took a few seconds for him to start bleeding, and then..."

"Yes, love. But don't go on distressing yourself about it. Try to think who would want to attack Stinky like that."

"Who? Nobody. It would be a tramp or one of those young muggers. But the local police wouldn't hear anything like that. I suppose it was easier to call it an accident than to start looking for the one who did it."

"That's what you reckon, is it? That it was a tramp or muggers?"

"There was nobody owed Stinky a grudge big enough to kill him."

"I'll believe you, love. But think for a moment. Why would a tramp or a mugger kill Stinky?"

"Why? Well ..."

"Don't stop, love. Go on."

"To pinch something, I suppose. Or vandalize something."

"Was anything missing? Anything smashed up?"

"No. Nothing like that at all."

"So the cops were probably right in thinking it wasn't a tramp or a mugger. And besides, how many tramps or muggers do you reckon could have seen off Stinky? He was a big bloke. A trained fighter. You say he was fit. And at the first hint of trouble he could have armed himself with one or other of the tools from the bench—a hammer, wrench or mallet, perhaps even a length of timber."

She seemed bemused by Green's logic. "I agree no single chap could have seen Stinky off, unless that chap was very fit or took him by surprise. I suppose tramps aren't often very fit, are they?"

"Very few of them. But muggers tend to be younger, though they usually hunt in groups. Did the police ask your neighbours if they'd seen a gang of youths in the village that day, or a vagrant?"

"I don't know what they did."

"Your neighbours haven't told you what questions were asked?"

"No."

Green grimaced. "Then none were asked," he said. "Most people can't keep things like that to themselves. You'd soon have heard about it if the police had done a house-to-house investigation." He paused a moment before continuing. "What explanation did they give for the doors of the garage being almost shut and the light not being on?"

Mrs Miller gave an exclamation of disgust. "They said that the wind had swung it to. And when I said our garage doors didn't swing shut on a still morning when there wasn't even a breath, they said sudden breezes did come along even on the calmest days. Either that's what happened, they said, or I'd been mistaken about exactly how the doors were. I hadn't noticed properly, because I was upset at the time. All that sort of nonsense. I just had to give up in the end because they had an answer for everything, or else they didn't believe me."

"Did they actually say that?"

"As good as. They told me straight out that if I insisted they should start looking for somebody who had attacked Stinky, they'd start with me."

"And?"

"They said there was no sign of anybody except me and Stinky ever having been in that garage, so if anybody had killed him in there it must have been me. Then they said it usually turned out that way with killings—members of a family doing each other in." She breathed deeply. "I'm telling you, Bill Green, those coppers blackmailed me into staying quiet about what I thought. Threatened me, in fact, if I didn't accept what they said, even though I know it wasn't true. Coppers! I've seen cats dragging better rubbish out of dustbins than that lot."

"It doesn't sound too good," agreed Green. "Who were they—the cops, I mean—who dealt with you?"

"The County ones, I suppose. What's it called round here? South Central, is it?"

Green nodded. "That sounds as if it could be right but I meant the names of the police officers. Can you remember what they were called?"

"Can I. I'll never forget them. There was a Detective Inspector Putrey and a Sergeant Cheshire. What do you want to know for?"

"Well now, love," said Green quietly, "I'm employed by the Government."

"Civil Servant?"

"Sort of. I'm what's known as an SSCO. Not that what I do need concern you, really, but I don't mind telling you that I know one or two senior policeman up in London. There's a liaison bloke at the Home Office and a detective chief superintendent or two. One in particular. I think I ought to mention this business to them, don't you?"

"Will they be able to do anything?"

"They won't be able to bring Stinky back."

She thought for a moment or two. Then she said: "He'd want it cleared up. He didn't like untidiness. And as for me, well I didn't like the way they treated me. I'd call it threatening, the way they spoke to me, and Stinky would never have allowed that."

"What would he have done?"

"He'd have told them. And if that hadn't worked he'd have found somebody to say something. He knew a lot of people he'd served with. Big names, you know. Besides solicitors and journalists and others who'd have advised him. I mean, look, there's you. You've offered. You're an old mate, just come out of the blue and you know people."

"Perhaps Dave Frampton..."

"I don't reckon so. Not Dave. He's all right, of course, but I don't think he's got much clout, as Stinky would call it. Not a school teacher."

"I see. Where does Dave live, by the way?"

"In a place called Oriel. It's quite a largish market town..."

"I know, love. On the Thames, somewhere up Marlow way."

"That's it. I've never been there, but he told us it's pretty. An old sort of cottage place. Been in the family for several generations. His grandad was born there, I think. 'Course there's lots of big expensive property round there now. Bourne End, Maidenhead, Marlow, Henley. But he says his cottage is fine. It's still standing and he's prettied it up. Even got a grant, I believe. One of a small row. Number four Withy Lane. Stinky and I were going

86

to go for a week this summer. He didn't have us up there before now because he only moved in about eighteen months ago, after his mum died. He was lucky, you see. After his mother died and the cottage came to him he managed to get another job in a school near there. Art master, he was. Still is, or was when he and his missus came down for Stinky's funeral."

"He's not retired then?"

"A couple of years to go, I think."

"I see." Green got to his feet. "He was never a great pal of mine, as I said, but I might drop in on him if I'm round his way. I get about a bit, you know, and the chance could arise sometime."

She stood up and looked out of the window. "Have you got a car with you?"

"I left it near the church. I didn't know my way around all these private roads, so I did a recce on foot."

"They are difficult. Stinky used to say he couldn't see the point of the barriers. He reckoned that no road block was any good as a deterrent unless it was covered by a machine gun."

Green smiled. "That's what we were always taught. They had to be in the primary firing arc of one gun or the secondary arcs of two."

"You still remember?"

"Some of it. Not the lot, because I wasn't a professional, like Stinky."

Masters and Reed were nearing Clacton at half-past five. The fifteen miles of road after Colchester had comparatively little traffic to impede them, but as they approached the town there were more vehicles and progress was slower.

"Rush hour, Chief," said Reed, as he negotiated a roundabout, the centre of which had been newly planted with flowers for the coming summer.

"It's not too bad," replied Masters. "But finding Wadham's address could be something else. Ah! Slow down a bit. There's a sign there pointing the way to the railway station. A few enquiries there, among taxi drivers, might be of use."

The station at Clacton, like that at many seaside resorts, is a terminus, set well within the town, close to the residential areas and the main shopping streets. As they passed along the front of the buildings they saw another sign indicating the cab rank.

"Chapman Road," murmured Reed, manoeuvring the big Rover across the line of traffic and pulling in opposite the six or seven taxis lined up waiting for fares.

"Carisbrooke Road?" The cabby gave Masters the directions. It was no distance at all. It took Reed about four minutes to fetch up outside Wadham's house.

"Car in the garage, Chief. He could be home from work by now."

Despite his recent illness, Wadham looked hale and hearty. He was still in his business suit when he came to the door and was inclined to be a little wary when Masters announced his rank and name.

"This is not a criminal matter, Mr Wadham. It in no way concerns you personally, but I was given your name by a Mr Jason Burnett, a solicitor with whom you served in the army during the war."

Wadham's manner thawed a little, but he still did not invite them to enter. "Jason Burnett? How is he?"

"Very well indeed. I went to see him concerning a soldier who served in your battery in the old days. The man is apparently in trouble and we want to help him."

"What sort of trouble?"

"We think his life is in danger."

"What's his name?"

"This could sound silly to you, Mr Wadham, but we don't know his name. He wrote to a colleague of mine—also known to you. When you knew him, he was Sergeant Green of C Sub."

"Sergeant Bill Green?"

"Now a detective chief inspector."

"A good hand, Bill Green. A bit dour perhaps, but a really reliable bloke whatever the state of play."

"He would be flattered to know your opinion, Mr Wadham. Evidently this former soldier thought he could trust Bill Green, too. At any rate he wrote to him—tentatively, without giving his name, in case the letter fell into the wrong hands. We are engaged now in trying find the man, who is, we think, in some danger. Colonel Peter Penn-Northey has given us some help. So has Mr Burnett, and he suggested you might be able to help us further."

Now the door was opened wide.

"You'd better come in."

As Masters and Reed entered, a woman's voice called: "Who is it, dear?"

"The police."

As they went into the sitting room, Heather Wadham appeared, slightly agitated. "Did you say police, Philip?"

"Yes, old girl. Scotland Yard to be precise."

"Scot...Phil, what have you done?"

"Nothing, Heather. Don't alarm yourself." He introduced Masters and Reed to his wife who said, surprisingly, to Masters: "I've heard of you. I read the papers a lot, being at home alone all day. You're very well known, aren't you?"

"My name gets mentioned now and again, ma'am."

"And so does your wife's. I read a column about her in one of my magazines. She's interested in adoption, isn't she?"

"She helps one of the societies."

"Heather," said Wadham, "we'd better not hold Mr Masters up."

"Oh, right. Can I bring you a drink?"

"No, thank you," said Masters. "No alcohol, at any rate. We shall be driving back to London shortly."

"Does that mean you would like coffee or tea?"

"Coffee would suit us very well, thank you."

When Mrs Wadham had left them, they got down to business.

"This is strictly confidential, Mr Wadham."

"I understand."

"The unknown warrior who wrote to Bill Green as-

89

serted that he had seen murder done. From his description of the murderers, we think he has unwittingly witnessed a crime by a couple of very dangerous criminals. I think he sensed this himself, hence his reluctance to sign his letter, lest it should in some way lead the murderers back to him."

"Was the letter genuine."

"Bill Green thinks so. His correspondent made a number of references to incidents which only members of your battery would know. He asked for a reply in the *Telegraph*. We put one in the personal column. His response to that was to send Green this drawing." Masters produced a photocopy of the Scafati bridge cartoon and handed it to Wadham.

"Recognize it, sir?" asked Reed.

Wadham paused before replying. "I don't think I recognize this particular sketch, but I do think I recognize the style. By that, I mean I think I have previously seen a number of similar efforts from the same hand."

"The hand being . . . ?" asked Masters.

"A chap called Frampton."

"David Frampton, who was at one time a member of your surveying team?"

"That's him. He was always ripping off sketches like this on the backs of message forms and handing them out to the lads. Usually funny. Sometimes he just drew voluptuous nudes. They were very popular, I can tell you. To men, some of whom hadn't even seen a woman for months and years, those drawings were coveted items. The equivalent of the pin-ups in barrack rooms at home."

"So this cartoon wasn't necessarily sent to Bill Green by David Frampton?"

Wadham shook his head. "I can't say positively, of course, but I should say the chances are that it wasn't. As I said, those sketches were scattered around like confetti. Somebody hung on to this one, and is now using it as . . . well, as a sort of authentication for something."

"Quite. That is what we supposed. So now we want to try to trace Frampton, to see if he can remember the person to whom he gave it. Mr Burnett said that as Frampton was in your team, you would be the officer most likely to be able to help us."

The door opened, and Mrs Wadham came in with a tray. "I've put some home-made biscuits out for you." She turned to Masters. "They'll help to keep you going until you get back home tonight."

"Thank you, ma'am."

She smiled graciously on him and left, as she explained, to get on with supper.

Although he added no sugar to it, Wadham stirred his cup of coffee reflectively. Then he put it down untouched.

"I can't tell you where Frampton lives or if he is even still alive. But I will tell you what I know about him."

"If you please."

"When the war was over, every soldier had to be given a written reference—as from one employer to another, prospective one. At the same time, every unit had to appoint a Careers Officer whose job it was to collate all the millions of pamphlets that poured out of the Ministry of Labour telling of job prospects, training schemes and so on.

"As I was a budding personnel man before the war—very budding actually—I found myself with the job of Careers Officer. And I had to write the references for my own men. Mostly the references were stereotyped affairs saying that the man had done yeoman service, was of exemplary character, and not much more. But those who hadn't got jobs or trades to return to came to me for advice and help.

"One of these was Frampton. He wanted to become a teacher. You won't remember, but in 'forty-five the country needed thousands of teachers, and there was a scheme afoot to produce them quickly. Standards of entry were, I'm afraid, lowered, and the usual training college course of two years was cut to one year for these mature men.

"Frampton wanted to be an art teacher. In those days, people couldn't rush about claiming to have three or four O levels as they do today. Students had to sit the complete

School Certificate Examination, and if they didn't satisfy the examiners in English, Maths, a foreign language and several other subjects in a balanced core curriculum, they didn't get a certificate or the right to claim any passes."

"All or nothing," said Reed.

"Just so, Sergeant. Frampton had actually sat for his School Certificate and had the usual documentary proof that he had succeeded in parts of it. With his drawing ability, too, there seemed every prospect of him getting taken on for one of the short teacher training course. But I can recall telling him at the time that he had a mental blockage when it came to putting his mother tongue into writing. It seemed as if he could get his ideas down extremely well in the form of sketches, and he was quick-witted enough to think of titles and captions for them. But having said that ... well, I wasn't surprised he had failed to pass in his English essay, for example. When it came to writing applications, I had virtually to write them for him. Certainly I had to edit them heavily and then get him to rewrite them. And another thing. For an artist, he had an execrable fist. His actual calligraphy was almost indecipherable. But he was an intelligent fellow, and he'd served long and hard, and I had no qualms whatsoever in helping him and backing his application. He succeeded, too. He got taken on and I learned about a couple of years later that he had passed muster and had a job as a teacher. But I haven't any idea where he was working or where he lived."

"Thank you," said Masters. "Maybe we can trace him in one of the schoolteachers' associations."

"Is that the lot?"

"There is just one other thing. Your mentioning Mr Frampton's illegible writing and general lack of ability to put words on paper and would seem to rule him out as Bill Green's correspondent."

"Just as I suggested?"

Masters nodded. "The man who sent the letter wrote flowery English, and used a number of words not usually found in the ordinary man's vocabulary."

"Impedimenta," said Reed. "Chagrin, indigenous, ruinous, fickle moon, that sort of thing."

"Not many of the people in our battery—of any rank—would use words like that."

"The writing, too," said Masters, "was full and flowing. A very good hand. No hint of script. Almost Victorian is the best way I can think of to describe it."

"Pot hooks?" asked Wadham.

"I believe that is what the old writing training was called."

"Then I can probably help you."

Masters almost held his breath in anticipation.

"The real battery clerk, the trained one, that is, was a bombardier—a two-striper. Actually, ours was a local lance-sergeant, promoted so that he could use the mess. But his assistant was somebody who would fit the job. There always was one available, you know. A chap who wouldn't fit into the business of manning and maintaining a gun, but who by nature and upbringing was more at home and, indeed, of more use, working in the battery office. Some of those boys used to learn typewriting and bookkeeping at night schools in those days. Called evening classes now, I believe. Others had civilian jobs which fitted them for the office work. Ours, for instance, had had two or three years' experience in a bank or an insurance office—I can't remember which—before coming to us after initial training.

"His name was Pearce. And he was flowery. The only son of elderly parents. Carefully nurtured, taught to speak properly, not allowed to play with other boys, put into a good safe job with built-in security and then, wham! pitched into a world war just like that."

"You can imagine how he talked when I tell you he was known to one and all as Bung-ho Percy. Or was it What-ho Percy? No matter. He talked with a bit of a plum, and he had a vocabulary. He'd never say 'rations up' like everybody else. He'd report that the victuals had arrived. And his writing was to match. A good, legible, flowery script, taught by a elderly mother who'd learned to write

93

in the 'nineties. He, I suggest, could be the man you are looking for. Other than Pearce, I have no suggestion as to who would fit the description of Bill Green's correspondent."

"Thank you. He sounds a distinct possibility. Do you by any chance, remember his Christian name or names?"

Wadham thought for a moment or two and then shook his head. "I can't say I ever knew them, although I must have seen them on documents."

"Nothing at all to help us?"

"Nothing, except..."

"Except what, Mr Wadham?"

"Pearce had a cast in one eye. A very noticeable one if he took his spectacles off. Not that it impaired his vision except that he had to wear his specs—the old, army, tinsided ones, supposedly designed to go on under a gas mask. That's all, Mr Masters. I can't even tell you the colour of his hair, so I suppose it was more or less brown."

"And you don't know where Pearce lived or the area he hailed from?"

"From his voice I'd say south of Watford and within easy reach of London. But that's only a guess."

Masters got to his feet. "In that case, sir, we'll leave you to change for supper. Thank you for being so co-operative. You really have been a great help. Could I ask you to say goodbye to Mrs Wadham for us, please, and to thank her for the coffee?"

— 5 —

Reed made good time back to London now that the worst of the rush hour traffic had gone. He did the journey in about an hour and a half and so it was only a minute or two after eight o'clock when he deposited Masters at the end of the narrow road leading down to the little house where the DCS lived.

To Masters' surprise, when Wanda met him in the hall with her usual kiss of welcome, she told him that Green and his wife were in the sitting room.

"Had to come, George," grunted Green apologetically. "Something you ought to hear tonight in case it affects your plans for tomorrow."

"Glad to see you both," replied Masters. "Had you not been here I'd have rung you."

"Struck oil have you?"

"Shall we say the test-boring looks promising?"

Wanda handed him a drink. "Have this, darling, then go and change. You and William can talk over supper."

He put his arm round her waist. "Meaning, I suspect, that you and Doris would like to hear it all."

"That's right, George," said Doris. "We were in at the beginning and we are interested."

"In that case, if you'll excuse me, I'll take my drink upstairs with me. I'll be down in about ten minutes for nosh."

"Nosh?" demanded Doris. "You're getting to be as vulgar as Bill. When I think of the beautiful way Wanda always prepares and serves your food and you call it nosh..." She breathed out heavily in disgust. Masters

95

grinned, kissed the top of his wife's head, released her and left the room.

"That's what I call being courteous to your host," said Green. "Poor chap comes in after a long day's work, finds you here, welcomes you and then you kick him in the teeth."

"I didn't do any such thing."

"You told him off in his own house."

"He was belittling Wanda's food."

"Not he. Everybody calls food by other names." He turned to Wanda. "George Bernard Shaw said that old soldiers always carry grub in their packs while young ones carry ammunition. Then there's one by some bloke who wrote a verse about chub, pub and grub. And Shakespeare . . ."

"Don't go on," said Doris, "because you'll never find one that mentions nosh or connor or any of the other common words you people use."

"No, love," replied Green contritely. "But common or commons . . ."

"Have another drink, William," said Wanda, "while we wait for George."

"Who is in high fettle," said Green, rising to help himself at the corner drinks cabinet. When he had replenished his glass, he raised it to Wanda. "He gets about, does George."

"He also gets results," said Doris scathingly. "Which is more than I can say for some people who spend more time talking and eating than achieving."

No reply was necessary from Green, because Masters appeared in the doorway and said, "Seeing you're doing so well with the gin bottle, Bill, you can give me a refill, too."

It was just as well Wanda had prepared a cold supper, for they sat over it for a good two hours while both men reported their respective interviews in great detail.

"Bung-ho Percy," mused Green. "I do remember him—just. But never when we were actually fighting. Only when we were back home here from Italy. We used to parade on a sort of cinder patch outside the battery office in those days. He used to flit in and out...oh, yes! Now I've got him fixed. I had a bit of a run-in with him, I remember. Certain chaps like the quartermaster and battery clerk never did guards, for obvious reasons. But their understrappers got the idea they were excused, too. Guard duties came round quite often enough without all the hangers-on being excused. Besides, blokes like the battery-office staff sat on their backsides miles behind the lines when we were fighting, and then when we came out of action, it was the gun teams that copped all the guard duties. Or that was what they thought should happen. They reckoned their job was to sit in the office with the list and decide who was next for duty. We got the battery sar' major to put a stop to that. Anyhow, one night when I was guard commander, Percy was to be one of the sentries. The inspections at guard mounting were the most thorough we ever had, and a wise guard commander went round his men pretty carefully before the duty sergeant paraded the guard, inspected, called the role and handed over to the orderly officer for his inspection. I looked my lot over that night, and Percy was...well, you could tell he'd never been a practical soldier. He wasn't mucky, but he wasn't spruce, and there were birds' nests in his rifle barrel. If I'd paraded him in that state I'd have been in front of Penn-Northey next morning and been given an extra ten guard duties. So I kicked his backside and told him to go into the nearest billet and beg, borrow or steal a decent set of webbing and a clean rifle—and to be back before I could say his name or he'd be on the highest possible hook available.

"Course, he didn't get back. Fortunately, we always paraded a spare man. The idea behind that was that the smartest bloke on parade was then excused stag—the actual sentry bit—and could have a night's kip. His only duties were to get the guard's meals from the cook-house—supper and breakfast. But I had to report one short on guard parade and that caused trouble because it was the duty sergeant's job—not the guard commander's—to ensure they were all there. So two of us were a bit hot under the battledress collars."

"Actually, the orderly officer acted reasonably. He wasn't prepared to cause trouble for two senior NCO's on account of the likes of Bung-ho Percy."

"What did he do?"

"I think he made Bung-ho parade with the guard every night for a week—fully spitted and polished—just to ensure he got his kit up to scratch. But it wasn't really Percy's fault, you know. He hadn't had his backside kicked, being in the office all day. The battery clerk was a lance-sergeant, but he was a clerk, not an NCO."

"So Pearce had cause to remember you, Bill."

"I suppose he had, but not with affection."

"A thing like that wouldn't rankle after all these years. It can't have done, otherwise he wouldn't have approached you."

"If it was him who wrote the letter," said Doris.

"True," admitted Masters. "We don't know for sure, but he sounds like a very good possibility. And Bill has found out where Frampton lives, so we are keeping the ball rolling. However . . ."

"Now what?" asked Green, taking an apple from the fruit dish and biting into it viciously.

"There's something which is not quite clear in my mind. Miller came to join you for a few weeks at the time of Mareth. He came from another battery."

"Right."

"Pitkin said that Miller had the Stuka drawing at that time."

"Right."

"Pitkin also said that it had been drawn by one of Miller's friends in his original battery. Yet Frampton was in your battery. That means that Pitkin should have known Frampton, yet when we saw him yesterday he knew nothing of the artist, despite the fact that he is reported to have strewn his cartoons about like confetti."

"I was in the same battery, and I didn't remember Frampton," said Green. "George, you really have no idea how isolated the sub units were. A chap could join the other troop in the same battery and you wouldn't meet him for six months. And as I said, the lay-out of the battery in action meant that there was a battery command post somewhere behind the two gun troops, where chaps like Glencross and Wadham worked with their surveyors—like Frampton—and signallers under the nominal control of Jason Burnett. But the administrative headquarters—the battery office vehicle, the mess vehicles, the Q bloke's waggons and so on were all in the B echelon, miles behind the line, under the control of the regimental quartermaster. That's where men like Bung-ho Percy spent their days unless and until we were pulled out of the line for an appreciable period, and that didn't happen often. It did at Tripoli, and it did after Tunis, before we sailed for Salerno. But those were the only times in that last year in the desert. So, like me, Pitkin wouldn't see much of Percy and I can tell you, Pearce hadn't so much going for him that he'd stand out in your memory for forty years."

"I'll accept that, Bill. The best argument of all is that if you, with your prodigious memory, had forgotten him, then there is no wonder that most others had. But Penn-Northey! Pearce was in his office. They must have been in close contact at times."

Green shook his head. "Penn-Northey had an office room separate from the office staff when we were out of action. And he dealt always with either the battery sergeant major or the battery clerk proper, not with the underlings. The battery commander wouldn't have known much about Pearce, not to remember him by. Glencross and Wadham would though, because as soon as we came out of the line their fighting, command post and battery HQ became one. They would then be the officers responsible for people like Pearce."

"I understand that now, I think. But what about Pitkin saying Miller's artist friend was from another battery?"

"He could have made a simple mistake."

"Yes?"

"Or he could have been right."

"Very clear," said Doris. "He was either right or wrong."

"It's true, love. At the time of Mareth, Frampton could have been in Stinky Miller's original battery. Remember Frampton was a Specialist and they weren't all that thick on the ground. The regiment had to balance its resources, and that meant moving people like surveyors around occasionally. Sickness and casualties meant that one battery could be virtually depleted of surveyors whereas another could have a full complement. Matters had to be adjusted. So, though Frampton may not have been with us at Mareth, he could have been by the time we sailed for Italy, because just before then there had naturally been a big sort out."

"Fair enough," said Masters. "Our main jobs now appear to be to interview Frampton and to locate Pearce. I think he won't be able to give us much more than Wadham did." He paused for a moment and looked at Green. "And then there's Miller's death," he said quietly. They waited for him to continue. "Bill, you gave me the distinct impression that you felt Mrs Miller was giving you a true picture and that she genuinely deserves to be taken seriously."

"That's precisely what I believe."

"I will ask you a further question. Do you think his death, if it was not an accident, is in any way connected with the business we are concerned with at the moment?"

"You've answered that yourself," replied Green, taking out a crumpled packet of Kensitas and selecting a cigarette. "You wouldn't have asked the question otherwise. Let us assume that Stinky was murdered. You're not the man to ignore any case of murder we stumble across in the course of investigating another crime whether it is immediately connected with the business in hand or not. You have to know whether it is part of our show or merely fortuitous or circumstantial or whatever. So, if Stinky was murdered we have to look into his death, now, in case it is important to our current project.

"So far so good. But we don't actually know whether

100

Stinky was or was not murdered. That won't be good enough for you. We have to know for sure. If we decide he was, what I have already said applies. If we decide he wasn't..." Green shrugged. "...then we'll have wasted a bit of time on the say-so of Mrs Miller and my misreading of her story. But you won't mind that, because we waste a lot of time in a good many of our cases. It is inevitable. It is part of the job, to go haring after false clues, making futile guesses, and producing faulty theories.

"So we have to investigate Stinky Miller's death. My answer to the question as to whether it is in any way connected with our present project is, yes, if he was murdered, his death is relevant. I, like you, would find it hard to believe that it has just cropped up in the course of our investigations and yet remains totally divorced from what we are about."

Wanda gave a little clap of applause when Green came to the end. "I am sure you are right, William," she said. "Don't you agree, George?"

Her husband nodded. "Bill put it admirably well. But it raises all sorts of snags. How do we investigate a case that the local force has already wrapped up to its own satisfaction? To do it secretly will be almost impossible. Our actions will be bound to cause comment. To do it openly will not only contravene the orders I have been given concerning secrecy but...well, quite frankly, I don't think the South Central Constabulary will let us meddle. Certainly not without a capful of strong facts to back up the request, and even then they would want to do it themselves."

"Which would be no earthly," grunted Green. He sat up straight in his chair. "Look here, George, I went out of our ground today really."

"With the best of reasons," murmured Masters. "You were visiting a bereaved woman. A courtesy call, unconnected with duty."

"Nuts. I went there to see what I could get. And that's what you've got to do. You're worried about her. Want to reassure her by going for a little chat. Nothing more. It's a nice area where she lives, so while you're there you have a look round like any other visitor. If you happen to see something...well, you don't mention it to the local bobbies because they've already dealt satisfactorily with the case and you're not the sort of chap to want to cause them any embarrassment by even suggesting there was something they might have overlooked."

"I know the answer to that one," replied Masters. "It's as short as the one you just gave me."

Green looked across at Wanda. "Any more coffee, love? I've talked so much I'm clammed."

"More coffee for everybody?" asked Wanda, getting to her feet.

"Yes, please."

"As I said, Bill, your argument is specious. However, I'll buy it, because I have no choice. But we can't go down there in strength. You and I must go alone, in one of the ordinary civilian cars, and wearing some sort of leisure gear. Slacks, sweaters and windcheaters. We're out for the day or on holiday or something. I don't want some bright village bobby to see us and suspect anything."

"Fair enough. I know Wanda can't come because of young Michael William, but is there any reason why I shouldn't take my missus down to see my old mate's widow? Doris would make good camouflage."

"Thank you very much."

"You wouldn't mind doing that for George, would you, love?"

"For George, no. For you? I'll give you camouflage."

"I'll gladly accept your offer, Doris," said Masters. "Bill, don't bother to come in first thing tomorrow. I'll pick you up at your place at ten. Before that I'll brief Reed and Berger. They can go to see Frampton. I've noted his address. They may have to hang about till he finishes school at a quarter to four or thereabouts, but Berger knows about your visit to Mrs Miller and Reed was present when I spoke to Wadham, so they can bring each other fully up to date."

"Fair enough."

102

"Coffee," announced Wanda. "Boiling hot." As she poured, she said: "I wish I could be with you three tomorrow. I do so hate being left out of things."

Mrs Miller was very surprised to find Green on her doorstep again the next morning before twelve o'clock.

"You again, Mr Green? I didn't expect to see you so soon, if ever."

Green looked hurt. "I promised you I'd have a word with somebody about things, so I did. Last night. Now I've brought my wife to see you. This is Doris..."

"And I'm Dinah," said Mrs Miller. "Pleased to meet you."

"And this," said Green, "is Detective Chief Superintendent Masters of Scotland Yard, and to prove it he'll show you his identity card."

Masters did as Green had suggested and shook hands with Mrs Miller who, finally, invited them into the house and the regimentally correct sitting room.

"Are you really from Scotland Yard?" she asked Masters. "I mean you really have come to ... well, I don't know what..."

"Don't get worried, dear," said Doris. "Mr Masters really is a very important man, and he's a very clever detective. So just you sit down and hear what he has to say and answer his questions."

Mrs Miller sat and then jumped up again. "Oh," she said, "I should be getting you some coffee."

"Please don't bother, Mrs Miller," said Masters. "But before we begin to talk, have I your solemn promise that you won't talk about this visit to anybody? Not to members of your own family, neighbours, friends, anybody?"

"You see, Dinah, love," said Green, "the DCS shouldn't be here. If the local bobbies were to get wind of his visit there'd be reactions and he would be in serious trouble for trying to help you."

"I won't breathe a word."

"Thank you. Please tell me exactly where on the head your husband was injured."

She put her hand flat on top of her crown. "Right in the middle here."

"Not on the temple, to the side?"

"No. A drop of blood had run down one side, but he hadn't been cut there at all."

"That is clear. Now, tell me how you knew your husband had been hurt on the top of the head."

"He was bald just there. It was as easy to see as if..." She sought for words. "...as if a child in short trousers had fallen and cut its knee."

Masters nodded. "May I see the stone you showed Mr Green yesterday."

"I'll have to get it from the other room."

"Why the insistence of where it hit him?" demanded Green.

"Because blows to the temple may lacerate the artery in the groove in the bone just there. When that happens there may be a short period of unconsciousness, but that is often followed by a period of normal consciousness which our forensic friends call the 'lucid interval' which can last for an hour or more before the return of unconsciousness and eventual death."

"Is that important in some way?" asked Doris.

"Very. You see, Mrs Miller told Bill there was no weapon near the body other than the stone, but even more important, there were no tools nearby, which there would have been had Miller been working there. But this might have been explained if there had been a lucid interval, because he could have put them back on the bench during his period of normality."

Dinah Miller returned and handed Masters the painted stone. Without a word, she took her seat.

Masters weighed it reflectively in one hand. "Is this the size of the one that is supposed to have fallen on him as near as you can judge?"

"Within an ounce," she asserted. "Stinky went to great trouble to get them all the same shape and size." She looked round the room. "You can see what he was like. Everything just so. He told me when he was collecting them—and it took him several days to match them up—that it was a calibration job. I didn't ask him exactly what he meant because I guessed what he meant."

"I can answer that, George," said Green. "Nominally our shells all weighed twenty-five pounds. But, of course, they didn't. They were all weighed at the factory and marked plus one, plus two, minus one, minus two. Plus one meant it was at least four ounces overweight, plus two, eight ounces. Minus one, four ounces underweight and so on. Weight affects the range. Variations didn't matter when we were plastering the enemy, because we wanted to hose them about a bit. But when we were calibrating the guns, getting them all to shoot exactly the same distances with the same ranges on the scales, we had to sort the ammunition. For strict testing, all the rounds had to be the same weight. If we had time, we even weighed them on scales to try to iron out even those four-ounce units. That's what Stinky was doing with his stones."

"Thank you, Bill." Masters turned to Mrs Miller. "The head is a funny thing when it comes to impacts. Blows from blunt objects such as clubs or iron bars will fracture the skull, but it has been known for a blow from a fist to cause injury. So there is no exact way of measuring what will or will not be dangerous. But, in my opinion, unless your husband had a particularly thin and brittle skull, a stone like this, dropping from a height of a foot or so, would do no more damage than cause a bruise or a slight laceration of the scalp. Enough, probably to cause no more than a headache at worst."

"I knew it," said Dinah Miller.

"Please do not take what I have said as absolute fact, Mrs Miller. There are many variations of head injury. For instance, a relatively slight impact such as the one your husband is alleged to have suffered may not cause immediate unconsciousness or any hint of skull fracture, but it can still be dangerous. However, such injuries have very, very slow results. By that I mean they don't produce any symptoms for weeks, maybe months, after the original blow has been suffered.

"Such a course would not have caused me any surprise. But your husband died immediately. This suggests that the blow was—as you have maintained—a more serious one than has been supposed."

Dinah Miller looked him full in the face. "And what are you going to do about it?"

"For the moment, nothing. So far, I have only produced an opinion, not fact. Now I want to get on to something else."

She sat back, ready to answer his questions.

"Was your car in the garage when your husband died?"

"No. It was outside at the kerb."

"Why was that?"

"Because Stinky had been out earlier that morning and he left it out because he knew he'd be working in the garage."

"Good. There is an electric light in the garage?"

"Yes."

"Was it working that morning? The bulb hadn't fused?"

"It was perfect. Stinky made sure of that. Besides, I switched it on when I went in and found him."

"When you went out—left the house to do your shopping—were the garage doors open or shut?"

"Wide open and held back by snecks on the posts. He had to open them to take the car out, and he always left them open if we were in the house and the car wasn't back in."

"Did you positively see them open?"

"Yes. I went out back to tell him I was going off. He had bits and pieces of glasshouse laid out on the lawn and the garage was wide open with the cardboard boxes the bits came in open on the floor."

"Was the light on?"

"No. There was no need for it with the doors wide open on a bright day when he wasn't actually working inside. Stinky wasn't mean, but he wasn't a one to waste electricity."

"Thank you. Now may we go outside and see the garage?"

"If you want."

Mrs Miller unlocked the garage doors. Masters and Green opened them and fastened them back against the stub posts with the hooks and eyes. There was an oldish Morris Minor inside. In impeccable order, the woodwork frame of the bodywork was highly varnished, the paintwork without blemish.

"Do you drive, Mrs Miller?"

"Yes. I learned in the ATS. Do you want it out?"

"No, thank you. I can manage." Masters switched on the light and moved down past the offside of the car. "Is this the shelf?" he asked.

"That's it. The stones are still there."

The shelf barely cleared Masters' head. He stopped to gauge distances and to see what else was stacked there.

"Would a hammer drill jazz the stones, Bill?"

"They're rounded on the faces. Not too stable, I'd have said. They could have moved."

"And the tins of paint?"

"If they're full, they'd be too heavy, but those small things like that carton of rooting powder, they'd have gone for a burton if the stones did."

"Was anything else off this shelf on the floor, Mrs Miller?"

"Nothing. And I haven't touched anything up there since. Not straightened anything, I mean."

Masters nodded and passed on to the front of the car and stopped in front of the work bench. "Have you tidied this?"

"Yes. I put things in the places Stinky had for them. I had to, you see, because a neighbour came in and finished putting up the greenhouse for me. He used the tools, but he wasn't like Stinky. He just left them lying about."

Masters continued to look about him. Then he turned and asked: "What is that, Mrs Miller?" He pointed to a board, over a foot long and six inches wide. The two ends had deep V-cuts. Round the board, using the cuts to prevent slipping, was wound a great mound of strong, discoloured twine. From this main length hung shorter lengths, probably a couple of dozen or so, each ending in a large sea-fishing hook embedded in a wine-bottle cork.

"That's Stinky's layline."

"His layline?"

"And those two metal rods are the anchors."

"What exactly is a layline?"

"For fishing overnight."

"Please explain a little more fully."

"When the tide times were right, that is when the water went out in the early evening, say about five o'clock, Stinky would put his layline down about eighty or a hundred yards out, on the sand left uncovered by the ebb. He'd stretch it out, tying it each end on one of those rods which he then drove into the sand. The hooks are tied on alternately down each side. He used to bait them, stretch them out and then leave the whole thing for the next tide to cover over. Then early next day, at about six in the morning, when the tide had gone down again, he went to pick the line up. And the fish, of course. He caught a lot that way. We never had to buy fish, because he could do it most of the year round except when there was a gale or the tides were all at the wrong times."

"You say he caught a lot of fish that way?"

"Never knew him get less than four or five. Dabs, flounders, sometimes sea bass or codling. If he got too much to use there and then he'd fillet it and put in in the deep freeze. Very useful it was, too, because he liked his fish."

Masters leaned forward to where the line was propped against the wall at the back of the bench and removed one of the protective corks. "Some hook," he said. "You could take a whale with that."

"Hardly," replied Mrs Miller, "but the little things were no use. Not big enough to hold the bait secure. Use them and the crabs could just nick the worms off every one before the fish could get a sniff. Stinky tried them. Besides, the eyes on the little ones are so small you can't get a line stronger than button thread through them. A good, strong fish could break away as easy as kiss your hand. Stinky didn't like the idea of them swimming off with hooks in. He thought it was cruel, because they wouldn't be able to feed properly."

"I see. Did the crabs ever manage to take the bait off these big hooks?"

"Always. Off some, that is. Three or four every lay, perhaps, but there's two and a half-dozen hooks on the line, so that didn't matter much." She turned to the other wall of the garage. "That's his fish bass, hanging up, next to his bait fork. He used to dig for worms you know, out on the wet sand."

Masters only gave the indicated items a cursory glance. He continued to look at the tools still on the bench and in the wall racks. The others stood quietly by as he peered and weighed in his hand a hammer, a spanner and a very large screwdriver, with a big round knob of a handle, which he held by the blade as if testing its suitability as a cosh. Then he picked up the layline from where it stood upright, at the back of the bench, leaning against the wall.

"What's this?" he asked Mrs Miller quietly.

"I'm sure I can't tell you. I've never seen it before."

Green leaned forward to peek at the object. It was a circular slab of lead, three inches in diameter and an inch thick. Protruding from the top was a wire loop, looking like a half-driven staple. To this was knotted an inch or two of double nylon line.

"Blob," said Green. "Blob for the end of a sea-fishing line. Not for a sea rod. You'd never be able to cast with a weight like that. For a line you'd drop over the side of a boat anchored offshore. Bigger version of the things on those little lines they sell to kids at the seaside. You must know the things, George. A little wooden frame with a few yards of orange cord, a hook and a sinker. They catch crabs and seaweed with them usually. This is a more workmanlike job. Home-made, of course. I expect Stinky chopped up a bit of old lead piping and put it in a tin lid on the gas ring. When it had melted he took it off the heat and stuck a loop of wire in the middle, then when it had set he knocked it out of the tin. I've made similar things myself scores of times."

"When?" demanded Doris. "I've never known you do it."

"When I was a kid," replied her husband. "We used to make our own lines then. Couldn't afford to buy them."

Masters said to Mrs Miller. "You say you've never seen it before. Does that mean that Stinky didn't go line fishing from a boat."

"Not to my knowledge, he didn't. He hadn't a boat, and I don't think he knew anybody who had. There's certainly no boats down on our bit of beach, but I have seen sailing dinghies being got ready there. People bring them down and put the masts up and the sails and things before pushing them into the water. But not often. I've seen one about three times. Stinky said they probably belonged to a sailing club a few miles along the coast, and instead of towing the boats there they'd sail them along, in good weather."

"That seems very clear, Mrs Miller. But if your husband didn't do any line fishing, why should he have this sinker?"

"I honestly don't know. I expect he found it on the beach and brought it home."

Masters nodded his appreciation of so likely an explanation for the presence of the sinker, and put it back behind the lay line.

"Were you thinking of it as a weapon?" Mrs Miller asked. "The thing they hit him with."

"Not really. Of course, swung on a piece of cord it would make a deadly weapon. But if somebody did use something other than the stone to club your husband with, they would have taken it with them and not left it here to be found and tested. It's mere presence here would give the lie to what they sought to achieve. Nobody would accept that the death was an accident if the weight that killed Stinky was later found hidden away behind the layline. No, I think we can rule it out as a possible weapon."

Masters turned, and they all filed out of the garage. He

switched off the light, and as they were locking the doors he asked: "On the morning he died, Stinky had been out earlier. Where had he been?"

"To pick up his layline."

"He brought home some fish?"

"Quite a lot. A couple of quite big plaice among them."

"He used the car to get to the shore?"

"Yes. There's one of the private roads runs down that way. It just peters out above the line of stones, but there's room enough to turn there."

"He could get past the barrier quite easily?"

"Yes. It just lifts. We have the right of way, being residents. Besides, there was a lot to carry. There was the line, a tin of bait, the fish bass, a pair of gum boots and probably the fork."

"But when you went out round the village you didn't take the car?"

"Sometimes I did, sometimes I didn't. If I was just dittering about the village and going somewhere for a cup of coffee I walked—when it was nice, that is. It's not far if you use the little lanes."

She ushered them indoors once more.

"It's gone one o'clock," she said. "Let me get you something to eat and drink."

"Please don't bother," said Masters. "We've got to be on our way. I've been very interested in all you've told me and what Mr Green told me of his talk with you. I can't promise anything will come of it, but I shall certainly be doing something more about it. Everything depends on your keeping quiet about our meeting, Mrs Miller. If one word about it gets out, we shall be stopped from proceeding."

"You can trust me, sir. Stinky was my one and only and we had the best part of forty years together. I want the one who stopped us making that fifty."

Doris Green said: "You can trust the chief superintendent to do anything that can be done. And my old man, too."

After driving only a few miles, Masters pulled in at a pub. "I imagine we can all do with a drink and a sandwich."

"Just the jobbo," said Green, rubbing his hands. "I've got a thirst I wouldn't sell for fifty quid on a Saturday night."

"Bill!"

"What's up, love?"

"The way you put things."

"Sorry, love, but you both know what I mean and that is the art of good communication which all the buffs say is so important these days." He stood aside to let his wife go before him into the pub. "What's it to be?"

When they were settled with drinks and a plate of sandwiches, Green said: "You weren't very talkative in the car, George."

"He was driving," said Doris. "Keeping his mind on the job."

"Keeping his mind on the job, maybe," grunted her husband, through a mouthful of food. "But I know George. He's been having thoughts."

"About Mrs Miller?" asked Doris.

Masters smiled. "Actually, it was about the case, but not exclusively about Stinky and his missus."

"Out with it," said Green. "Some earth-shattering thought that nobody else has considered."

"I don't know about earth-shattering, but we certainly haven't considered one very important aspect of this case."

"Oh, yes? What's that?"

"Bung-ho Percy or T. A. Lamief said in the original letter that a very senior police officer was consorting with, and was even dominated by, a couple of murdering crooks. What we have not asked ourselves is what is the nature of the business in which they were co-operating?"

"There's blackmail, for sure," replied Green. "Our senior colleague just daren't report that murder."

"Why? Because he was there and party to it?"

"Partly. But he was only present because he had to be, I suspect. Our information is that he didn't play a major

112

part, so he obviously wasn't the instigator. Which means he was there under threat of some sort. Which in turn means that he had been guilty of some pretty illegal practices which gave the crooks a hold over him."

"Good. So he's guilty of illegal practices. What sort of practices?"

"Being a cop, it could be turning a blind eye to some sort of villainy..."

"For money?"

"What else?"

"Corruption, in fact?"

"Corruption, perversion of justice, leaking information about police activities. There's any number of illegal things he might have participated in."

"Which means he was privy to what Dringle and Swabey were up to."

"And guilty by association, you mean?"

"Not quite. What, I should like you to tell me, were our two villains up to, that they needed and could afford to have police cooperation?"

"Their racket, you mean?"

"Yes."

"I don't know."

"Just like that?"

Green shrugged. "It could be anything from hijacking lorries to kidnapping for all I know. In fact it could be an average cross-section of all types of villainy."

"You mean they weren't fussy what sort of crime they committed as long as it paid off?"

"Why not? According to records they'd tried their hands at any number of things, and most of them had come off or, at least, they weren't sent down for them."

Masters didn't reply. He lifted the plate and offered Doris another sandwich. As she took one and thanked him, Green said: "You see it differently, I suppose, George?"

"Yes, Bill, I do. I'll tell you why. According to our records, they have dropped out of sight for a period of several years. That is what you discovered, isn't it?"

"Yes."

113

"So, if we were, at one time, continually running up against them and we are no longer doing so, it must be for one of only two reasons. The first that they have reformed their ways and are going straight. The second, that they have moved outside our area."

"The likes of Dringle and Swabey are pathological villains. They could never go straight. They could never be non-violent. And, unless we've been wasting our time this last day or two, we are pretty sure Bung-ho Percy's letter confirms they are still operating."

"Agreed. They are still operating. But not in the smoke where their usual pickings are, but in an area where they have a senior police officer sewn up. They carry on in his area only, and they are not picked up like they used to be. But, Bill, if they were to move out from under his protection, into any other area to do a few jobs, it is almost certain their activities would draw police attention. They'd have been picked up just as they were in the old days, even though they may have continued to get off in court."

"So you reckon they are operating solely within the one police area."

"That's my theory."

"But there wouldn't be enough pickings in just one area. I mean even a senior jack can't hide the fact if every big house in his manor is burgled. Or if lorries are only hijacked as soon as the main roads cross his boundary. He'd have to produce some results to keep his job or else explain his failure pretty convincingly."

"Quite, Bill. And that is an important point. A rapacious pair of pathological crooks would soon become known in the area, despite police protection, if they were involved in any sort of villainy based on theft of any sort—burglary, hijacking, kidnapping, turkey gobbling, cattle rustling or Christmas-tree lopping."

"Why?" asked Doris. "All those things go on in London—probably not stealing live turkeys and Christmas trees, but I've heard about meat stores being raided. So if it goes on in London, it could go on elsewhere, partic-

114

ularly in big towns and cities."

"Very true," replied Masters. "But for Dringle and Swabey to need police protection means they are operating in a big way. Yet they are not working a highly populated district."

"You don't really know where they are operating, do you, George? Isn't that one of the things you are trying to find out?"

"Don't take him on at his own game, love," cautioned Green.

"I'm not taking him on."

"Doris is quite right, actually, Bill. I've been guilty of jumping the gun. Because in their profile of T. A. Lamief the sergeants said that hedgerows built up on dykes were a feature of the south and south-west of England, and because Mr Lamief was taking his pictures near water over which he would have to look southeast or south and because Lamief was near enough to London to travel there twice in quick succession to post letters and because all our other contacts in the case seem to have been in the southern part of the country, I had jumped to the hasty conclusion that we were going to find Lamief somewhere along this south coast."

"Oh yes," said Green sceptically. "You don't jump to hasty conclusions, George. You get fanciful ideas which lead you into theorizing in all manner of ways, but you never reach conclusions till you're sure. That means you know something we don't."

Masters shrugged. "As I said a minute or two ago, Bill, I don't think Dringle and Swabey can be engaged in concentrated crime that involves actually lifting material possessions from their rightful owners—not just in one police area. It would certainly get known. But two chaps like that wouldn't move out from under the protective wing of a corrupt senior officer once they had suborned him. Neither, according to you, are they capable of curbing their criminal activities. So how are they earning their living?"

"I'll get us all another drink," said Green. "You two can

115

carry on talking among yourselves."

"You didn't answer George's question, Bill."

"I don't have to, love. He's got all the answers."

When he returned with the drinks, his wife again tackled Green. "George may know what you meant, but I don't. Not without you telling me straight out."

"He's been going on about Dringle and Swabey not thieving things."

"I heard that. What I didn't hear was your answer about what they actually are doing."

"If they're not nicking things and they're not clever enough to run computer fiddles or big frauds, which they aren't, then they're probably using the sea."

"What for?"

"Smuggling, love. It pays off a treat, but you don't rob anybody, except the customs people. George realized this was a possibility, so he located them near the sea."

"Was that his hasty conclusion?"

"Yes, love."

Doris picked up her drink. "It sounds a very likely answer to me. Logical, I mean."

Reed and Berger reached Oriel soon after half-past two in the afternoon. They left the car in a public car park and set off on foot to find Withy Lane. After several enquiries, mostly of people who claimed to be strangers in the district, they saw the public library.

"Street map in there," said Berger. "Let's go and look it up, because short of asking a local cop I don't think we shall find Withy Lane. And the Chief told us to steer clear of the local force at any price."

"Even to the tune of not asking them the way?"

"I suppose he thinks even a beat bobby would be able to recognize us as cops. Sort of ESP, I suppose. Anyhow, I'm not prepared to do what he's expressly told us not to do."

"Not on your flippin'," agreed Reed. "We can see the local voting register in there, too. It might be as well to see if Frampton really does live at number four and whether he has his missus living with him."

"According to Bill Green he had at the time of Miller's funeral."

They took their time about it, and so it was nearly half-past three by the time they were knocking on the cottage door. There was no response, but the woman next door came out to tell them that Mrs Frampton would not be home until half-past five and if they were selling anything they needn't bother to try it on with her because she didn't buy from people who came selling at doors.

"Actually," said Reed mildly, "it was Mr Frampton we came to see."

"Double glazing is it?"

"If I were to tell you, you'd be as wise as I am."

"He'll be here about four o'clock," she snapped and retreated into her cottage.

"You're getting as bad as old Bill Green," accused Berger as they strolled away.

"She's a nosey old bag. I had to choke her off or tell her some downright lie, and I couldn't think of a plausible one at the time."

"I know. I was praying you wouldn't say yes when she asked if you were selling double glazing, because as like as not she'd say Frampton had got it and then we'd have been scuppered for the next call."

"If she pops out again," aid Reed, "I'll tell her we're making plans to demolish the cottages to make way for a supermarket. That should replace her curiosity with indignation."

Berger laughed. "If she heard a titbit like that you'd not need a demolition squad. What she'd have to say would bring the whole lot tumbling down round our ears."

"Okay," replied Reed, "I'll just say we're house agents, come to offer Mr Frampton eighty thousand for his cottage."

Berger laughed again. "You seem determined to send her mad somehow. If not with anger, than with greed." He looked up. "I suggest we stop here for a fag. The old dear can't see us from her window, but I can see Framp-

117

ton's front gate. We'll know when he arrives."

He arrived just as four o'clock was sounding from a nearby church. A VW Beetle drove past them and up to Frampton's front gate.

"Here we go," said Reed. "Ah! His neighbour has come out to warn him we called."

"The old so and so is pointing to us. Yes. He's coming to meet us."

"Good afternoon. I understand you called at my house half an hour ago."

"Mr David Frampton?" asked Reed.

"Yes."

"We're police officers, Mr Frampton. No, I won't show you my identity card just now, because your neighbour is still taking a great interest in us, and I'd rather she didn't know anything about the reason we've called on you."

"What is the reason?"

"Actually it is nothing that concerns you directly, Mr Frampton."

"Oh, Lord! Don't tell me Gary Smith has been sending rude drawings to the mayor again."

"Nothing at all like that. Actually it concerns a man who served in the same battery as you in the war. We're trying to find out his name and to locate him."

"That's a pretty tall order, after forty years."

"It's a pretty tall story, too, Mr Frampton. Do you think we might go along to your house and talk indoors?"

"Of course. Come along."

As soon as the door was shut behind them, both sergeants produced their identity cards.

"Metropolitan Police, Scotland Yard?" asked Frampton. "That's a bit high-flown, isn't it?"

"If we could explain..." began Reed.

"Sure. Sit down. I'm all agog."

They sat.

"When you were in the army," said Reed, "there was a sergeant, called Green."

"Thick-set chap?"

"Yes."

"Bill Green?"

"That's right. C sub sergeant."

"What about him?"

"He is a detective chief inspector at the Yard."

"One of your bosses, eh? It's just as well I didn't say anything nasty about him."

"We like him well enough."

"So did we. A dour chap, but sort of reliable. We could do with a few more like him about these days."

"DCI Green got a letter at the Yard a day or two back. From a chap who knows he's a policeman and reckons he served in the same battery in the war."

"Now you come to mention it, I knew Bill Green was a copper before he got called up."

"But you haven't written to him?"

"That's a funny question. You've got the letter. You should know who wrote it."

"Bill Green's correspondent didn't sign his letter. But he did send him a wartime drawing—a sketch of the bridge at Scafati. You are an artist, Mr Frampton."

Frampton laughed. "Thanks for the compliment. I used to think at one time that I could be an artist." He shook his head. "Dreams fade. I am an art teacher, capable of sketching a bit and drawing third-rate cartoons." He scratched an ear. "The bridge at Scafati, you said? That seems to ring a bell."

"It should do, sir. You drew it."

"I've no doubt I did, if it's a wartime sketch and has come from someone in the old battery. But I'm trying to remember the occasion—the reason why I drew the bridge at Scafati."

"The caption you put on it was: 'A hit, a very palpable hit.'"

"How very quotatious of me."

"Come again, sir."

"Sorry. In-joke. At the school. The Head of English referred to one of her new male assistants as quotatious after reading something he'd done. Like the old lady who

119

loved seeing *Hamlet* on the stage but found it rather too full of quotations."

"Have you remembered the Scafati sketch yet, sir?" asked Berger.

"Frankly, no. Not entirely that is. But at the back of my mind . . . wasn't it something to do with a lucky shot? A sort of one in a million chance?"

Berger nodded. "That's the one. Colonel Penn-Northey—Major as he was then—was on this little pack bridge in his tank when Bill Green landed a round on the parapet."

"Got it," said Frampton. "A momentarily noteworthy event I deemed worthy of illustrating at the time." He laughed. "I suppose it was a dreadfully immature effort."

"Not at all," replied Berger. "We looked at it carefully and at the Christmas card you drew. We admired them."

"Nice of you to say so."

Reed brought the conversation back to the matter in hand. "Can you remember to whom you gave that sketch, Mr Frampton?"

"Oh, Lor! Now you're asking! Any one of a score of people, I suppose."

"Your friends in the battery command post, perhaps?"

"Almost certainly one of them."

"Or the battery office personnel."

"Unlikely. The office was usually so far back that . . . wait! Wait one moment."

Reed and Berger sat silent as the schoolmaster's brain ticked backwards to bring memory into focus. Then—

"We were in the Salerno bridgehead at the time. It was too small an area for anybody to be miles behind the lines. We were hugger-mugger till that day when we broke out. The battery office, the mess trucks and Q wagons were all cheek by jowl with the command post. There was no room to get the usual dispersal of vehicles as protection against air attack. Fortunately the RAF were managing to fly Spitfires off a grass runway to protect us." He looked up. "Yes, I could have given that sketch to a chap in battery HQ. In fact, I think I did."

"You remember his name, sir?"

"I could be leading you astray."

"Never mind that, sir."

"A chap called Pearce."

"Christian name, sir?"

"I think it was Stanley. I don't really know for certain, because everybody called him Bung-ho Percy, because of the way he spoke and the rather old-fashioned expressions he used."

"Was he a friend of yours, sir?"

"As a matter of fact, he was, in a sort of way. You see I'd been with the regiment for some time, but in a different battery. Then I was posted to this other battery a few weeks before we sailed from Tripoli for Salerno. I went over to my new battery with my kit and had to report to the battery office. Pearce was on duty. We got talking, and after I'd seen the sergeant major, Pearce showed me where to kip. It was in his bivvy. Orders had gone out that we were all to sleep in bivvies with mosquito-netted ends. Two men to a tent. Formerly we'd always slept in the open, but mosquitoes had started being troublesome round Tripoli and they were expected to be even worse in Italy. So we slept in bivvies and had to take those ghastly anti-malaria pills—Atabrin and Mepacrin.

"Anyhow, I kipped with Pearce. Battery HQ and the command post were all together in any case. We got on quite well. I think he'd felt a bit isolated before I joined him because, quite frankly, he didn't speak the same language as the other men. He was an only child of elderly parents, I think, and he hadn't been allowed to get about much before he was called up. I suppose my chatter was the nearest to anything he heard that he could really understand. He was a bit flowery, you know, but I must confess I found his conversation a pleasant change from what usually passed for conversation among the lads."

"I can understand that, sir," said Reed wryly. "The one-adjective boys. Strictly limited vocabulary."

121

"Quite."

"And you think you gave that particular sketch to Mr Pearce."

"I can't be sure that I did, but he used to like them. I got the impression that he regarded them as the nearest thing to culture he could get at the time. He always asked for them if he was about when I ripped them off."

"That seems fair enough, sir. Now, you wouldn't know where he lives, would you?"

"Before I answer that, can I know what the trouble is?"

"Not in detail, I'm afraid, sir. And I must ask you not to talk about our visit, or even the fact that we are policemen. Suggest that we came to try to sell you some insurance."

"I'll respect your confidence."

"I'm sure you will. Briefly, then, Bill Green's correspondent witnessed a serious crime. Furthermore, from where he was hiding, he heard a couple of names mentioned. Some sixth sense must have warned him to be very cagey about anything he said or did, so he wrote to Bill Green who he knew was at the Yard—he'd seen him briefly in a programme on telly. But he didn't sign the letter, in case it didn't reach Bill Green for some reason, and he'd mentioned the names of the criminals. So DCI Green was faced with the problem of finding the chap who wrote the letter. Not only to sort out the alleged crime, but because he knew the letter-writer really was in great danger. The two names he had mentioned were those of a couple of the nastiest criminals at large. Our first priority, then, is to find and protect the writer. But not one word of what we are doing must get out or his life will be in even more danger."

"And the drawing? Where does that come in?"

"We think he sent it to authenticate his story, sir. We've taken his letter—a fairly long, flowery, and very circumstantial one—word by word, and discovered a few clues to help us. We've spoken to a lot of people. Penn-Northey, Lewis Pitkin . . .

122

"I remember him."

"Jason Burnett, Philip Wadham, Mrs Miller whom you know, I believe, and now you, among a lot of others. We had got as far as learning that Mr. Pearce was a possible, because Mr Wadham, I think it was, remembered that he was a bit pedantic. But nobody has been able to tell us where Pearce lives. So if you can help us, Mr Frampton...?"

"I can certainly tell you where he lived and worked four...no, five...years ago."

"And where was that?"

"Chinemouth. You know what that's like. One of the biggest seaside resorts with a town centre full of shops and theatres and gardens and crowds."

"Only about thirty miles west of where Mrs Miller lives," said Berger quietly.

"That's right. My missus and I went to Chinemouth for a fortnight. We enjoyed ourselves—sitting on the pier and a show of some sort to go to each night, even if it was only the ice-follies or the swimming spectacular, so called, on some nights. But was it hot! About eighty every day. So I used to run about in old slacks, sandals, a depressed-looking bush shirt and an even worse depressed Panama hat. I know I looked a disreputable old duck, but I felt even more so one lunchtime when we were in the town centre, wandering around looking at expensive jewellery and clothes, when a very smartly dressed gent in immaculate office suit, a beautifully ironed white linen hat and shoes shining to glory stopped me and said: 'Excuse me, but are you Mr David Frampton?' I knew immediately by the plummy voice and his eyes—he had a cast in his right eye, which his glasses did nothing to hide— that it was Pearce. We only had a couple of minutes' conversation, because he was out and about on business and in a hurry. But our talk was just long enough for him to tell me that he lived and worked in the town. Something to do with insurance. I think he said he was a broker, but I can't be sure."

"Thank you," said Reed. "Somebody told us he was either in a bank or in insurance in the old days. It is nice to have it confirmed. You don't happen to know his full address, by any chance?"

Frampton shook his head. "We didn't arrange to meet or anything like that. I'm surprised he stopped to talk at all when I looked such a tramp. Funny, isn't it, how you can be friends at sometime and then, if you meet many years later, there's none of the old spark left? We met for a couple of minutes and I don't think either of us wanted to prolong the meeting or to renew our acquaintanceship over a drink or anything like that."

"It happens," agreed Reed, getting to his feet. "Thank you, Mr Frampton. You've been a great help. You've cleared up several points for us, and our bosses will be duly grateful."

"Pleasure. Can I offer you something before you go?"

"No, thank you, sir. We'll be off before Mrs Frampton gets back, and that will save you a few explanations. Besides, we've got to get back to London."

"I'll drop you both off at home if that's all right," said Masters.

"It's only three o'clock." said Green.

"I realize that, Bill, but I hope you'll come over for a conference tonight. Both of you. We might as well chat at my place as in the office."

"We'll be living at your house soon," said Doris.

"I'm sorry about asking you to come across this evening, but I have a feeling that we should push on with all speed. And before we can talk with any great confidence, we must know what the sergeants have learned from David Frampton. We shan't know that until probably half-past six, which means we can't do a proper job now. So put your feet up for a couple of hours, Bill, and then come over."

"I didn't mean I wanted to be left out," said Doris. "I want to come. But won't Wanda mind?"

"Not you two, she won't. You know she regards you both as members of the family."

"You're on," said Green. "On the understanding that as soon as I get in I can ring Wanda and tell her we'll have fish an' chips for supper and I'll go out for them. There's that nice shop not a lock of perches away . . ."

"Bill, you can't tell Wanda she's going to have fish and chips. She may not want them."

"I can try."

"It's a good idea, actually," said Masters, "because I would really like the sergeants to be present, too, so that we can go over everything quite thoroughly."

"Can I tell Wanda that?"

"Yes, please, Bill. And get round when you can, though I may not make it with Reed and Berger till seven."

"I'll give her a full run-down," said Green, "and tell her to fill the vinegar bottle."

"Bill!"

Masters laughed and brought the car to a halt outside the Greens' semi.

"Tea, George?" asked Doris.

"No, thank you. I've one or two things to do."

Doris went up to the door. Green stayed behind to ask quietly: "Going to make a few enquiries of the Drug and Narcotics brigade?"

"I think it would be as well, don't you? And I thought about asking how the illegal immigration trade is prospering."

Green shrugged. "Might as well. There's no mileage in watches since the chip came in and nothing in brandy either since this duty-free lark became common."

Masters drew away and made for the Yard.

Ten minutes after he arrived in his office, Chief Inspector Hebditch knocked and entered. He carried a heavy compartmentalized file which he plonked on the desk.

"We don't often get you asking about drug trafficking, sir. Have you got something which could do us a bit of good?"

"Sit down," invited Masters. He was filling his pipe from a brassy tin of Warlock Flake, and took his time before continuing.

"Actually, Hugh, I want to pick your brains rather than give you information. At the moment I am on a funny sort of case."

"Murder, as usual, I suppose, sir?"

"We think so. Not proved yet, of course. We're only just getting to grips with it. But we have a whisper that two heavies who used to operate round here in the smoke, but have, of late, dropped out..."

"Names, sir, please," said Hebditch reaching for his file.

"Dringle and Swabey. But I don't think we've ever connected them with drugs."

"No mention," conceded Hebditch, disappointedly.

"Not to worry. As I said, we've heard nothing about them round here for years. But we reckon we've now relocated them in the South Central Counties area."

Hebditch waited for Masters to continue.

"We think they are connected with continuous villainy down there. By that, I mean they're not the types to do a job and then lie low. We think they're always up to something. But the point is, they're not doing a lot of blagging. There's nothing to show that our two stalwarts are pillaging country houses or anything of that sort."

"I'm with you, sir. You're wondering what they are doing for bread."

"That's it. If they're not robbing people, houses, banks or conducting a protection racket, what are they doing?"

"And you thought that because South Central Counties area includes a good long stretch of coastline, they were fetching in something across the beaches pretty frequently?"

"Could be fetching stuff in. Not were."

"I knew it," said Hebditch.

"Knew what, Hugh?"

"Well, sir, even if you are not in touch with us very often in your line of business, you must read in the papers how most of our hauls of the hard stuff are at major

126

airports and seaports. You know, the usual stories. Customs seizes three million pounds' worth of heroin concealed in a consignment of figs at Liverpool, or three pounds of the stuff in the false bottom of a suitcase at Heathrow."

Masters nodded.

"I don't have to tell you, sir, that no matter how much we grab in that way, we're not getting upsides with the problem."

Masters nodded again.

"There's a lot gets through the air and seaports that we don't catch. Passengers will conceal it anywhere, and how are the customs lads to know that the busty blonde going through is really as flat-chested as Wee Willie Winky without her falsies overstuffed with uncut hashish? You can't ask everybody to strip to the bare buff, can you?"

Masters shook his head in agreement.

"But I'll say this for those lads, their presence there, and the fear of detection by them, is a real deterrent, simply because they—and we—do have our successes. So though those routes are not entirely closed to them, the people who ship it in are always on the look-out for easier, less dangerous routes.

"The point is, thank heaven, there aren't a lot of methods open to them, but there is plenty of space. I'm referring to coastline, sir. The British Isles have a lot of it, and those boyos know that it is relatively easy to come ashore unseen. Most people pooh-pooh that idea because of coastguards and the like. But there aren't all that many coastguards nowadays, and you've only got to remember that our lads could land unseen in Europe every night of the year even though the whole of the German army was on guard to see they didn't, to say nothing of mines, barbed wire, searchlights and radar."

"You are telling me that drugs can easily be brought in this way?"

"Are being brought in, sir," corrected Hebditch. "I've known it for a long time."

"Through the South Central area's coastline?"

"I couldn't pinpoint it as being there, exactly, sir. I just know it has been coming in. In a sort of organized way, if you take my meaning."

"Please explain."

"When you get to know it, you can sense there's a sort of pulse about the drug scene. If the market is only being served with irregular—or even regular—big supplies, there comes a time, just before each new delivery, when there's an actual shortage or the signs of approaching shortage in case the next big consignment doesn't get through. It's just like ordinary life, sir. Let housewives hear a whisper that there's going to be a sugar shortage and most of them are out, lick for laddie, combing the shops for sugar they neither need nor want, and if they didn't hoard it, there'd never be a shortage.

"Much the same goes on in the drug world, sir. But of late, that pulse has been missing, even when we've intercepted huge packets of the stuff. The big lots are still coming in. The fact that we stop them occasionally proves that. But I reckon there's been a steady extra trickle coming in."

"There's an excess of supply over demand?"

"No, sir. The big boys don't like that. It could depress the market price. No, just enough to iron out the pulse. A steady extra trickle, as I said. And a steady supply, no matter how big or how little, takes organization."

"I get your point. Picking it up at an arranged time, at an arranged place, bringing it in at the arranged spot for pick up, arranged dispersal, arranged disposal and so on?"

"That's it, sir. In amounts just large enough to make it well worthwhile, but not big enough to clog the market. And it could come in anywhere from the northern isles to the south coast, wherever there's a convenient beach. In fact, I had supposed it did come in at widely differing spots."

"By night, presumably?"

"Not necessarily, sir. Let me give you an example. Say you bring a boat from France to Cowes, where there's

128

always hundreds of them sailing in and out from everywhere. You sail in and declare you've 'come foreign'. The customs inspect you and you're clean. You don't tell them you've met a Cowes boat fifteen miles out and done a transfer of goods. The Cowes boat sails back in after a jolly good day's cruising, but she hadn't 'come foreign' so she's not inspected. And getting a few pounds of extra baggage across in the car from the Isle of Wight is no sweat, because there's no customs inspection between there and the mainland. All done in broad daylight, sir. It would look a fishy business if done by night."

"I see. Thank you, Hugh."

"You're not going to give me anything else, sir?"

"I am— when I've got it. But please don't start anything until I give you the word, otherwise you'll blow everything sky high. And, Hugh . . ."

"Yes, sir?"

"Forget we've ever had this conversation. Every word of it. Until I get in touch with you again, that is."

"When is that likely to be, sir?"

"Within a week, I'd say. But I'll repeat what I've just said. Don't even go looking up those two names in records or on a VDU. Not a word to your colleagues."

"It sounds important, sir."

"It is. Outside my team and the AC Crime, you're the only chap who knows anything about it. The implication of that should be obvious to you."

"It is, sir."

"Now, if you'd care to stay for a few more minutes, I'll have some tea sent up. Can you spare the time?"

"I reckon I can just about manage to squeeze enough time to drink a cup of tea, sir."

Masters lifted the internal phone.

It was ten-past six when Reed and Berger reported to Masters' office.

"Didn't know whether you'd still be here, Chief, but we thought we'd better look in before we phoned you at home."

129

"I'm glad you did. Now, give me the briefest of brief summaries. Then I want you to push off home if you want to freshen up, and try to make it back to my place by seven-thirty for fish and chips and a full review of the case. Use the car and bring it round with you so that you can take the DCI and Mrs Green home when we've finished."

"Well, Chief," said Reed, "we can give you the answers in two sentences. Frampton is almost a hundred per cent sure he gave the drawing to Pearce, who made quite a collection of them."

"Good."

"And five years ago, Pearce was living and working in Chinemouth. He was an insurance broker."

"Five years ago? Not now?"

"No reason why he shouldn't still be there, Chief. That was the last time Frampton ran into him."

"I see."

"Chinemouth is the sort of place scads of people retire to, Chief, so there's no reason to suppose Bung-ho Percy has moved out now he's finished work."

"And we ought to be able to trace an insurance broker, Chief," said Reed. "Even if he is retired, his firm could still be going. And if it isn't, every other broker in the place will have known of him."

"I beg your pardon? Oh, yes, quite. He'll be easy enough to find, I've no doubt. I was just wondering how far Chinemouth is from Caldenham village."

"Funny you should wonder about that, Chief. We mentioned the same thing. The distance is just over thirty miles. Thirty-three, actually, by road."

"Thank you. Is that it?"

"That's it, Chief."

"In that case, off you go."

— 6 —

The two teams reported to each other over the fish and chips. Masters insisted on great detail at such sessions so that everybody should be as well informed as everybody else.

When both sides had finished, Reed said: "The fact that Pearce lives at Chinemouth seemed to give you great satisfaction this afternoon, Chief, and that the distance between there and Caldenham is only thirty miles also seemed to please you."

Wanda and Doris Green had, so far, stayed out of the conversation, as though they recognized that this was a working review. But now Wanda asked: "Why should the fact that Pearce lives at Chinemouth cheer you any more than it would were he to live in Blackpool? Apart from the fact that it is nearer to home?"

"Nearer to Caldenham," said Doris.

"What's that got to do with it? Oh, I know you three went there today to see Mrs Miller who is convinced her husband did not die naturally. But this case—Bill's case, if you like—concerns Mr Pearce and goings on, presumably, in Chinemouth. Mr Miller has been dead some time. Mr Pearce's man died only last week. They are two separate incidents. The only thing linking them is that the two men served together forty years ago. Now one is dead and one isn't. So why should the fact that Chinemouth and Caldenham are thirty miles apart please George?"

Doris spread her hands to show she disowned all knowledge as to why Masters was pleased by this geographical proximity; she merely knew he was.

Wanda looked round at the men, other than her husband, seated at her supper table. "Doesn't any one of you want to know the answer?"

"We all know the Chief," said Berger to Wanda. "You better than any of us. He gets funny ideas. It's what the Germans call having a sixth finger."

"And the rest of you just blindly accept whatever funny ideas he gets?"

"Apart from him being our boss, yes. Though blindly accept is not the way I'd put it. Experience has taught us to respect his ideas. The DCI calls him jammy. He declared a few weeks ago that you fed the Chief exclusively on Tickler's Plum and Apple, whatever that is."

"Last week it was William Percy Hartley's Golden Plum," said Reed. "Not that I've ever come across either of them. But the point, although the DCI never points it out, is that in order to get jammy—on your face or your fingers—you have first to be able to nose out the jampot."

"I am being fobbed off," said Wanda. "William, can't you help me?"

"I think I can love. I think probably the sergeants misled you slightly. What I mean is, that George is delighted at finding—or at the prospect of finding—old Bung-ho Percy in Chinemouth. For a number of reasons. Some of them quite minor ones, such as the fact that there is a frequent and fast train service between there and here, so the problem of how letters could be posted in London disappears. But there are bigger reasons for George to be happy about Chinemouth. For one thing, it is a large town and houses the headquarters of the South Central police. So Bung-ho's claim about a senior cop being involved could be quite valid. And for another thing, George hasn't yet told us how he spent the latter half of the afternoon. But I happen to know that he is at least half convinced that Dringle and Swabey are drug trafficking. Not smuggling through airports or seaports, but across open beaches. So to have a seaside resort, as it were, confirmed as the home of Pearce and, presumably, the centre of operations of the two villains, with the added presence of senior coppers of whom at least one could be corrupt, appears to suggest to George that it is all coming together nicely. Hence his pleasure at the news the lads brought him at tea time today."

Reed and Berger added nothing. Wanda seemed satisfied with this lengthy, if less than convincing, explanation. Masters entered the fray to say that Green was right about the drug trafficking, and went on to recount his afternoon's conversation with Hebditch.

"So where are we?" asked Green when Masters had finished.

"We are at the point where we can go and confront Pearce and get the complete story out of him," replied Masters. "He has to show us the scene of the incident and then I suppose we have to do some illicit digging ourselves to discover if a body is actually there."

"Then what?"

"He must contrive to identify the police officer he saw."

"And then?"

"The whole shooting match goes in absolute secrecy to the AC Crime."

"Who will," said Reed, "as likely as not, hand it straight back to you, Chief."

"No," said Masters. "He will have to get on to the local Chief Constable. Don't forget there are two distinct operations here. My orders are to establish whether the crime described in the letter actually took place. That is the first phase. The second—the actual investigation of any crime—is the duty of the Chief Constable of South Central. The AC Crime has no power to hand it over to us or anybody else."

"But..." began Doris. "But surely it should be your job, George. To complete the whole case, I mean. Nobody would think of handing it over to anybody else."

"I'm afraid they would, Doris. Local forces have a fierce pride in their ability to cope and in their statutory right to be responsible for the handling of crime within their areas. It depends upon the character of the Chief Constable of course. But should we discover a body and Anderson has to ring the CC at Chinemouth, what do you think the reaction is going to be? How will the news be received?"

Green answered for his wife. "I hate to think what it will be, George. First off, the local CC will get all high an' mightly because Anderson set us on to make sure there had been a crime in his area. He'll maintain the information should have been passed to him at the outset so that he could have had the pleasure of what we've been doing for the past few days."

"If he could have done it," murmured Reed.

Green continued. "Then there'll be the psychological shock of hearing that one of his senior officers is alleged to be a crook. Nobody likes hearing news like that, nor do they like the prospect of a full-blooded investigation of their own force."

"And that's only for starters," murmured Berger. "There's the fact that there's been organized drug trafficking going on in his area for yonks without him knowing anything about it. I'll bet any CC would love to hear a titbit like that."

"Right, lad," continued Green. "So when he gets all this good news from Anderson, we can't count on the CC feeling all that matey towards the Yard. His instinct will be to tell us to take a running jump at ourselves and leave him to sort out his own midden."

"Is that really right, what Bill says?" asked Doris.

"It's the way of the world, I'm afraid. Like the old custom of cutting off the heads of bearers of bad news. But as I said, it depends upon the character of the Chinemouth CC. He could be the sort to face the fact that with alleged corruption in his own upper echelons, he would be wise to say nothing to anybody else and ask us to carry on in secret. Or he could be almost the opposite type. One who is so crushed by the news that he wants to hand it over to somebody else at any price. In which case we could again be asked to carry on."

"So what are the chances of your seeing it through, George?" asked Wanda. "About evens?"

"About that, I'd say, poppet."

"So, just in case you are asked to carry on, have you a plan?"

"Plans depend on events."

"I realize that. But after the guilty senior officer has been identified, shouldn't he be taken out of circulation immediately so that he can't contact Dringle and Swabey? And I don't just mean suspended from active duty."

"I certainly think he should be detained for immediate questioning."

"When?" asked Green. "What's the timetable for tomorrow?"

"We'll go down to Chinemouth first thing in the morning. We'll use a civvy car, not the Rover. I want to be inconspicuous."

"Two hours' run, Chief. Two and a half in the rush period," said Reed.

"Set off at seven. Arrive soon after nine when everywhere is open so that we can start to locate Pearce. With luck, we should have found him by eleven and have the location of the grave by lunchtime."

"We can't dig in broad daylight," objected Green. "Not if we're to keep it secret."

"We'll use the afternoon for identifying the guilty copper. After dinner we'll start to dig—by dark. If we're successful we get on to Anderson."

"Disturb him while he's having his nightcap?"

"Why not?"

"I like it. Then what?"

"I suppose we shall have to stand by until he's done his diplomatic bit with the Chief Constable. He may do it there and then, no matter what the time."

"In which case, what do we do?"

"Wait for Anderson to ring us back. If the CC doesn't want us, we go to bed and return next day. If the CC does want us to carry on, we go to see him and immediately thereafter take up the senior officer Pearce identified for us earlier."

"All in the middle of the night?"

135

"If needs be."

"I knew it," said Green. "No sleep."

"We shall book in at a hotel tomorrow morning, Bill. You can have a siesta in the afternoon while we're identifying the naughty bobby. It won't take all of us to do that job."

Green grimaced. "Seven in the morning, you said?"

"It'll be a quarter past by the time we get to you."

"In that case, it's time we weren't here."

"He needs his beauty sleep, you see," said Doris. "If he misses it he gets bags under his eyes and his complexion suffers terribly. Goes all muddy."

Green got to his feet in silence. Then he said: "If you make any more cracks like that, love, I'll tell them about that hair net you sleep in and the nice new plastic bowl you've bought for your teeth. The one with the bunnies on."

"We're well up to time, Chief," said Berger. "The last sign said thirteen miles to go and its not quite ten to nine. There's just one thing. Chinemouth is a big place. There's about five roads into it."

"A car park in the town centre is what we need to begin with, I think."

"In that case, Chief..." Berger consulted the road map again. "If we leave the dual carriageway just short of the town, there's a smaller road which leads right up on to the cliff front on the eastern side. That's where all the decent hotels are. They've all got big car parks. We could use one of those. Book in, too, while we're there. Then it's just a step downhill into the shopping centre and not far from the business blocks."

"If you know the way," replied Masters, "we'll leave it to you. You know what we want, basically. In detail, we shall each do the following jobs.

"Bill, we shall need a street map of the town. Estate agents will usually provide one..."

"The best place, Chief, is the publicity centre run by

the council. It's a wooden shop place, near the entrance to the public gardens. The brochure has a pull-out in the back. It's a street map of Chinemouth and Ponde."

"Yes, Ponde," exclaimed Reed. "I'd forgotten Ponde."

"What about it?" demanded Green.

"Ponde is a town in its own right. But it's joined on to the west of Chinemouth. A conurbation."

"Like Brighton and Hove?"

"Something of the sort. Ponde has a big bay, almost enclosed. There's a chain ferry across the mouth and then the road leads on to Gossage. It's a big area we've got to play with, Chief."

Masters turned to Green. "See what you can do, Bill." He addressed the sergeants. "I'd like you two to spot what insurance houses you can, preferably brokers. Go in and ask if they know where you can find Pearce—Mr Stanley Pearce. I shall go to the town hall to inspect the electoral roll. If I have no luck there I'll go to the public library. I'll consult the telephone directory there—there won't be any in booths, I suspect. I'll get the address and number if Pearce is listed. In that way we ought to learn what we want to know and even have it confirmed in pretty quick time. Is there a good, central spot for us to meet up, Berger?"

"Yes, Chief. The entrance to the public gardens. The DCI will be quite close and the rest of us not far away."

"Thank you. Meet up as a matter of haste please. Once you've got something, that is."

"Left at the next junction," warned Berger.

"George," said Green. "Yesterday you said you thought we should waste no time. That's why you called last night's meeting. Now you're at it again. Haste, speed, hurry. What's got into you?"

"Stirrings, Bill."

"Stirrings?"

"Mental stirrings. Call them a quickening of the grey matter if you like. Urging me on."

"You're uneasy?"

"Slightly. Not in a panic exactly, but I don't set off on jobs at seven in the morning unless something is goading me on."

"But you don't know what it is that's bugging you?"

"Actually, I do. Or think I do. A couple of nights ago when I went to bed, I studied the copy of Pearce's letter again. Something you once told me years ago came into my head."

"Blaming me are you?"

"Not seriously. Who could blame anybody for anything on a perfect spring morning like this, especially as this road is so much quieter and prettier than the one we've just left. Do you realize we haven't seen another car for several minutes?"

"No you don't," said Green.

"Don't what?"

"Get out of telling me what's bugging you by trying to divert us with a lot of hogwash about the scenery."

"Oh, sorry! Years ago, when we were investigating the deaths of five women that a madman had buried in the form of a cross, to help us discover them, you did a bit of survey work to tell us where to dig."

"I remember."

"You were very successful. While you were doing it you told me that when you brought guns into action day by day, you put them down with a gap of about fifty yards between them. But when you put them into positions at night, even though you counted the paces to get the distances correct, when daylight came the guns were always much closer together than they should have been."

"Right. It's very difficult to judge distances in the dark."

"You said the same applied to time. Particularly if you were alone in what was perhaps a dangerous situation."

"Correct. A minute could seem like an hour, and every bush and every shadow was a Jerry."

"Pearce was in a panic that night, I suspect. He said he waited a long time, listening for a car to start up. Now sound travels a long way on clear moonlit nights."

"True. What are you getting at, George?"

138

"I have been worried lest he should have been too impetuous. Did he really wait long enough? Or did he stumble away over the fields making enough noise to waken the dead?"

"To warn the three villains is what you really mean. You think they realized they'd been spotted and are looking for Pearce."

Masters nodded.

"And we've got to get to him first."

"That's about the strength of it, Bill."

"It hadn't struck me that way, but I'll respect your feelings. Anyway, we should reach him in the next hour or two."

"Panda car ahead," said Reed. "Chief, I think there's been an accident. There's a body in the road."

"Pull up to see if we can help the constable," ordered Masters. "Go across and offer, Berger, but don't reveal your identity."

"Right, Chief."

Reed drew in short of the scene of the accident, on the other side of the road. Berger got out and trotted over. In a very few seconds he was back again.

"How is he?"

"Bad, Chief. There's an ambulance on its way. But there's something else. I think the DCI should come and have a look."

"Why?"

"He's a man about sixty-five, Chief. There's a smashed camera in the road and a pair of binoculars round his neck."

"Go on."

"His spectacles are off and smashed."

"And?"

"He's got a very noticeable cast in his right eye."

Green was out of the car and lumbering across the road almost before Berger had finished speaking. He knelt beside the body opposite the constable who was holding the man's arm, applying pressure to the artery.

"Nothing you can do, sir," said the constable.

139

The words seemed to rouse the injured man. He opened his eyes and peered upwards at the DCI's face above him. For a moment there was nothing, and then weakly he murmured: "Sergeant Green."

The eyes closed. What little life there had been left seemed to slip from the body, like water thrown on to a shiny surface seems to withdraw. It was almost visible.

"That's it," said the constable, lowering the arm. "You knew him, sir?"

Green nodded.

"He called you Sergeant Green."

"Yes. We were in the same unit in the army during the war."

"Can I have his name and address, sir, please?"

"Name is Stanley Pearce. I never knew his address, except that he lived in Chinemouth. I think he was an insurance broker there." He rose to his feet. "We weren't pals, you see. In fact I hadn't seen him for years."

"Thank you, sir. I've got that. Could I have your name and address?"

Green gave the details, referring to himself simply as William Green, with no mention of rank.

"What happened?" demanded Green.

"Hit and run, sir. Had to be. I came along from the town and found him, just before you arrived."

"Which way was the bastard going?" demanded Green.

"Away from the town."

"We haven't passed a car since we left the main road some miles back."

"He'd have gone down a turning, sir. There's several a bit further on."

Green nodded. "I think I hear your ambulance. Is there anything else I can do?"

"No, sir, thank you. We'll have to trace his wife and family. It should be easy enough."

"Nothing in his pockets with his address on?"

"Only this, sir." The constable produced a sheet of paper. "It looks like a list of birds."

Green looked at it. "I seem to remember he was a bird

140

watcher. Used to photograph them."

"Yes, sir. His wallet just has money in it. No identity."

Green shrugged and moved to the grass verge as the ambulance pulled up. He stood silently by while the body was put on the stretcher and loaded. Then he crossed slowly to rejoin his colleagues.

"Pearce?" asked Masters quietly.

"Yes. It was old Bung-ho. And I saw the writing on a list of birds from his pocket."

"The same?"

"The same hand. And the same flowery stuff. Every ordinary bird's name had its Latin name alongside it."

"Hit and run?"

"Going towards the main road. The constable said it could have turned down a side road."

"Get in, Bill."

"Where are we going?"

"To Chinemouth."

Green stared at him.

"We must get to know where he lived, Bill. And get the map. But that's all. We'll be going back to London after that. The game has changed, so we must change our tactics."

Reed started up and they moved off towards the town.

"You foresaw this, George."

"That he was in danger, yes. As I told you a few minutes ago."

"The hit and run?"

"Too coincidental to be anything but intended, Bill. I feel sorry for Pearce, but at any rate his death confirms that there's something seriously wrong down here. He started the hunt. We've got to finish it."

Green nodded. "We'll get the bastards. Old Bung-ho was as inoffensive a man as one could hope to meet."

About an hour later they met at the entrance to the floral gardens. Green had selected a bench in the sun. By means best known to himself he had managed to keep it free of other people, so that all four could sit down and be able to talk without fear of being overheard.

141

Reed was reporting. "I saw the GPO, Chief, so I thought I'd have a glance at the yellow pages. His company is still going strong even though he's retired. Pearce and Watson. I got the address and went to find it. Guess where it was."

"You seem quite excited about its location," said Masters. "That means it is relevant to the case. Which in turn means that it solves something, confirms something or explains something." He thought for a moment. "I suspect Pearce didn't live above the shop, because the address I have for him is The Limes, Worcester Avenue. That doesn't sound as if it could be in the middle of the business area. So, the office is close to something of importance or somebody of importance . . . I'll guess that it is so situated that out of his office window he can see the entrance to the main HQ police station and consequently can see the comings and goings of all the top brass in the division. This explains how he could be so sure that one of the men he saw that night was a senior police officer. He saw the man every day, but probably didn't know his name."

Reed laughed. "I ought to know better than to play guessing games with you, Chief. Remind me never to come to one of your son's birthday parties if you're going to be there yourself."

"It's a useful discovery," said Masters. "Somebody—it may have been me—raised the point of how many of our citizens would ever recognize a local police bigwig, and wondered how much store we could set by Pearce's claim to know the identity of one in Chinemouth." He turned to Berger. "What did you manage to discover?"

"I got his address from the phone book, Chief. The same as the one you got. Then I had a thought."

"What about?"

"I wondered why Pearce should be three or four miles out of town, on foot, at nine in the morning. Remember we saw a bus going out that way, later. It occurred to me that probably he'd gone out on an earlier one."

"Please go on."

"Then I wondered if perhaps he hadn't a car. Was a

142

non-driver because of his eyes or something."

"A good thought. What did you do?"

"I got his firm's phone number from the yellow pages. I rang them and said I had a Volvo, the same year and capacity as Mr Pearce's and he had suggested that if I were to ring them and mention his name they'd be able to give me a better price for third party, fire and theft than I'd got at the moment."

"What did he say?"

"Quite a bit, actually, Chief. But the only bit that concerns us is that far from having a big Volvo, Mr Pearce has never had anything on four wheels in his life. I rang off when I'd got that info, Chief. But I reckon it means that his activities would be confined to a strictly limited area."

"Got it," said Green decisively. "As the battery clerk's assistant, Pearce was the despatch rider. That means he rode a motor bike. Quite a powerful one. A BSA 500 if my memory serves me. Not in the desert, of course. Nobody could ride a bike there. But bikes were issued for various people before we went to Italy. Despatch riders were among them."

"Thank you, Bill. When we get back to the Yard, Berger, check with the Swansea computer to see if there was a motor cycle licensed in his name."

"Right, sir."

"What about you, Bill?"

"I got a couple of maps from the holiday enquiry centre. And I had a look at the model they've got in there."

"A layout of the town?"

"Yes. In relief. You can see at a glance that the east of the town is hilly and has cliffs. The west, running into Ponde, is low, and so is the other side of the ferry. And there's a point to consider there, George. Where all the front of Chinemouth runs east and west, the direction changes beyond Ponde harbour. The coastline down to Gossage is almost north and south. So if Bung-ho pointed his camera almost east that night, there's a chance he was the other side of the ferry."

"Out of Chinemouth altogether, in fact?"

"Yes."

"We'll remember that point, Bill. Thank you for raising it. Now, for my part, I looked up Pearce's home address in the phone book, and then went to consult the electoral register. I wanted to know if there is a Mrs Pearce or indeed any children living at home. I assumed that any children Pearce might have had would by now have been of voting age. There is no other Pearce other than Mr Stanley Pearce registered at that address. No wife and no kids. There is, however, at the same address, and listed above Pearce, because her name begins with B, a Mrs Mary K. Brunton. She is the only other person registered there."

"Can't be his widowed sister," grunted Green, "because Bung-ho was an only child. Could be a cousin, I suppose, or simply a living-in housekeeper, unless, of course, the house is divided into flats."

"I think we ought to look into that," said Masters. "Not today. The police will have been round there by now, to tell her the news. But tomorrow ...Bill, as he recognized you, and that young constable probably told Mrs Brunton that he mentioned your name just before dying ..."

"I know," said Green resignedly. "I have a very good excuse for calling at the house to offer my condolences and to suss out the situation. She may even be expecting me to call—the man to whom the last dying words were said."

"Sorry, Bill, but it does seem ..."

"Don't apologize, George. None of the rest of you has any reason to call at the house. I have, and I was the one who knew him."

They were on the way back to London before noon.

"You said we would have to change our tactics, George," said Green, who still appeared depressed. "That sounds to me as though you know what you intend to do."

"I think we should talk matters over now."

"Before we begin, Chief," said Berger. "Can we know

144

why we are returning to the Yard, only to come down again tomorrow if the DCI is going to call on Mrs Brunton."

"Somebody's moved the goalposts, lad," said Green. "We've got to go and tell the team manager and sort out a new playing formation to cope with the new situation."

"The DCI's got it absolutely right," said Masters. "I shall now have to report to the AC Crime and get his blessing on how we go about things from now on. Our original objective, remember, was to find the author of the letter and then to learn two things from him. The site of the grave and the identity of the police officer he saw with Dringle and Swabey. Having got that information we were supposed surreptitiously to open the grave and discover whether it did, in fact, contain the body of a murdered man. If we had got that far, the matter would then have been reported to Mr Anderson so that he could make the necessary diplomatic moves between us and South Central. After those had been completed, we could have been asked to hand the investigation over to the locals, or we could have been asked to take it on as an overt murder enquiry."

"I think we all understood that, Chief."

"Then why ask why we are going back, lad?" grunted Green. "We found out who wrote the latter. But he's dead. So he can't tell us where to look for the grave or who the bent copper is. In other words, we can't complete the first phase, and that means we've no facts with which to start the second."

"So it's all over. Is that what you're saying?"

"No, lad. But the first plan has gone wrong. So we've got to have another one. Not an easy matter when we've still got to work in great secrecy on other people's ground."

"That's the state of play," agreed Masters, "and it could be that, without the firm evidence Pearce could have supplied, the AC will decide to call it off."

"But?" queried Green.

"Although the inclination to do so may be there—after all, we are only investigating on the flimsy premise of an anonymous letter, if one looks at it in cold blood—the death of Pearce may convince him that we ought to carry on."

"The AC will take your word for that, will he, Chief?"

"That and a few more things will, I hope, convince him."

"Such as?" demanded Green.

"Our agreed belief that drugs are coming ashore in this area, backed up by Hugh Hebditch's conviction that an organized trickle is entering the country by a route other than air and seaports."

Green grimaced. "No really hard facts there, George. Not enough to swing a decision."

"What about if we could, as near as dammit, prove it?"

Green stared at him. After a pause, he said: "You've got something, otherwise you'd never had made a remark like that."

Masters took out his pipe and tin of Warlock Flake. "Stop at a suitable hostlery, when you see one, Reed. The DCI is going to buy me a drink."

"I am?" demanded Green. "What for?"

"As recompense for what I'm just about to ask you to consider."

"We're listening."

"Stinky Miller was murdered."

"Is that it? I had that idea myself."

"You mean you don't want to hear what I think were the why's and wherefore's?"

Green settled back and lit a cigarette. "Let's hear it," he grunted.

"My belief is this—and it explains why I was so pleased to hear that Chinemouth lies only about thirty miles from Caldenham. I think Dringle and Swabey import their goods over any flat, open beach where a motorized inflatable can be brought ashore and where there is a convenient road running down to that shore so that the craft can be either deflated and stowed or shoved on to a roof rack, with the engine in the boot or hatchback.

146

"When I say any beach, I mean any suitable beach within the South Central area and usually within thirty or forty miles of Chinemouth."

"Why?" demanded Green.

"Because I think that the inflatable always sets out from the Chinemouth area. A perfectly normal thing. People get used to seeing it go off, that's if anybody bothers to note it, because there are always hundreds of sailing dinghies, powerboats, inflatables and the like sculling around the resort. But it doesn't return to Chinemouth with its goods. The car goes by road to pick it up at the pre-arranged spot. And that spot is always an open beach, served by a road and within the cruising distance of the inflatable—that is, within thirty or forty miles. The car waits, in view from the inflatable as it approaches land ..."

"Probably with some form of signal, Chief," said Berger. "Show a red flag or something if they want it to hold off."

"Could be. Or headlights. But that is a detail which needn't worry us at the moment."

"Caldenham was one of their beaches?" asked Green.

"I think so. There are so many suitable spots round here that I suspect they never needed to use any one of them more than once or twice a year. In that way they wouldn't attract too much attention or give the idea that there was a regular business."

"They were hot on security. They had a police brass hat in their pockets, they dispersed their landings, they had the car to give warnings and so on. But there was one more precaution they felt they had to take. And that was to have a drill for ditching the drugs should the need arise."

"All they'd have to do is shove it overboard."

"In essence, yes, Bill. But with powerful glasses it is easy to see people going through the motions of throwing parcels overboard. We've often seen reports to that effect."

Green grunted his assent.

"Furthermore, parcels don't always sink when you want

147

them to. A couple of pounds of white powder carefully wrapped in great thicknesses of paper all enclosed in a waterproof plastic packing could bob about on the surface for a long time. And it could be picked up by the wrong people."

"So they had to weight the parcels," said Green.

"Just so. But I also think that though they had to be prepared to ditch the stuff, they also had hopes that should they have to do so, they might be able to retrieve it. The tide round here ebbs a great distance. If they ditched something a couple of hundred yards out, it could be left high and dry on the next ebb tide. But that is speculation."

"Isn't it all?" asked Green innocently.

"Hear me out and then decide. I think our friends had their drugs handed over to them in relatively small, sausage-shaped, waterproof packages."

"By a craft out at sea, Chief?"

"Yes. Each package was attached by a length of strong nylon string—probably a yard long—to a large lead sinker." Masters turned to Green. "Stinky's blob, in fact."

Green nodded without speaking.

"The inflatable then set off for shore with the sinkers inside, on the floor of the craft, the strings going over the rounded sides, and the sausages submerged under water. In other words they towed them in, and all that needed to happen should they be forced to ditch was that the sinkers had to be slid surreptitiously over the side. They'd go down, unnoticed by any watchers, taking the drugs with them."

"But they didn't reckon on Stinky's layline," said Green. "Is that it?"

"That's exactly it. They came in, trailing their sausages when there was still a foot or two of water over the line. The crabs had stolen the bait from some of the hooks, and one of them caught in a package. Before the man or men in the craft knew what was happening, the sinker whipped overboard and sank. They would know the area roughly, but it is awfully difficult to know exactly where

148

something has sunk. However, they weren't worried. They'd made provision for this sort of thing and the tide was on the ebb. All they had to do was stow the dinghy and engine and the rest of the drugs and drive away from the scene, leaving one man concealed somewhere, ready to go out and pick up the sausage as soon as it was left high and dry by the ebb."

"No danger there," agreed Green. "There's always stuff being cast up on beaches. People are always picking things up. Even if anybody saw him it wouldn't cause comment."

"Quite. But to the watcher's dismay, a car comes down the road and stops there. Out gets Stinky. The layline hasn't been uncovered yet. There's still six inches of water over it. But that doesn't worry Stinky, because he has gum boots in the car and he knows exactly where his line is. He can recover it from six inches of water. This he proceeds to do. He finds not only fish on his hooks, but a sausage-shaped parcel attached to a big sinker. He doesn't stop to examine it. He puts it into the fish bass with the fish and returns to the car."

"All of which has been seen by the watcher, Chief?"

"So I believe. The watcher returns to his mates who are parked somewhere close by. They decide they have to retrieve their property. Stinky's car is an easy one to trace. They quarter the village and find it parked outside the house.

"Stinky has said nothing of his find to his wife. There's no reason why he should have done. He probably picked up something on the beach almost every time he went there, so it was no great event.

"He goes indoors and has breakfast. Then out he goes again to the garage to finish putting up his greenhouse. I don't think the villains had located him before that time, otherwise they might have gone into the garage and picked up the sausage."

"You're sure it was there, Chief?"

"Almost positive. The garage was open, remember, because Miller had taken the car out, and he was in the

149

habit of leaving the doors stapled back. I can't think that he would take a wet and smelly layline into the house. He'd dump all his stuff on the bench before going indoors. The parcel of drugs would be there, but he would have taken the fish in to be cooked or frozen."

"Fair enough," agreed Green.

"So Stinky goes to the garage to put the corks on his line and generally clear up—he was that sort of man. There is his find. He handles it and thinks it is of no value to him, but the lead sinker might come in handy some time. So he cuts the string and puts the sinker at the back of the bench, leaving the sausage just lying there. Then he tidies up his line on its board and he puts that away at the back of the bench, hiding the sinker. The villains have now located him, but they can't do much because Mrs Miller is about. They wait until she has said goodbye to Stinky and then they move in. I make no guesses as to what was said, but one of them bashed him on top of the head. Right on top. You can draw your own conclusions as to what they used to get the impact right in the centre of the crown."

"Hammer maybe," said Reed. "Their own. They'd come armed with it."

"Very likely. Then one of them has the bright idea of using one of those stones to give him another blow in exactly the same place—probably when he was already on the ground. Then they leave the stone by the body, with blood traces on it and so suggesting that it had fallen on to his head, cracked his skull and killed him. They seize the sausage off the bench, not noticing the sinker wasn't there, unlatch the doors and close them and make off."

"Leaving Mrs Miller to find Stinky and the local police to make a dog's dinner of the investigation," said Green bitterly.

"That's how I see it," said Masters. "Is it worth...?"

"A drink? Yes."

"Worth putting up to Anderson was what I was going to ask you."

"You don't have to ask, George. You may be—probably are—miles out in the details, but the essence of the thing is right. It fits. Anderson will buy it every time."

"In which case he will ask us to carry on. And then we shall have a job on our hands. We shall have to find the grave."

"Nice-looking pub coming up, Chief."

"How very convenient. I'm looking forward to my drink."

Green and Masters were with Anderson.

The AC Crime heard them out and then sat silent for a moment or two. Then he said to Green: "You used the expression, a can of worms, to describe conditions down there. I'd call it a pit of snakes." He then turned to Masters. "Are you absolutely convinced that this chap Pearce was deliberately murdered this morning?"

"I firmly believe he was killed deliberately, sir. Absolutely convinced? I should need firm evidence to go quite so far as that."

"And Miller?"

"The same, sir, though I think I have a deal of evidence in his case, and I have been told by our forensic people that a blow from a smooth stone weighing a pound and falling only a foot or so would be unlikely even to break the skin of the scalp. The height from which it would have to fall to cause a depressed fracture of the skull would be many times that distance."

Anderson nodded his agreement and then asked: "How do you intend to proceed now?"

"You are authorizing me to go ahead, sir?"

"I don't like multiple murders and I don't like bent cops being involved in them. Particularly senior ones. The commissioner has given his unconditional approval for this investigation, so I'm now telling you to carry on. But the need for secrecy grows greater, George. Three men killed already. On no account must there be more, and certainly not because of us."

"I'm going to search for the grave, sir. The sergeants—

at Bill Green's instigation—are trying to buy several composite maps of the area."

"Scale?"

"One over twenty-five thousand, sir," said Green. "They show every hedgerow. But we're also getting copies of the six inches to one mile. They show every tree and bush."

"You're going to comb the area?"

"Pearce's letter gave us some clues as to how to proceed," said Masters, "but it is still a big job."

"Very big, George. Will you manage it?"

"If we could have the services of two policewomen who won't mind posing as outdoor types, sir."

"Hikers? That sort?"

"Exactly that sort, sir."

"How long for?"

"Several days at least, I'd have said, sir."

"To stay down in Chinemouth?"

Masters nodded.

"In that case they'd better be unmarried. Anything about looks?"

"They are to pose as the girl friends of Reed and Berger. One will be masquerading as Bill Green's daughter."

The AC grinned. "In that case, Bill Green can pick 'em."

"I'd rather they were nominated, sir. If Bill has several up for inspection it might start speculation among those not picked."

"Leave it to me. They'll report to your office at four. I shall tell them nothing. You brief them and stress the security angle."

"Thank you, sir."

"Anything else?"

"I don't think I need bother you any further, sir. We're going off in three cars as holiday parties. Women and all."

"Right. Good luck, and keep me informed, George."

Reed and Berger were showing Masters and Green the maps. Masters, not as familiar with the products of the Ordnance Survey as Green, was enthusing over the detail

152

that the sheets gave him.

"They're not maps, Bill, they're plans."

"The big ones are. They're for business purposes, really, not for finding your way along a motorway."

A timid knock at the door.

"Cover them." ordered Masters, and waited till the maps were rolled before inviting the caller to enter.

Two callers, in uniform.

"WPC Clegg, sir," said the blonde.

"WPC Tippen, sir," said the brunette.

"First names, please."

"Muriel," said the blonde.

"Irene," said the brunette.

"From this moment on," said Masters, "you will be known exclusively by your first names. So, Muriel and Irene, have you any idea at all why you are here?"

"No, sir," said Muriel. "We were told to come here by Commander Smith, and not to tell anybody we were reporting to you."

"Commander Smith said you may want us for a special job for several days, sir," said Irene.

"Right," said Masters. "Now to start with, Muriel and Irene, you are not to address any of the four officers in this room as sir during the coming operation. Is that understood?"

Both girls nodded. Masters said: "Have a seat or perch on the desk if you like, because everything from now on is going to be very informal. It has to be that way, because you two are going to be part of a holiday party going to the seaside for a few days."

The two faces lit up. "That sounds marvellous...er marvellous."

"To work," said Green.

"Yes."

Masters turned to Green. "Which will pose as your daughter, Bill?"

"It had better be the brunette," said Green.

"Good. Irene, you will refer to Mr Green as dad and nothing but dad from this moment on. Sergeant Berger will be Tom. He is your boy friend. All clear?"

"Yes, Mr Masters."

"Good. Muriel, you will be Sergeant Reed's girl friend and you will call him Paul."

"Yes, Mr Masters."

"The assignment starts from this moment. Paul has arranged an unmarked car for you, Muriel. You will take it when you leave here and drop Irene at her home. Then you will go home. You will both pack cases for a week at the seaside."

"Excuse me, Mr Masters. We both live in the WPCs' quarters behind Oxford Street."

"So much the better. You have no families to explain matters to, and as for social engagements...well, please plead unexpected duties, but make no mention of going away."

"Cancel them for tonight?"

"I'm afraid so. To get back to where we were. You will go to your quarters and pack. You will be masquerading as hikers. That means strong shoes and country clothes of one sort or another, at any rate for daytime. You can of course pack what you like for the evenings.

"You will do that immediately you leave here. By half-past six, you will report to my house. Paul will give you instructions as to how to get there when you leave to get the car.

"At my house you will be briefed. You'll also get a bite of supper, too. But it will be a long session and please wear casual clothes. And talking about casual clothes, don't pack any items of uniform to take to the seaside except your identity cards.

"Tomorrow morning, early, we shall be starting the job proper. I stress that you will not talk to anybody about anything I have said. Is that clear?"

"Yes," said both girls together.

"Now, money. Don't worry your heads about hotel bills. They will be taken care of for you. Tomorrow morning you will each be given a float of a hundred pounds to

154

cover incidental expenses. That money has already been drawn and so you need not approach the finance office for any reason to do with this project. Your overtime will be signed in at the pay office in the normal way at the end of the month. Nobody will know what the overtime was for." He paused for a moment and than asked: "Any questions, Muriel?"

"No, Mr Masters."

"Irene?"

"No, Mr Masters. Not questions. But you...and Mr Green and Paul and Tom...are one of the big murder squads. Are we going to help to investigate a murder?"

Masters smiled. Green said: "It could be quite exciting, love. Your old dad will tell you all about it tonight."

Irene smiled back. "Thanks, dad," she said pertly, and swung herself to the floor. Muriel said: "We're looking forward to working with you awfully, Mr Masters."

"Thank you, Muriel."

"We seem to live here these days, love," said Green to Wanda.

"It's very nice to have you and Doris at any time, William. And at the moment it is a bit special. George was telling me he just daren't hold a briefing meeting at the Yard. Not one involving Doris and me, that is. There'd be all sorts of speculation and he says he must avoid that at all costs."

"True, love, true. And he's running up to form. Had some good ideas as usual."

"I'm pleased to hear it. Doris is in the kitchen if you'd like to see her. She's cut a mountain of sandwiches and while I was putting Michael to bed she cooked enough sausages for eighty, not eight."

"That's what I like to hear."

"Help yourself to a drink. It's all laid out on the dining table as we shall be having a stand-up fork supper."

"Do you mind if I push the booze all to one end of the table, love. I shall want it for spreading maps on."

155

"Of course, William. Do as you like. George didn't tell me..."

"The maps are my department, love. Up to me to ask you for the space to show them."

"I love you, William Green," she said, and much to his surprise and delight, kissed him on the cheek.

"What's all this?" demanded Masters, coming downstairs after his bedtime visit to his son. "And him with a brand-new daughter!"

"I'm longing to meet her, William."

"Any minute now, love. Those two lasses are so scared of George here they'll ring your bell as Big Ben strikes half-past. And I'd watch him if I were you. Some of those bits of capurtle at the Yard think he's the cat's miaow."

"You mean I've got competition?"

"Not you, love. Nobody gets into the final with you. But the old preliminary-round winner might fancy her chances."

"Scurrilous," said Masters. "That's what it is. But I'm pleased to hear him running on like that."

"Why?" asked Wanda. "Does it pander to your vanity?"

"Well..."

"Well what?"

Masters grinned. "It shows Bill is back in form. He was a bit down earlier in the day."

"Oh? Why was that, William?"

"You'll hear all in good time, love. Now I'll go and get that drink."

"Get me one while you're at it, Bill. I'm going to be here by the door, waiting for..."

A ring at the bell interrupted him.

"...the girls," he said, and opened the door. As he did so, Big Ben struck in the distance.

Berger introduced Irene to Doris, her new mother, and insisted that Doris should refer to him as Tom, her prospective son-in-law. It was all very jolly for a few minutes, then Masters asked them all to crowd into the tiny sitting room where the sergeants and the two girls had to sit on the floor.

"Muriel and Irene know nothing of our present operation," he said. "Doris and Wanda are not up to date with today's events. In order that they should all be fully in the picture I am going to give the whole business another airing. This will be the second time today for Bill and myself and I'm sure the rest of you who have been in from the beginning will be a little bored with it by now, so I'll make it as brief as possible without cutting corners."

He spoke for rather longer than twenty minutes and finished by saying that Anderson had told him to push ahead in secrecy. Then he invited questions. They came thick and fast from the four women. He and Green answered them exhaustively. At last the examination came to an end.

"It's about eight o'clock now. We'll break for supper and a drink and then continue later."

"Now I know why you were depressed, William. I feel very sorry about poor Mr Pearce. I realize he was not exactly a friend of yours, but he had called on you and, in doing so, had done the right and proper thing."

"I know, love. But if only he'd told us who he was he could have still been alive."

Wanda left him to see to her guests. She needn't have worried overmuch. The two girls were offering the food around and were doing famously. Masters was pleased to see it. His team was rapidly welding into an homogeneous whole.

He called for order after a half-hour's break.

"We are operating in secrecy in other people's territory," he began. "That means we must not only show no signs of being a police team, we must show positive signs of not being a police team. To this end we are travelling to Chinemouth as three distinct holiday parties, and we will act as such. Mr and Mrs Green will have their daughter and her boy friend with them, all in one car—the one we used today. Muriel and Paul will go down as a courting couple in a second car. Wanda and I with Michael will be in a third car. We shall all stay in the same hotel and we will get to know each other slightly when we are there. Enough to have a drink together of an evening. Nothing more than that. Just sufficient, in fact, to pass brief orders and information.

"Each pair will have a portable radio. It will be carried out of sight, but easily get-attable, in the pocket of a rucksack or in a bogus camera bag. It will not be switched on if other people could be within hearing distance were a transmission to come over."

"We have to keep switching on and off, Mr Masters?"

"If you pass groups of people, even single persons, you will switch off. You will not just press the send switch to prevent your set from receiving. That would kill the air-way for everybody else. You keep your set at receive when out of earshot of others, and you maintain radio silence except in an emergency. And by emergency I refer to warnings of danger or announcements of success only.

"Mr Green will be control. Tomorrow he will be one hundred. I shall be one, Paul will be two and Tom three. The three outstations will keep their numbers throughout, while control will change daily. As the county cricket games have started by now, tomorrow our call sign will be Middlesex. So, if control wishes to call me—and I am code sign one, remember—he will say: 'Middlesex one hundred for one'. My only reply to that will be the single word: 'One.' If on the other hand I wish to call control, I shall say: 'Middlesex one for one hundred'. Is that all quite clear?"

"Just like cricket scores?" asked Reed.

"Exactly. On Tuesday control will call himself Lancashire and his code sign could be ninety-three. So on that day should any calls be necessary from control they will be: 'Lancashire ninety-three for three'. From Tom they will be: 'Lancashire three for ninety-three'." He paused for a moment and then asked: "Has everybody in the room got that procedure clear?"

"No," replied Wanda.

"Right. In that case we shall have ten minutes' rehearsal. Bill, will you and Doris please assume control and give us a bit of practice in the procedure?"

By the time Green had taken each group through the routine three or four times, everybody felt competent to cope. He then added one last instruction.

"If anybody wishes to speak to all stations," he said, "the figure four will be introduced. As control, I shall say: 'Middlesex one hundred for four'. You will say: 'Middlesex four for one hundred'."

"Everybody will be four, you mean?" asked Doris.

"Yes, love."

"But how will you know who spoke?"

"By adding a little bit. Gatting made one. Or two or three, according to who sends the message."

"Gatting?"

"We will give you the name of a different batsman to mention each day."

Masters got to his feet. "I want everybody to practise the procedure on the way down tomorrow. I want it perfect and so succinct as to be unlikely to arouse outside interest. Police nets are very close. Even if they overhear anything, I don't want the locals to understand. For that reason, nobody will use the sets for sending except in dire emergency."

They murmured their understanding. He continued. "If you have to send, think out or, even better, write out your message before you go on air. Usually one word followed by a map reference will be enough. For example: 'Danger, one, two, three, four, five, six'. Or, 'Success, one, two, three etcetera', should be enough."

"Map references—those numbers," said Doris. "I don't know what they all mean."

"You will very soon. Bill is going to take us through to the dining room now and show us how to use the maps he has got for us."

Green gave each pair a set of the 1/25,000 maps. "You will see that these maps are so large-scale, that you need three to take you from east of Chinemouth and along the coast to beyond Ponde. They are large bits of paper to use, so I want everybody to cut them down by taking off the top half away from the coast. Do that later." He stretched a set out on the dining table so that they joined to depict the whole area. "You will see that these show everything in the way of little tracks, hedgerows, small copses and so on. Away from the town, that is. And these are the ones I want you to use for finding your way about.

"Make use of everything on the ground for checking your position at all times. For instance, this line with sort of pylon signs on it is the overhead power cable. If you're using a track or following a hedgerow that it crosses, note your position at that time. And trust the maps. They are correct."

Doris said: "There are all sorts of little things shown."

"You can read at the side of the map what they are, love. There's this little table."

"Oh yes."

"Each map is divided into squares, numbered across top and bottom and both sides. They are one thousand yards square. You heard of map references a minute or two ago. They are always to be in six figures. Here's how you get them. Read across the map from west to east first, just like reading a book." He put one podgy finger on a line. "This is three four. And so those are the first two figures. This house, standing alone near the middle of the square, is about seven tenths of the way across the square. So the third figure is seven.

"Now we go up the map from bottom to top. The square we're talking about is sitting on line seven two. So those are the fourth and fifth figures of the reference. The house is about six tenths of the way up the square, so six is your last figure. The whole reference thus becomes: 'three, four, seven, seven, two, six'."

He looked round. "Don't worry, we'll be going through it all again, several times. But to help you get the third and sixth figures—that is to help you measure how far across and up a square it is, I've got some roamers. These are only little bits of card marked off in distances one tenth of the distance across the square. If you put the corner of the roamer on the spot on the map, line up the roamer so that its sides are parallel with the lines on the map, you can read off exactly what the third and sixth figures should be." He demonstrated as he spoke.

"We'll practise that in a minute or two, but first I want to show you these other maps. Six inches to one mile in scale. They are more like plans than maps, and we need a great many of them to cover the area. So we are not going to work from them as a general rule when moving about, but to use them for detail if needs be."

He stood back. "Right. I'm going to do one more map spot for you, and then I'll be testing each pair."

More than half an hour passed before Green was satisfied that every member of the team was reasonably competent with the maps.

"Right," said Masters. "Everybody get a drink before final instructions.

"We shall travel in convoy tomorrow morning. The meet will be at the Greens' house at seven-fifteen. Irene, you will use the car you have at the moment—the one we used today—and pick up Tom in good time to get you to the RV on time. Paul, you will reverse that and pick up Muriel, also in good time. You will have spare room in your car, so if there is anything that's a bit much for the others to load, please be prepared to take it should you be asked to do so.

"Paul will lead the convoy, with Tom next and I shall bring up the rear. Please try to keep in touch visually. It is not always easy to do, but it can be done. We shall pull up in a lay-by on the minor road into Chinemouth. That's one half a mile from where Pearce was killed this morning. There we shall have a chat before we finally enter the ring."

Green said to Reed: "When you go to draw up your car, make sure you get three of the telescopic probes and a couple of shovels. Oh, and some good lamps. If we have to dig at night we won't be able to show a light, but we may need one if we find a doings."

"You can't see to dig in the dark."

"Don't be daft lad. I dug slit trenches and gun pits in the dark hundreds of times in the last struggle."

Doris said suddenly: "What about Michael? The little love knows Bill and me. He can't pretend not to."

"Good thinking that, man," said Green. "You and Wanda will have to pretend to chum up quite quickly—meet on the beach or something. Me, as hanger on, I'll just follow suit and become pals with the choker."

"I'm sure we'll all manage famously as long as we remember the need for caution," said Masters. "Now, everybody, off home with you. Don't forget to take your maps and don't forget to cut them down so that only the coastal area remains. Then fold them in such a way that they're easy to use."

As the sitting-room clock chimed for midnight, Masters bolted the front door behind the last of his departing team.

— 7 —

They reached the lay-by in good order soon after nine o'clock.

"We shall use one of the biggest of the hotels in Chinemouth," said Masters. "The Tivoli."

"Are we booked in?" asked somebody.

"Don't worry. They have plenty of space. A judicious phone call yesterday afternoon made sure they were able to provide the rooms. Just a speculative enquiry as to their ability to house a party of twenty-three Americans should they decide to come this way."

"The Tivoli! It sounds more like a theatre than a hotel," said Reed.

"So does The Savoy," grunted Green, "but you can get a passable bed and breakfast there."

"Paul, you and Muriel will book in as soon as we arrive. The DCI is going to have a word with Mrs Mary K. Brunton whom we assume to have been Pearce's housekeeper. After that he, Doris, Irene and Tom will book in. Wanda and I will appear at lunchtime."

"Then what?" demanded Reed.

"You will take the west half of Chinemouth. Tom and Irene will take the east, with the DCI and Mrs Green in the middle and in attendance of course. My wife and I will go further west, taking in the area of the ferry. No, don't get your maps out now. But remember what you are looking for and work systematically. A hedgerow not far from the sea."

"Parallel to the coast?"

"Not necessarily. Say one were to be at right angles to

163

the beachline, a tripod could still be set up in a gap to look south and east. But it is a double hedgeline you are looking for. It may not be very noticeable as such if it has not been attended to for years.

"I want you to look at every possibility and to cross them off on your maps as you do so. That's all I want to say. You must use your own initiative. We shall meet, this evening, by chance, in the hotel bar." He turned to Green. "This afternoon, Wanda and Michael will be on the beach in the flat area of sand within two hundred yards of the north end of the ferry. Should you and Doris happen to pass that way any time between two and four, you might make their acquaintance."

Green nodded. "I'll unpack my sandshoes, just in case. And I can tell Wanda anything I get from Mrs Brunton."

"Excellent. Right, away you go, Paul. We'll give you a few minutes' start."

Masters, holding his toddler son by the hand came to a halt a yard or two from the water's edge.

"Oh, bath!" said Michael, indicating the English Channel with his unencumbered hand.

"Lots of water, darling," said his mother. "Like your bath, but much bigger."

Michael indicated that he would like to get a little closer to this new phenomenon. When his father led him down close enough for the incoming wavelets almost to reach his feet, he was delighted. "Oh, bear!" he said ecstatically, delighted by the gentle movement. "Oh, bear!"

Nearly everything was referred to as Oh, bear. Everything for which Michael had neither noun nor adjective. The channel was Oh, bath. He knew that much. Its description was Oh, bear—a particularly long and drawn-out Oh, bear, to signify the high level of his approval.

Masters was not surprised by his young son's description of the rolling sea. Everything was prefixed by Oh! Flowers were Oh, fars! The detective in Masters had discovered this much when a rose in a vase had suddenly shed its petals. Michael had made the event momentous by uttering, for the first time, "Oh, far!" a word nobody realized he knew.

"Oh, bear, it is, old chap. Marvellous, isn't it?"

"Does he like it?" asked Wanda, coming up behind them.

"Apparently, sweetheart. He has given it the ultimate accolade."

"I wondered whether he might not be just a little frightened at first."

"No sign of fear, but a deal of pleasure."

"Are you going off now?"

"Yes. On foot. I'll leave you the car. Have you got your keys?"

"In my bag. But you are disobeying your own orders, George. You said nobody was to go off alone."

"Let's not tell anybody. I'm proposing to cross on the ferry for a quick shufti the other side."

"I could put Michael in the buggy and come with you. He'd love to go up on the top deck and see the boats passing."

Masters grinned. "And you?"

"Oh, I'd like it, too, and the sand on the other side looks clean and golden."

"Right." Masters scooped up his son. "We're going on a ferry...a ferry...a ferry..." He jogged over the sand back towards the road where the car was parked.

"Oh, bear!" said Michael.

"Mrs Brunton?"

She was, guessed Green, about fifty. She was plump and neatly—almost tightly—dressed in a pale-pink-and-blue-striped summery frock.

"Yes."

"My name is Green. Bill Green. I saw Mr Pearce yesterday morning as I came..."

"You're the gentleman the policeman mentioned? He said Stanley recognized you and said your name."

Green nodded. "I didn't come yesterday because I thought you'd be having a number of callers and a lot to do."

"I was all at sixes and sevens," she admitted, "but it's not so bad today. It will get bad again I expect after the inquest. But you'd better come in."

"If you're sure..."

"I was going to have some coffee."

"In that case..." Green stepped inside.

She led him through to the kitchen. A neat, well-planned, modern room. "Do you mind being in here?"

"Not at all. My old mother always used to say you could show your friends into the kitchen and others into the front room."

As she pulled a chair out from under the melamine-topped table and offered it to him, she said: "Your mother was right. You were a friend of Stanley's, weren't you?"

"No, love, I can't claim that."

"No? He told me he was writing to an old friend of his. Sergeant Green, I think he called you?"

"That's right. We were in the same mob together during the war, and Stan did write to me. But we weren't close friends. We hadn't seen each other for years."

"I see."

"What's up, love? Is there something you want to say."

"He'd been a bit worried this last two weeks, but he said it would be all right when Bill Green came."

"Did he tell you what the trouble was?"

"No. But it worried him. And he wasn't the one to be worried."

"When the policeman came yesterday and mentioned me, did you tell him Stanley had written me and expected me to call?"

"No. Should I have done?"

"I'm pleased you didn't."

"Why?"

"Are you a relative of his, love?"

"Sister-in-law."

"He married your sister?"

"Veronica. She died about ten years ago. Cancer, it was. It cut him up, naturally. You see they'd no children and he had no near family to turn to. Ronnie was a good bit older than me and we weren't all that close ourselves. But I lost Fred—my husband—three years ago. It was then that Stanley . . . well, he was in insurance, you know, and he seemed able to see to things. He did everything for me and then, well, somehow it just happened. I came to keep house for him, and I must say I was surprised at how nice he was. Fred and I used to think he was a bit of an old stick, though Ronnie thought the world of him. I got to know why—a bit too late, perhaps."

"Perhaps," agreed Green. "But you made him comfortable and fed him well and so on, didn't you?"

There were tears in her eyes as she nodded.

"You make the coffee, love. We can talk while you do it."

She took two cups and saucers from a cupboard. "You didn't tell me why you were pleased I didn't mention you to the police."

"Well, love, it would have been very inconvenient for me."

"Oh, why?" There was suspicion in her voice now.

"Keep a secret?"

"Of course I can."

"I'm a copper myself."

"Oh? From round here?"

"No, love. From London. And I'm off my patch, so I'd rather the locals didn't know, otherwise they could get stroppy. You see, we're not allowed to work in other people's areas without them knowing."

"So you're a policeman. A sergeant, like Stanley said?"

"No, love, I'm a detective chief inspector. I was a sergeant in the army when I knew Stanley."

She eyed him thoughtfully. "Stanley wasn't in trouble with the police, was he? No, he wouldn't be. Not Stanley."

"Not in trouble, love. He'd got to know something not too nice that he thought involved a local policeman. He wanted to talk to me about it."

"I see." She poured boiling water into the two cups. "But you didn't get here soon enough to talk to him." The tone was accusatory.

"Because he didn't give me his address, love. I've had to comb the whole country to find him."

"Didn't give his address?"

"No, love. You see, he wasn't sure I hadn't retired and that the letter wouldn't go to somebody else at the Yard."

"Scotland Yard?"

"Yes, love. Any sugar about?"

She got up to get the bowl from the cupboard.

"He was silly. Couldn't he have rung you?"

"He didn't, at any rate."

"Who was the policeman he wanted to talk about?"

"He didn't give me his name, love. So I'm up a gum tree, unless you can help. Did he ever mention any police officers?"

"Never. I didn't know he knew any."

Green grimaced. "That's that, then. I'll be getting back to London as I can't do any good here."

"Isn't there anything . . . I mean, didn't Stanley give you any idea what he wanted to talk about?"

"None. And just as I get here he's knocked over by a hit and run artist. Miles outside the town."

"The local police say they don't know whether they'll get whoever it was."

"They're difficult cases," agreed Green. "But what was he doing out there? Hiking?"

"He'd gone to do some photography. On his motor bike, you know."

"There was no bike anywhere near when I saw him."

"The local police have found it. He'd left it behind a pub. He'd left it there before."

"I see. The locals have it, I suppose?"

"Yes. I don't know what for."

Green offered no opinion. He said suddenly, as though the thought had just occured to him, "Stanley did tell me a bit about his hobbies in the letter. He said he'd been out to get a shot of the moon on the water."

"Oh, yes. But he didn't get it."

"Why not?"

"He said something had gone wrong with his camera and he couldn't see in the dark to put it right."

"Not having a car he couldn't go inside and put the light on to see by."

"No. He was out on his bike, but he'd left it a good way away, he said. Too far to go back and switch the light on to see."

"Where was all this?" asked Green nonchalantly. "On the cliffs out to the east?"

"I didn't ask him, and he didn't say. But it couldn't have been that way, could it, because it's built up along there and there's street lighting along the marina walk? It would have meant he could have seen to put the camera right, because there couldn't have been much wrong. He was using it again next day."

Green got to his feet.

"I won't hold you any longer, love. Thanks for the coffee. And don't worry too much."

"Apart from him going like that, I've got nothing really to worry about. He's left me the house, you see, and I have a bit of money from selling my own house when I came here. I'm nicely off, in fact, but there, so I was before, and I shall miss having him around."

"There's nothing this side at all," said Reed, pulling the car up. "The main road runs as close to the cliffs as it can without actually dropping over the edge."

Muriel examined the strip of map on her knees. "It does diverge here and there. Oughtn't we to try..."

"We've got to try, flower, but it's not on. Pearce's description of the murder, I mean."

"How do you mean?"

"I mean if three murderers are going to take a fourth bloke to a spot where they're not only going to kill him, but also bury him, it's got to be more private than anything we've seen round here. Not in the few yards between the main road and the cliff edge."

"Too risky?"

169

"Yes. Not only that, Pearce's letter suggested to me that there wasn't a road handy. The car the villains used was out of earshot and there were hedges and fields and things. There's nothing like that round here."

"There's a sort of hiccup in the road up ahead. About a mile away." She pointed to the map. "There's an inlet here, called Seth's Cove. The road turns quite sharply in and then out again and from the V there's a footpath marked running down to Seth's farm and beyond it to the cliff edge on the south of the inlet."

"How long?"

"Altogether its more than half a square. Say between five and six hundred yards."

Reed inspected the map. "There are some hedges, as one would expect at a farm, but ..."

"But what?"

"Old Pearce said he left the spot by another route. If the villains used the track ..."

"Which they might well do. They'd leave the car at the V-junction, hidden probably, and then walk down. Six hundred yards. I don't think Pearce would hear a car start up at that distance, would he?"

"I wouldn't think so. But which way did he use? He'd steer clear of the track. There's no other way marked."

"Couldn't he go across country?"

"Where to? It was dark, remember."

"Moonlight, actually."

"Okay, but he must have had some means of getting there. Bill Green says it was probably a motor bike. Where would he leave it? Because that's the way he'd have to go."

"He'd take it as far down the farm lane as he could, wouldn't he?"

"I would."

She turned to him. "So he couldn't have left by a different way from there."

"No."

"So what do we do? Skip it?"

"No," said Reed, "we take a look."

170

"Because Mr Masters says we do?"

"That. And because if you look at the east point of the cove—it's the south point on the east side, actually, you'll see the map has got the word Ruin printed there. And Pearce was going to have included a ruin in his picture."

Berger asked: "Did you get anything from Mrs Brunton?"

Green, who had just returned to the car which had been parked round a corner safely out of sight of The Limes, said: "He was definitely out on his bike that night. He was yesterday morning, too, but he'd left it at a pub and then gone off on foot."

"That was his pattern of action, you reckon?"

Green nodded. "Bung-ho Percy was the sort who'd have a set pattern for everything he did."

"Nothing else about that night?"

"Only that he told his sister-in-law, who kept house for him, that something minor had gone wrong with the camera—as an excuse for not getting the picture he'd gone out for, that is."

"Reasonable enough, I suppose."

"It could be confusing," said Green. "Mrs Brunton said he couldn't have gone to the east of the town, because there's a coast road with lights on it for miles, and he'd have been able to see quite easily to adjust his camera."

"That helps, doesn't it?" asked Doris.

"Not really, love, because so far as we know the camera didn't go wrong. Bung-ho Percy only said it did. So Mrs Brunton's guess is one based on false information." Green turned to Berger. "You're a bit of a photographer."

"A bit of one," agreed Berger. "I've done the official course and I take all our shots of dabs, scenes of crimes and like. Some of my pictures have been known to come out."

"No need to be sarky, son. Just use your knowledge to answer me this. Would those street lights along the coast road spoil a night shot of the moon?"

"No. Not if the camera was between the lights and the sea. It might mean that any object in the foreground—

tree, fence, or house, even—would stand out a bit more clearly if they were near enough to reflect any of the light."

"So Bung-ho could have operated to the east."

"Quite easily, I'd have said. Particularly as he mentioned something about getting a building and a tree in the shot."

"Okay, lad, start her up and let's get ourselves booked into this Tivoli place."

The ferry, loaded with vehicles, including a public transport bus, drew itself, along the chains laid on the seabed, across the two or three hundred yards of water at the mouth of the bay.

Michael, up top with his parents, watched the small pleasure craft that came and went, but seemed more interested in those under sail than the faster, powered ones. He gave hardly a second glance to the small coaster making its way slowly towards the quay at Ponde. As far as Masters could tell, the open hold carried a cargo of sand, while a washing line, strung between the bridge and the mast, carried the crew's laundry.

"It's a beautiful day," said Wanda. "Clear and warm. No hint of cold, but not overwhelmingly hot and stuffy."

"That's the sea for you," replied her husband. "Go inland to the hills and dales in weather like this and you'd swear that nowhere on earth could be more perfect. And yet when you get to the sea—not the popular seaside— there's a sort of resounding cleanliness about it that you only ever get in an absolutely deserted indoor swimming pool. It has something to do with acoustics as well as sight and temperature and atmosphere."

"Oh, bath," said Michael, waving one arm.

"Quite right, old chap. Just like singing in the bath," said his father, lifting him preparatory to descending the companionway for disembarkation.

They tramped for ten minutes or so across the soft, dry sand beach backed by hummocks with marram grass crowns. Masters had Michael in one arm and the folded buggy in the other hand. Wanda had her bag of necessary bits and pieces.

"George."

"Yes, darling?"

"Can we stop just here, somewhere, please? It's just right for sandcastles."

"Fairly close under a dune for a bit of shelter?"

"Yes, please. Not that we need any shelter, but I can sit and lean..." She put down her bag.

"Is there anything I can get you? There are a couple of kiosks at the ferry."

"Nothing, thank you."

"I'll be away for about an hour. Then we'll go to the hotel, clock in and have a sandwich."

He struck off between the dunes, working due south. Before many minutes he was, as he had intended, walking parallel to the eastern coast of the promontory which extended the few miles down to Gossage and beyond before turning west to continue the general line of the south coast. Now he was between the road that the ferry traffic would take and the beach, and getting further from the latter as he progressed. He paused for a moment to consider his position. A tableland, not entirely flat, between the beach and the road. Perhaps only two or three hundred yards wide at the point he had reached, but growing wider as the tideline and the road diverged. A good many bushes and trees in full leaf around him, but no sign of farming or laid-out fields. He climbed a small hillock just to get a few feet of height for better viewing. He faced south. To his left the sea rippling and shining in the sun. To his right, the road with another ferry-load of traffic travelling in convoy. Beyond the road some semblance of agriculture. A field greening over with some young crop. A cottage or two and a sense that, despite the road, this area could be desolate at night except for those few weeks when holidaymakers arrived to set up clandestine tents among the dunes and hummocks.

He stood where he was, using binoculars and map for probably ten minutes before pushing on along the same line. Conscious of his promise to Wanda to be away for no more than an hour, he curbed his curiosity as soon as he reached a little unfenced footpath crossing his front. According to the map it joined the road and led to nowhere. He glanced left and right along it. Nobody in sight, but beyond it a change from unworked scrub and hillocks to an area that had been worked at some time.

He turned left along the path to walk the short distance to the shore and then left again along the water's edge. Wanda saw him coming from this different direction some minutes before he reached her.

"The ferry is coming across towards us," he said. "If we pack up now we can take the return trip. If not, we shall have to wait for half an hour."

They booked in at the hotel where Wanda fed Michael in their room while Masters bought sandwiches for the two of them.

"There's a machine on the landing at the head of the stairs. In return for a lot of money it will spew out a tin of tonic and a miniature bottle of gin. There's even ice if one wishes."

"One wishes."

"Right. There's no lemon."

"I'll bring one in this afternoon."

"Clever thing. Got a knife?"

"I've got Michael's complete set with me."

They were building a sandcastle in the place where they had first gone on to the beach when Bill and Doris Green strolled up to them.

"Got a light, mate?" asked Green, offering his packet of Kensitas.

The conversation developed from there. Before long the women were playing with Michael, and Green had his jacket off. He recounted his meeting with Mrs. Brunton.

"Bill," said Masters at the end of the report, "you didn't by any chance ask if you could look at Pearce's snaps, did you?"

"I thought of it, George, but I didn't reckon it would

be polite. There could be hundreds of them, in which case it would take hours to go through the lot and as I didn't know who I'd be looking for, I could have been faced with mug shots of thirty or forty blokes. How would I pick a winner out of that lot?"

"In circumstances like that, you wouldn't. But it occurred to me that Pearce could have taken a sort of sneaky shot of somebody. One which would be recognizably sneaky if you get my drift."

"I get your meaning. I'll give it a try tomorrow, perhaps. Going back there again today would be a bit too much." He sat up and stretched as two strangers passed close by. "Would the young man like an ice cream? There's a shop at the ferry."

"Ask Wanda, Bill. She may indulge him, but she's not too keen on sweets and the like."

"Strict rationing system?"

"Except for fruit."

"I'll be back."

Green returned with five vanilla blocks and the necessary wafers. "Wanda said she'd stretch a point as the lad is taking a working holiday."

Masters grinned and made his slider.

"What are your two young people doing?"

"A swift recce of the whole sea front of the town, just to satisfy themselves there isn't some open space of public garden that would fit the bill."

"To bury a body?"

"Pointless, I know. But they're making sure."

"I've got a feeling, Bill."

Green licked a runnel of ice cream from his wrist. "I thought you might have."

"The other side of the ferry. The road and shore diverge. The area between them—where it widens out appreciably—has been turned into fields and farmed, but is still pretty desolate."

"Ideal burial country, in fact."

"Fairly flat overall. Divided by hedges, giving uninterrupted views over the water to east and south."

175

"Have you seen a likely spot?"

"Not a spot. The area."

"You want to concentrate on it?"

"I want an opinion from you tonight, after you have heard reports from the others."

"Judge whether they have seen anything which would lead me to believe there may be possibilities in their areas? If they have, they continue. If they haven't we concentrate on your area, is that it?"

"Slightly more than that. We laid our scheme not knowing this part of the world. I want you to decide whether, after using today as a preliminary canter, we should change our plan. If you decide we should..."

"Meaning you think we should."

"Meaning that I have found an area which definitely offers. If the others haven't found likely spots... well, you're always saying that one should always reinforce success."

"And you want me to decide?"

"In case I favour too strongly my own view. You're the most impartial. And besides that..."

"What?"

"You're a great map buff, Bill. If you decide we should concentrate on the area the other side of the ferry, you should be able, by studying the maps closely, almost to pinpoint the actual spots we should examine. I know it's breaking away from our original plan, but with somebody who knows his way about a map as you do, there should be a number of pointers that will help. The villains had a car. Bung-ho Percy had a bike. Both were parked at, presumably, definable spots, but both, presumably within reasonable distances of the grave."

Green nodded. "There's something else. We've touched on it already."

"Bung-ho Percy said he left by a different route."

"Yeah! But different from what? From the way he himself came, or from the way the villains went? He doesn't make that clear in his letter."

"Oh, Lord, neither does he. I took it for granted that

he retired by a different route from that taken by the villains."

"That's logical," acknowledged Green. "But where had he left his bike? In the same parking place as the villains left their car? If so, he may have used a route out of his hidey-hole different from the one he went in by, but his objective would still be the same. He'd still have to fetch up at the place where he'd parked his bike."

Masters grimaced. "The villains could have spotted the bike there. Taken its number. Found out who it belonged to. Kept their eye on Bung-ho Percy for a day or two and then staged his killing."

"Good thinking," acknowledged Green. "That would account for the time lag between the murder Bung-ho witnessed and his own little accident. They probably had to wait until they could get him in open country before seeing him off. But we haven't exhausted the possibilities I might look for on the map."

"No. Because Pearce may have parked his motor cycle in a completely different spot from that chosen by the villains for their car. If that happened—and it could well be so, because parking a bike is a hell of a sight easier than a car..."

"You can ride one cross-country. Pearce might have got his machine up fairly close to his position in the hedge."

"Just so. And if that happened..."

"Then what he said in his letter meant that he took the same route away from his position as he'd used to get to it, but it was a different way from that used by the villains to get to and fro. Which is how we read it the first time."

"True, Bill, but it doesn't give us an easy answer as to how the villains got on to Percy."

"You reckon that's important?"

"Yes, I do."

Green let a handful of sand trickle through his fingers before turning back to Masters to say: "I've got an idea about that, George."

"Excellent. Let's hear it.

177

"It's your fault, actually."

"Everything usually is, according to you."

Green grunted. "I have to give you credit for something."

"Give me the idea, instead."

"Your insistence that the grave is the other side of the ferry..."

"Suggestion, Bill not insistence."

Green shrugged. "Whatever. If you look at the map you will see that you can take a road through Ponde which continues right round the bay or lagoon or whatever it's called. It goes through Gossage and eventually comes back to the other side of the ferry."

"A long journey."

"Ten or twelve miles, I suppose."

"Costing more in petrol than the ferry charge."

"Maybe. However, my idea is this. Stan Pearce would take his bike across on the ferry."

"I'll buy that."

"When he has to retire, after witnessing the murder, he thinks he'll avoid the villains by taking the long way home, by the road."

"Thinking Dringle, Swabey and our bent colleague would naturally take the shorter route and bring their car over on the ferry?"

"Right. But what he didn't realize was that blokes like that are cagey bastards. They knew that if something were to go wrong, people might remember their car used the ferry that night. You know how it is. Cars lined up. The driver in the car behind might notice—simply because he's sitting there waiting—the make and colour of the car in front. Who was in it. The number even."

"What you're saying is that they would avoid that risk, however slight, and remain unnoticed and unrecognized on a main road."

"They would, wouldn't they?"

"Of course they would. Then what?"

"Stan Pearce didn't hear their car start up. So they probably paused at the car before setting off. For any number of reasons. To argue, have a leisurely pee, smoke a fag ... anything. And while they were doing that they heard his bike coming on to the road from the general direction of where they'd just been operating."

"They couldn't take any chances—just in case he'd seen something—so they start up, get on the road—not going towards the ferry—and have a look at him."

"They catch him up and pass him?"

"That's right. They're not sure about him, of course, so they don't run him down there and then. Besides, they wouldn't want to draw unwelcome attention to that particular area. But they get his number and see he's loaded with photographic clobber ..."

"Go on."

"Then they trace him and events happen as we suggested before."

"Good. It's not foolproof, Bill, but it's ..." Masters snapped his fingers. "I think I know ..." He looked at Green. "I'm not much of a photographer, but I seem to remember that when anybody loads a camera, they have to tear off the top of a carton that contains the film or open a cassette or suchlike."

Green nodded.

"Pearce would have to do that, wouldn't he? Say he dropped a strip torn off a yellow carton or one of those little tube things. Easy enough to do in the dark."

"Spit it out," urged Green.

"Our villains are uneasy about Pearce, and try to establish if he is, indeed, a threat to them. So they decide to have a quick look-see, in daylight, to make sure their own handiwork is well camouflaged and to discover if there is any sign of Pearce having been in that vicinity."

"They follow his bike tracks in?" suggested Green.

"Maybe. If the ground is right for it. But they discover a piece of new photographic litter within spitting distance of the grave, and the marks of a tripod on the hedge bank in a gap overlooking the spot where they committed murder. They'd know then ..."

"They'd go to finish him," interrupted Green. "And I'll

bet they've laid on some plan to collect any films he may have taken for printing. They'd have to, just in case he'd taken a shot of them. They couldn't be sure he hadn't."

Master grinned at him. "We could be wrong, Bill. But I'm sure we're not wide of some of the marks."

"I'm going to assume we're right."

"Will the scenario we've imagined help with the map work you're going to do?"

"Too early to say yet, of course, but at any rate I'll know the sort of terrain to look for."

Soon after four o'clock, when Wanda had collected Michael's bits and pieces ready for taking him back to the hotel for tea, WPC Irene Tippen walked along the beach alone. As she slowly crossed their front, her feet sinking in the soft sand, Green said to Doris, "This looks as though our car had arrived."

Irene ignored them and went on her way.

"What time were you expecting her and Berger?" asked Masters quietly.

"Half-four."

"Then I think there's something wrong. Irene must have seen us, and made sure we saw her, but she gave no hint of recognition.

"Why not use the blower?"

"I don't know, Bill, but I think you should follow her and contrive a brief meeting."

Without a word, Green got to his feet and followed his temporary daughter. "Don't look after him, please," said Masters to Wanda and Doris. "Just in case we are under observation. Act naturally."

"He's coming back," said Doris a moment or two later.

Green rejoined them. "She's gone into the ladies at the ferry terminal. I think, love, you should pay a call, too."

Doris caught on. "Do I say anything to her?"

Green handed her a few small coins. "Only if she speaks to you."

Wanda was busy dusting the fine sand from between Michael's toes when Doris returned. She handed the coins

180

back to her husband. "There's been a car following them. Sergeant Berger thinks it's a police car or that it has policemen in it. He managed to lose it long enough for Irene to get out. She caught a bus to get here. She's going back the same way on the one coming across on the ferry now."

"We'd best join her," said Green. "If we hurry we'll make it."

"Right, Bill. See what you can make of it. We'll see you back at The Tivoli. I'll keep an eye open for you."

"Right. Come on, love, we'd better hurry."

"What does it mean, George?" asked Wanda as Masters carried his son towards the beach exit.

"Haven't a clue, poppet, but I don't like it."

"You don't think Sergeant Berger could have been imagining things?"

"Unlikely. He's a skilled chap."

"But you rather suggested something like this could happen. Could your warning have affected his judgement?"

"Of course it could have done. If not, I imagine we shall soon know."

Masters took a seat at an outdoor table, to the left of the wide entrance steps of the hotel. Before him was the long forecourt, probably a dozen yards wide, but at least four times that distance in length, fronted by a low, grey wall which in turn was pierced by in and out gaps at each end. His own car was parked, nose-in to the wall, close to where a notice requested this disposition so that oily fumes from exhausts should not dirty the stone. Only two other cars were parked here, most of the guests preferring to use the much larger rear park. He was filling a pipe when Green arrived with Doris and Irene in a taxi.

"I'll go up and see Wanda," said Doris.

"She'll be giving Michael his tea so she could be in one of the lounges."

"I'll find her."

"What's it all about, Irene?" asked Masters.

"Exactly as I told mum. Paul said he'd noticed a car

181

behind us for several minutes, so we began to keep watch. After we were sure it was tailing us we played one of the usual tricks—turned and went back to where we'd just been."

"And then?"

"Paul thought an explanatory message would be too long for the radio, especially if, having got to us, they were monitoring calls."

Masters nodded his appreciation of this point.

"So Paul drove back into the middle of town. He beat the lights and rounded a corner out of sight so that I could get away quickly. We'd made the plan because we knew where you were meant to be. I got out pretty near the bus station so I hadn't far to go to catch a bus that was going to the ferry. I got off one stop before, went down to the beach and walked past you. I didn't stop in case anybody was watching me, but I thought you'd guess I had a message. I went into the ladies so that nobody—a man, that is—could follow me."

"Well done. And where is Paul?"

"He said he'd continue driving round. Then, if he thought he'd lost them, he'd come back here."

"Thank you. I'll wait for him. Why don't you go and get some tea. You've earned it."

Irene rose to go. "Send a waiter out, love. Or better still, tell him to bring us a tray."

They were having tea when Berger nosed the car into the forecourt and drew it up alongside Masters' car.

"Oh, oh," said Green. "Here's trouble."

Another car came into the forecourt as Berger was locking his door. The conversation that ensued was fully audible to Masters and Green.

"Excuse me, sir."

Berger looked at the burly man getting from the passenger side of the second car. He waited.

"We've been following you."

"I'm aware of that. I've taken your number and I'm just going indoors to write a complaint to the police."

"Save yourself the trouble, sir. We are the police."

"In that case," said Berger nonchalantly, moving around to open the boot, "what are you doing on private property?" He took out a rucksack. "And don't get the idea that I shan't proceed with my complaint, Constable."

"Sergeant, lad."

Berger turned on him. "Address me as lad just once more and your feet won't touch the ground."

"Is that so?"

"Have you finished what you wanted to say? I want to catch the post."

"One of them, is he?" said the second man coming up.

Berger slung his bag over one shoulder and turned to head for the door.

"Just a moment. I haven't finished yet."

Berger waited.

"Is this your car? Are you the owner of the vehicle?"

"As a matter of fact I'm not."

"Stolen is it?"

"Borrowed would be nearer the mark."

"I see. And your name, sir?"

Berger took out his identity card. It appeared not to surprise the local sergeant, but he did say: "DS Berger. I thought your name was Green?"

"Are you accusing me of having false credentials now?"

"No, chum. Are you on duty in Chinemouth?"

"I'm on holiday."

"Holiday? Then perhaps you will explain why you are using an official Scotland Yard car for private purposes."

Berger paused. Masters said: "I think this is where you step in, Bill."

Green got to his feet and lumbered across to the trio. "What's your trouble, lad?" he asked the sergeant.

"And who may you be, sir?"

"My name's Green."

"Ah. The Sergeant Green who was a witness at this morning's accident."

"Wrong on two counts," grated Green. "First off, I'm a DCI from the Yard, and second, I wasn't a witness. I arrived after the accident had happened."

"Are you responsible for the private use that is being made of police property, sir?"

"If you mean the car, say so. And how do you know it's police property anyhow?"

"We're not quite as thick down here as you people at the Yard think we are."

"I'm pleased to hear it."

"The constable at the scene of the accident noted this car's number when it stopped."

"Clever of him. And you traced the car, just for laughs, I suppose."

"When official cars are wrongly used . . ."

"Cut it out," growled Green. He turned to Berger. "How long since you first noted this lot on your tail, Sergeant?"

Berger looked at his watch and did a rapid calculation. "Two hours and thirty-five minutes ago."

Green glared at the Chinemouth sergeant. "Do you usually tail suspect cars for over two and a half hours? No, lad, don't bother to answer. You slide in front of them at the first opportunity. So what's going on down here? Remember something, lad, when you've been a jack as long as I have, you develop a nose for stinking fish and I'm getting a pong of about five tons of rotting herrings right now. And it's coming from you. Who told you to tail this car?"

"In the course of my duty . . ."

"Who gave you the orders, lad?"

"I'm not bound to . . ."

"Don't try it on, or I'll bring the big guns in, son."

"My superiors wanted to know what officers from Scotland Yard were doing on this patch, sir. I was told to find out."

"What's wrong with a telephone? Or are your superiors as dumb as they've made you look?"

The sergeant flushed angrily but held his tongue.

"Or did they tell you to do it secretly? If so you made a pig's ear of the job, lad. DS Berger here was on to you as soon as you started, I reckon. Yes? I thought so."

"You still haven't told me . . ."

"There's no reason why I should, but I will," said Green wearily. "The girl who was in the car with DS Berger is a WPC and she's my daughter—they're courting. I've also got my missus with me, as you'll see if you consult the hotel register. We're all down here on holiday together. Yes, lad, in an unmarked car belonging to the Yard. With permission from the assistant commissioner who, on occasions, is prepared to lend them to senior officers for private use. We pay for the petrol. You can, of course, ring the Yard and ask the AC Crime to confirm what I've told you. You're a bit late for doing it today, but first thing tomorrow morning would be fine. I hate to think what sort of an answer you'll get. You'll never be the same chap again, but don't let that put you off. His name's Anderson, by the way."

"I don't suppose my superiors will think that necessary, Mr. Green. Seeing we have your word for it."

"I could be hoodwinking you, lad. You tried to do a thorough job chasing Sergeant Berger. Complete it by getting on to the Yard."

"As I said, sir, I don't think it will be necessary."

"It will," grated Green, "because I have superiors, too, lad, and they like reports of little incidents like this. So they'll be expecting an enquiry. So you'd better give me your name, Sergeant."

"I don't think that will be necessary either, sir."

"Refusing me the information, are you, son? I wonder why? The smell of stinking fish is growing stronger than ever. I mean, look at it from my point of view. A DCI asks a sergeant his name, and the sergeant refuses to give it. Now what disciplinary crime would you call that? Even worse, what reason do you suppose the sergeant could give for refusing so small and legitimate a request?"

"This is unofficial."

"No, lad, it is not unofficial. You've been acting very officially and officiously. And I'll tell your Chief Constable so tonight, when I ring him. Note the number of their car, Sergeant Berger."

The sergeant, reluctantly, produced his identification.

185

"Detective Sergeant Cheshire," said Green quietly. "Thank you. I'll remember that." He turned to the constable. "And your name, lad?"

"Berwick, sir."

"Thanks. Now let me give you two Charlies a word of advice. If I were you, I'd forget this incident, as I'm prepared to do because I'm on holiday and don't want to be bothered with it. You can ring the Yard tomorrow morning, just to show I've told you the truth. But if I ever get cause to think you've made a thing of it other than a simple check on the car, I'll know you're playing some bloody devious game and I'll have every jack in the kingdom drafted into this area to discover what it is. And I'll be here myself to make sure you don't get away with anything. And if you don't believe I can do that, just ask a few questions about my record when you do get through to the Yard. I crucify bent cops."

Green turned and stumped back towards the hotel entrance. Berger followed a couple of yards behind. Masters, who had remained at his table throughout the encounter, straining his ears to catch every word, allowed them to pass him without any sign of recognition. But as soon as Cheshire and Berwick left the forecourt, he entered the hotel, to find Green waiting for him in the foyer.

"We shall have to move fast, George."

"Agreed, Bill. First I must ring Anderson to put him in the picture in case they do get through to him. I'll use one of the public phones."

Green grunted his assent. "Don't want any of this to go through the hotel switchboard. I'll wait outside the box, just in case anybody wants to get nosey."

Ten minutes later, Masters rejoined Green.

"The AC agrees with the need for speed."

"He reckons whoever set those two on will not be satisfied with my explanation?"

"Would you?"

"No. But it was the best I could do."

"Nobody could have done better, Bill. If they're not

bent, but ring Anderson to check your story, he'll confirm it, and that will be that. But they are bent, aren't they?"

"Must be. Nobody would go to the lengths of checking up like that on somebody who arrived at the scene of an accident after their own cops had fetched up."

"And that young constable would mention the name Green in his report. They'd think it odd that somebody who knew Pearce should arrive literally at the last gasp. So they checked up, and they've discovered the same Green is a DCI at the Yard ... well, by now somebody will have sussed that Pearce had been in touch with you and you're down here to investigate."

"So?"

"They're not particular about removing people who know too much. We've got to work fast to find that body, Bill."

"Before they can lay on a plan to get rid of me?"

"You, mostly. But the rest of us will be targets, too—if they get wind of what we're really up to."

Green shrugged. "I'd best get looking at those maps."

"Please. Oh, by the way, Anderson is sending up some help. Hebditch and three DC's, all armed. They're coming hot foot. They'll be here before eight."

Master was towelling himself after a bath when there was a knock at his room door. Wanda, sitting at the dressing table, got up to answer it.

"Come in, William. Excuse our state of undress."

"Anybody would excuse you anything, love, just for looking like that in your slip."

Green was carrying a rolled map which he proceeded to lay out on the bed. Masters with a bath sheet round his middle joined him.

"Thank God we had that chat, George."

"You mean you've found a likely spot?"

Green looked up. "I don't like sticking my neck out, but ..." He laid a thick forefinger on the map. "That hedge is about thirty yards in from the shore and parallel to it. It's about the only real hedge like that for several miles.

There are clumps of growth ... but no real straight hedge other than that."

"Excellent."

"If you look closely you'll see a dotted line between this area of beach ..."

"Billings Sands?"

"Between the edge of the sands and the hedge. That's an unfenced footpath. Follow it along ... it's very faint ... for, oh, about six hundred yards, I reckon, and it joins another. The map calls the spot Palmland Cross, but there's nothing marked except unfenced brushwood."

"Meaning?"

"There's no building or anything there, but as it's grand enough to have a name, I reckon it'll be big enough to park a car and turn it, or even hide it in the bushes."

"The villains parked there and walked north-east along the coast path?"

"To this spot." Green was now using a pencil as a pointer. "I know these hedges are in very faint grey, but you can just see that one runs towards the water along here, and joins our first one at right angles. If you look closely, it actually crosses it and continues for about a sixteenth of an inch."

"I wish I had a magnifying glass."

"George, you've got to take my word for it. It's there."

"Let me look," said Wanda.

They moved aside for her.

"It's there," she said.

"Thanks, love." Green returned to the map. "And now look at this, George. A footpath with a hedge alongside it ..."

"Hellishly difficult to see it."

"I know. But it leads to the western side of this water course and then turns right to reach this house called Drylea. The water course, I reckon, is no more than a ditch. Probably a dry one. I reckon that's where Stan Pearce parked his bike. He's about a quarter of a mile from this unmetalled road, which in turn leads to the main road."

188

"And how far from the hedge where we think he set up his camera? Two hundred yards?"

"About that." Green straightened. "Now, if I'm right, Stan Pearce would go back to his bike and when he reached the main road, would turn left to take the long way round. I think he knew the villains would hit the main road to the west of him and that by going the way he did, he would actually pass the end of the track they would use. But I reckon he thought he'd waited long enough at the hedge and taken so much time getting back to his bike and then riding along the tracks that by the time he got to the road, they would be well clear. And that was his mistake. I think the villains were held up for a bit, and saw Stan Pearce cross the end of their track before they got on the road. They probably knew there had been no ferry that could have got him there at that particular time..."

Masters interrupted him. "You've got it, Bill. Those characters stayed on the track, waiting for a ferry load of vehicles to go through. They didn't want to be noticed nosing in off that track. So they waited until the convoy had gone through. I think they put one man out to look back down the road to see that all was clear and it was that joker who saw Pearce join the road about a quarter of a mile away. In open country like that they probably saw his headlights as he bumped across country from the spot they themselves had left only a short time before. And then he crossed their bows. So they followed him."

"Something very much like that must have happened," agreed Green. "In fact, that bobbing light theory...George, you've got to be as near right as dammit. We've been scratching our heads to decide how the villains got on to Pearce, and what you've just said fits like a glove."

Masters grinned. "It also supports the results of your map investigation, Bill."

"You reckon it's worth a try?"

"Tonight. After Hebditch and his men arrive. Everybody is to be fed and watered for a move at nine."

Green nodded.

"I don't want any of the women with us."

"No. Doris had better come and sit with Wanda."

Masters shook his head. "We'll take no risks, Bill. Irene will stay with Doris. Muriel will stay in this room with Wanda. On the half-hour, Irene will ring here, and on the hour Muriel will ring your room."

"You think there could be some hanky-panky in this place?"

"If they're watching the hotel and see all the men leave, they could just try something. I myself am not prepared to trust Dringle and Swabey."

"I've got to be here, because of Michael," said Wanda. "But why the calls?"

"Checks, love," said Green.

"There's slightly more to it," said Masters. "If the people receiving the call are all right..."

"All right?"

"If they're not answering the phone at gunpoint," said Green bluntly.

"I see."

"If they are all right, they will answer by saying 'Mrs Masters' room' or 'Mrs Green's room', as the case may be. If they are not all right, they will pick up the phone and say the one word, 'hello'. Both types of reply will raise no suspicion, but 'hello' will be the danger signal. Bill, will you brief Doris and the two girls?"

Green nodded. "And if a call is missed?"

"The WPC's have radios. The one not under duress gets hold of us. And we shall arm them. Now," said Masters, to kill the tension, "I'll just put on a dressing gown, arm myself with money, and go along the corridor to see what the machine can do for us in the way of providing a quick drink."

The two WPC's, on instructions from Green, had an early dinner and then came up to Masters' room to guard Michael while the DCS and Wanda had their meal. Hebditch had arrived and joined them. His three DC's preferred to eat at a nearby restaurant. So Masters was able to brief the newcomer over the meal. It was Hebditch who took two of the weapons he had brought to the WPC's, both of whom were trained in their use.

"They could be watching the ferry, Bill," said Masters as they prepared to leave as unobtrusively as possible. "So we'll take the long way round. If you'll navigate..."

"How many cars?"

"Just two. You, Reed, Berger and I in one of our Yard cars. Hebditch and his merry men in their own. I've laid it on."

"All informed?"

"Have we got spades and the like?"

"Yes."

"Everything, including plastic sheets."

"In that case, let's go."

Forty minutes later, Green said to Reed, "Turn off right at the track about a hundred yards ahead."

Less than ten minutes later the cars were stopped at Palmcross.

"Leave two of your constables with them," Masters told Hebditch. "One with a gun. You bring the other."

It was a silent, Indian file trek along the coast footpath, Green leading, using a torch sparingly in the darkness.

Green turned his head. "Nearly there, George. I've been counting the paces. I worked it out, allowing thirty inches a time."

A minute or so later he stopped. "Left, ahead," he said quietly.

"Make for the corner where the two hedges meet, Bill. Then we'll work down towards the shore."

They congregated in the leafy right angle.

"Use torches first," said Masters. "You're looking for rubbish, particularly glass, on an area that could have been turned over recently. Take it slowly."

Reed and Berger, with the remaining detective constable, between them did the searching. They moved, line abreast, towards the sea. It was the DC who said: "The

191

grass is yellow here, sir. And there's glass."

The turves were easily toed aside. The probe sank into the soil easily.

"Congratulations, Bill."

"Thanks. Just one more river to cross. I'll have him up."

"Not you. Let the four younger men do it. I have a fancy to find your friend's observation post."

The digging was easy. The spoils gruesome.

"He's here, Chief," Reed had warned when the body had first been located, and so they were all clustered round when the final scoops of earth had been taken from round the recumbent form by Berger and the DC, both lying on the ground and reaching down to do their task.

"Photographs please, Reed."

"Aren't you going to call a forensic man?" asked Hebditch.

"No. We've got the SSCO here in the person of Bill Green. I want to keep this as quiet as possible."

"Roll the plastic sheet," said Berger to the DC. "Then we'll get it under the head first and work it down under the shoulders from both sides of the trench. We'll be able to lift him a bit as we go."

It was no easy task. Reed lay alongside Berger and grasped the front of the clothing to help take the weight. The burial had been too recent for the fabric to have rotted, but it was a grisly business. The limpness of the body, the smell, and the difficult working conditions were nauseating. Then the lift, trying to grasp the slippery plastic. It took the six of them. At last the corpse lay in the open air alongside its grave.

"So far, so good," said Hebditch, wiping his hands on handfulls of grass. "Now what, Chief?"

"End of project one," said Masters.

"I don't understand."

"The first project was to establish that a crime had been committed as reported to Bill Green by Pearce. The discovery of the body proves that there was a crime—if only an unauthorized burial. And that ends project one. Project two is the investigation of the crime. Properly

192

speaking, it's the job of the locals. We should now hand over and bow out."

"God Almightly, Chief, you can't do that. One of them did it, according to Pearce. What do you think the answer would be?"

"Could be," corrected Masters. "They're not all bent. But I agree, if the wrong one is given the case he'll move heaven and earth to save his own neck by ensuring the truth never gets known."

"So?"

"I must consult the AC again."

"Why? I mean this late?"

"It's not yet midnight," grated Green. "As to why, the answer's a lemon. We don't know which cop it was that helped to put this poor sod underground. And that's the big problem now. We want the AC's up-to-date views on that."

"But why not..."

Masters interrupted him. "Walk along to the cars with Bill and myself. We can talk as we go. Reed, you three stay here."

"Right, Chief."

"There's a public call box in the village a mile or two back, Chief," said Berger. "On the corner outside the grocer's."

"Thank you."

They stumbled along in line abreast so that they could converse.

"Why not just arrest Dringle and Swabey and demand to be told the name of their colleague in the local force?" demanded Hebditch.

"No good, lad," said Green. "They'd never say, because if they did, they'd be confessing to murder."

"We have no evidence on which to arrest them," said Masters.

"The letter from Pearce."

"No good, I'm afraid. An anonymous letter isn't enough. Pearce himself is not alive to testify and back up what he told us. Besides, he did not name the policeman in-

193

volved. Dringle and Swabey have only to persist in claiming their innocence and swearing they don't know any policeman and we've got nothing. Can you imagine what the DPP would say if we were to lay what we've got in front of him?"

"He'd boot you out," said Hebditch gloomily.

"Quite. And I don't think the locals would be too keen to let us investigate further once the news broke officially."

"That's true, I suppose. But from what you told me earlier, it has already broken."

"I think not. Only the people who are interested in us know we're here. For obvious reasons, they'll have kept it to themselves. It wouldn't be in their interest to noise it abroad. And I don't suppose for one moment they know how much we know or what we have just done."

"So the local Chief Constable won't know?"

"Not unless he's the bent copper Pearce recognized. And I believe that to be unlikely. I tend to favour a somewhat lower rank, one of the more practical coppers, as opposed to the totally office-bound."

They reached the cars.

"Any trouble?" demanded Green.

"No, sir. We heard voices down the track a while back, but we reckon it was a young couple finding somewhere private."

"Right. Keep your eyes open. We're taking one car. We'll be back in about half an hour."

"Any ... any success, sir? Along there I mean?"

"If you can call a dead body a prize, lad, we've won it."

Masters drove. Green, from his back seat, said to Hebditch: "There's one thing his nibs has not mentioned, out of kindness to me or because Pearce was once a colleague of mine in the army."

"What's that?"

"That Stan Pearce could have killed that bloke and buried him there."

"But he was the one who told you all about it."

"I know, son. But murderers do queer things."

"You mean he wanted to let somebody know he'd killed a man? A show-off?"

"Stranger things have happened. And if you take into account the lengths he went to in order to hide his identity . . . well, one could make out the beginnings of a case against him."

"I think not," said Masters quietly. "He described events too objectively. Definitely from the onlooker's viewpoint. And now he's dead, too."

"I meant before he was killed," said Green. "You must have considered him, George."

"In passing. Never seriously."

The car drew up at the lighted phone box and Masters got out.

"Masters here, sir. Sorry to trouble you at home and at this hour, but we have found."

"Found, eh? Stabbed?"

"We haven't been able to examine closely. But he's above ground."

"What do you propose to do now, George?"

"What would you like me to do, sir?"

"There are only two courses open to us. You either make a clean breast of it and withdraw, or you keep silent and find the people responsible. I favour the latter course for obvious reasons."

"I've got a dead body on my hands, sir. I can't keep that hidden for long."

"That's easily taken care of. I'll send you a plain van and a shell. Tell me where, and it can be with you in a few hours."

Masters gave him directions.

"Have a man at the turn off from the main road at three o'clock."

"Right sir."

"And now, George, how do you intend to proceed?"

"I have an idea, sir. It may or may not pay off."

"Like that, is it? How do you rate your chances?"

"It is based on fact, sir, but there'll be a bit of bluffing involved. If that pays off, well and good. If not we'll have to think again."

"I'll leave it to you."

"We've plenty of time," said Masters, "but I'd like the grave filled in and camouflaged, and then we shall have to carry the body as far as the cars."

"I'll see if there's any rope in the cars, Chief. It'll be easier if there are some handles."

"Poles or planks," suggested Hebditch. "I don't know where from, but there may be a few somewhere."

Masters took Green and Hebditch aside. He spoke to them quietly for a few minutes, outlining the steps he proposed to take. When he had finished he asked Green: "What do you think, Bill?"

"It's good—if it works."

"I'll do my best," said Hebditch. "I ought to be able to manage it. I'll be on my own ground, at any rate. What I mean is, I'll know what I'm talking about when it comes to smuggling drugs. The rest is your pigeon."

"Quite. I realize what I am proposing is a short cut, but I can see no other way without a very long, unpleasant and wearisome investigation."

"In that case," said Green, "the sooner we get that body to the pick-up point and then get to the hotel for a clean-up, the better."

Reed joined them. "The grave's filled in, Chief. But I've got an idea."

"What?"

"Why not leave the body here till the van arrives with the shell. We can bring the shell here and carry it back in that. It'll take another half-hour or so, but it'll be easier."

Green replied. "It's a good point, lad, but we won't be able to afford the half-hour. It'll be getting light before the van arrives as it is."

"In that case, we'll be ready to move in..." He paused

and peered into the darkness. "Chief, I think there's a car coming along the track this way."

They waited for several minutes as the car bumped slowly along and finally did a three-point turn near the body. Berger got out of the driver's seat and came to them.

"Hatchback, Chief. I couldn't find any belts or straps, but if we let the back seats down..."

"You're sure it will take the body?"

"Angled across, Chief, yes. I'll take it back very slowly."

"In that case load it. And have somebody walking close behind."

"Right, Chief."

— 8 —

The Assistant Commissioner (C) arrived at The Tivoli Hotel, Chinemouth, some twelve hours after the body had been picked up by the van at half-past three that morning.

Masters, Green and Hebditch were waiting for him.

"I've booked a suite in your name, sir. They're just expecting a Mr Anderson for the one night."

"A suite, eh? You're doing me proud, George. I hope the finance department won't query my bill."

"It has a sitting room, sir. We need somewhere to talk."

"Of course. I'll check in. If you'll give me ten minutes before joining me I'd be obliged."

"Tea for four in a quarter of an hour?" asked Green.

"Excellent. But I've forgotten to ask? How are Wanda and Doris?"

"They're both enjoying life, sir. They are with Michael on the beach."

"In view of what's happened, they're not unprotected, I hope?"

"Two WPC's with them, sir."

"Good. I'll see you at ... yes, make it four o'clock."

When they joined him, Anderson had changed into grey slacks and cream bush shirt.

"I've arranged the chairs. Make yourself comfortable. We'll not mention the job until after the tea has come."

The waiter arrived a few minutes later. Anderson thanked him and said they would put the trolley outside the door when they had finished. As the waiter left he tactfully hung a Do Not Disturb notice on the outside knob.

"Now, George, all of it. In detail. I know I've got the gist, but I want to be word perfect when I call on the local Chief Constable. His name's Gore, by the way."

Hebditch was pouring the tea. As Green took his cup, he said: "George's hunch paid off."

"Ah, yes. It sounded a very reasonable assumption to me. We have to assume that, in normal circumstances, the chain of command is solid, link by link, from top to bottom. But if there's a bent link, somewhere near the top and perhaps another near the bottom, it is unlikely that all those in between will be bent. It sounds a simple assumption, but I didn't see it like that myself. And the presumption that the solid links could be bypassed as a corollary! Good thinking, George."

"We had a very useful bit of luck, sir. That helped."

"What was that?"

"When we got back here with the dawn this morning, WPC Irene Tippen, who had been sitting with Doris during our absence, reported that not long after we left last night, there was an outside call put through to Bill's room."

"What sort of a call?"

"Very ordinary, except that it came from the local DI. A chap called Putrey. He merely said he'd heard that Bill was staying at the hotel and would like a private word with him."

"Private?"

"Yes, sir. All the WPC could do was to promise that she would pass the message on. She got a phone number from Putrey. Two actually. Home and office."

"Go on."

"We'd heard of Putrey. He was the man who had been in charge of the investigation into Stinky Miller's death out at Caldenham. Putrey had obviously heard from DS Cheshire ..."

"The one who chased Berger?"

"The same. He'd learned Bill was here. When we heard he'd tried to phone Bill, we realized there could be two reasons. First, that the locals were still intent on discovering why people from the Yard were here or, second, that Putrey had some totally different reason for calling. Some personal reason, perhaps. The fact that he had asked for a private word seemed to us to indicate the second reason."

"So Bill rang him?"

"Not at four in the morning. In fact, not until much later in the morning. Not until after we'd seen the coroner who'd enquired into Miller's death."

"He was willing to speak to you? A lot of coroners wouldn't take kindly to a police enquiry into how they conduct their business."

"I merely asked him if he was willing to give me a little information, sir."

"Sorry to interrupt, George, go on."

"We got back here about four or soon after. We bathed and cleaned up and went down for an early breakfast. By half-past eight, the three of us were in Caldenham village. We went there because I thought it better to ask at the doctor's surgery for the name and address of the coroner rather than to approach the police."

"Quite right."

"I asked the receptionist. I told her I was a policeman, but she was a bit uneasy and fetched the quack himself. After I'd assured him that my business did not concern him in any way I got what I wanted because he wanted to get on with seeing his patients. Actually, he was Stinky Miller's GP and was the one Mrs Miller called to her husband. We found that out later when we called on the district coroner.

"He's a solicitor called Lambourn. We had to retrace our steps a bit to reach him, but that was all to the good as we were very conscious of time and the need for speed in getting back here.

"He works in Thorncliffe and covers the country areas round about, including Caldenham. He hadn't been long in his office when we reached there soon after nine and he agreed to see us when we announced our identities."

"Good bloke," said Green. "He must have known we had a good reason for calling and that it could affect him in some way, but he co-operated willingly from the word go."

"I'm pleased to hear it. I'll send him a letter of thanks when I get back. What line did you take with him, George?"

"I simply said that new information, which he could not possibly have known about, had come up concerning Miller. He asked me what it was, and I gave him a slightly edited version of my theory. He heard me out and then wanted to get on to Putrey immediately which, if you recall, sir, was what I had originally intended to angle for. But in view of Putrey's approach to Bill, I thought it better to head him off for a bit until I'd heard what the local man had to say when we got hold of him.

"You see, sir, the biggest difficulty had appeared to me to be the getting hold of Putrey alone, without his superiors getting to know about it. Had I rung police HQ here and asked him to see me, he could well have mentioned it to his guv'nor and either been primed as to what to say or told not to see me. And there would have followed the bogus complaint about the Yard acting in their area without permission. And then we'd have been obliged to withdraw."

"You were taking a chance on him not being among the bent links."

"I thought not, sir, but I couldn't be sure. You see, I reckoned that if he had been a villain, he'd have gone over Stinky Miller's garage with a small tooth comb to remove every bit of give-away evidence. And he would have known what that sinker was. He would neither have missed it nor left it."

"Good God, George, he should have combed that garage in any case."

"He probably did, sir. But if he wasn't a villain he wouldn't have realized what the sinker was. To an innocent jack, that lump of lead would have been no more important than any of the rest of the tools and impendimenta there. So I reckoned he was either a villain and a rotten searcher or a straight man. But I couldn't see a villain leaving a bit of criminal evidence like that lying about when he'd got carte blanche to do as he liked on the premises. So I took a gamble on Putrey. That was my hunch, as you know."

"Of course."

"We stopped Lambourn approaching Putrey with a promise to tell him a fuller story later. But I got him to chat about the case. His coroner's office is not a full-time one. They second a serving officer to him for each individual case. Being a country district, he usually gets the local village bobby for making his preliminary enquiries.

"This is what happened in Miller's case. The Caldenham bobby who was called to the scene by the GP acted for Lambourn. He informed his sergeant who had expected Chinemouth to send a DS. To everyone's surprise, they got not only DS Cheshire, but a DI as well—Putrey. Lambourn was quite happy with this, but for some reason, Putrey was suddenly recalled to Chinemouth."

"Ah! I wonder why and who by?"

"Statements were taken from the GP and the police surgeon. According to Lambourn, both expressed some surprise that so light a stone should have damaged Miller's skull, but both stated that some skulls are like eggshells and can be broken by blows which wouldn't give another man a headache. Then the police submitted a report. No strangers had been seen in the village. All the men in the houses round about away at work. The stone had Miller's blood on it. The stone matched the depressed fracture. No fingerprints other than hints of Miller's own on the stone. No other likely weapon anywhere about. Several other stones teetering on the edge of the shelf above and so on. They said Mrs Miller had made an hysterical statement so full of wild assertions that much of it could be discounted, though the rest bore out the other findings."

"A whitewash, in fact?"

"I think so, sir, particularly as Lambourn got a message at the same time as the report saying that as a result of their investigation the police had no reason to suspect foul play and, therefore, recommended the coroner to conclude the enquiry. Faced with this, Lambourn did not hold an inquest, but wrapped the thing up by issuing his Pink Form..."

"That's the certificate of cause of death for the purpose of registration, isn't it?"

"Yes, sir. Form 100 Part B. Death due to blow to the head by misadventure, resulting in...and then all the technical terms for the actual injuries. Then he issued a cremation certificate, and that was that."

Anderson helped himself to another cake and handed his cup over to Hebditch for a refill. "And the coroner was quite happy, was he?"

"To do him justice, I don't think he was, sir. But as both doctors had said death from the falling stone was a possibility and the police had decided on accident, he didn't think he would gain anything by conducting a full inquest with jury and all the trappings."

"No pathologist's report?"

"He would have had one had the police not virtually squashed his enquiry. But he thought it would be of little value merely to have the other doctors' reports confirmed—probably confirmed I think he meant—in view of the police assertion that nobody else was involved."

Anderson helped himself to sugar. "Who initiated the police message that accompanied the report?"

Masters grimaced. "Detective Chief Superintendent J. B. Shepherd, sir."

"Who presumably withdrew DI Putrey from the case before he could enquire too deeply into it."

"That is what we believe, sir."

"Believe or believed?"

"Both. When we heard it from Lambourn, we believed we'd got the name we'd been wanting."

"And now?"

"We have had what we believed confirmed, sir."

"How?"

"By observation and by word of mouth, sir."

"Observation?"

Masters turned to Green. "Your show, Bill."

Green nodded. "I reckoned the man we were after would be getting uneasy, sir. Villains can sense things. Particularly a senior cop with long training. If he turns rogue he's got a nose start, if you'll pardon the expression. I don't think Sergeant Cheshire chased our car yesterday for a couple of hours just for laughs. He was set on."

"Detailed to do it, you mean?"

"Yes, sir. And my name was the link. The uniform constable at the scene when Pearce died made his ordinary routine report. He mentioned me because Stan Pearce had recognized me. And he noted the car number as a matter of routine. His report wouldn't normally go straight up to a senior CID officer. His own, uniform branch officers would deal with a traffic accident. But for a CID sergeant to be tailing my car meant a senior CID officer had seen the traffic report and had taken some interest in it, like getting to know from the computer at Swansea who actually owned it, and then issuing instructions to the sergeant to locate the car and keep it under observation.

"I reckoned that if a senior CID officer went out of his way to get hold of the report of a traffic accident as soon as that report came in, it could be because that senior CID man was on the look-out for it. And that, in turn, suggested he was expecting it to happen."

Anderson said: "I follow your train of thought, Bill. But a DCS arranging a hit and run incident to kill a man? That's almost unbelievable."

"I didn't say he arranged it, sir. I said he expected it."

"You mean he had been told it would happen?"

"That's it, sir. I doubt whether Shepherd actually killed anybody himself. But, according to Pearce, he was an onlooker when the first chap was knifed, and according to Lambourn he fudged the enquiry into Stinky Miller's death—which we think was again murder by his pals. So why not the same when Stan Pearce was rubbed out? They told him they were going to get Pearce and he, Shepherd, was to do his usual job of making sure there

204

was no evidence found to link the job with those who carried it out."

"But you thought the killings would be making him uneasy?"

"If I'd been in his shoes it would have made me pretty edgy, sir. And then when I discovered that there was a link, no matter how small, between Pearce's death and Scotland Yard, I'd be distinctly jumpy."

Anderson nodded. "I'm with you, Bill. What use did you make of your conclusions?"

"I tried to think like Shepherd would be thinking. Nobody at the Yard could possibly have known that Pearce was to be killed, or could have been present at the time, so that death was not a problem. Nobody could suspect a DCS of being involved in a hit and run when he was sitting in his office miles away. So he was safe on that score. Stinky Miller? He'd reckon he was safe there, too. The coroner had come to a decision based on a perfectly reasonable police report. Even if somebody did dredge up new evidence—which was unlikely—the worst that could happen would be that Shepherd would be considered as having been ill-served by his junior officers investigating the case. It was his job to make a recommendation on the evidence presented to him at the time, and he'd done just that so he was safe on that score, too. But there was a third body. The one buried under a hedge out near the coast. That should be safe, too. Nobody would ever dig four or five feet down under a hedge and discover it. And yet it was the only one that could conceivably pop up and cause difficulties and there was that niggle that there were Yard men in the area, even if they said they were only here on holiday."

Green helped himself to a cigarette. They all waited in silence for him to continue.

"If you're uneasy, sir, and there is just one item that can bring you down, I think your mind demands that you make sure all is well concerning that particular item. Your brain may tell you to leave well alone and steer

205

clear of having anything to do with the trouble spot, but it's a mental conflict that lots of villains have lost. Just a journey in a motor car and you can reassure yourself that all is well. You haven't got to do anything. You just stroll nonchalantly past to see that things are as they should be. No harm in that, you're giving nothing away, and you are taking action to calm your uneasiness."

"I think I see your move, Bill. You've had the grave watched."

"Right, sir. Reed and Berger and Mr Hebditch's three constables. All strategically placed to watch for his coming and to observe the grave. Reed and Berger had the cameras from our murder bags—with those long-distance lenses on. They actually covered the grave. The other three watched the approach roads. All out of sight."

"And?"

"He came, sir. He left his car at exactly the same spot as we parked in last night."

"Confirmation of your good map appreciation, Bill—if any were needed, of course."

"Thank you, sir. The constable near there said he noticed immediately that there'd been some activity there. Tyre marks and so on. He looked about very carefully before taking the coastal path."

"He must have been in a lather," said Hebditch. "We'd had a car along there, too. There'd be tracks in the sandy patches. He'd see them."

Green nodded. "I reckon he'd be in a stew. I know I would have been. Anyway, sir, he got to the grave. We'd put it back as best we could last night, and the lads had done a bit more clearing up early this morning when they'd gone out there. But, according to Reed, they couldn't hide the fact there'd been some digging and tramping about there recently. And that probably explains why Shepherd only had a short look and then hurried back to his car but the lads had got shots of him examining the grave and so on. They'd earmarked one of those shops that will develop and print in an hour. They rushed the film in there and waited for the shots. They

206

got back here about half-eleven, just about the time we got back. Of course we didn't know the chap was Shepherd, but we'd got the mug shots and the number of his car, so identification wasn't too difficult."

"Well done," said Anderson. "I'm sure the photographic evidence will help me a lot when I see Chief Constable Gore—apart from the fact that it will be of use in court. I hope you got written statements from the five observers."

"Not yet, sir," said Masters. "But they'll be there."

"Where are the men now?"

"I told them to rest, sir. They've all had a long stint."

"I see. Now, George, you said your belief had been confirmed by observation and by word of mouth. I've heard about the photographs. What about the verbal reports?"

"Just one, sir. From DI Putrey. As soon as we got back from seeing Lambourn, Bill rang Putrey. By this time we were pretty sure he was a straight link in the chain so we felt Bill could suggest a meeting. Putrey came here. Bill had said that as it was a private meeting it would be as well if it was not mentioned at HQ in case it resulted in harassment similar to the tailing that took place yesterday afternoon. Mentioning the privacy was merely a precaution, in view of the fact that Putrey had rung up at a non-businesslike hour last night to ask for a private word."

"So you're sure nobody knew he came to see you?"

"Pretty sure. Putrey seemed confident he was not spotted, and during the course of conversation he mentioned that Shepherd had gone out earlier this morning—as we know he had—and had not, by that time, returned to his office."

"Good. What did you learn?"

"Initially very little. I think that finding myself and Hebditch here as well as Bill shook him a little."

"I've no doubt it did."

"Anyway, Putrey at first tried to give the impression that all he wanted to see Bill for was to apologize for the behaviour of Cheshire and Berwick yesterday afternoon.

But it was very obvious there was more on his mind. When Bill asked him if he had given Cheshire the necessary orders, he confessed he hadn't. And when asked what sort of a report Cheshire had made to him, he told us that he had heard the story from Berwick. Cheshire apparently had gone straight to Shepherd with it. I felt that was probably an important fact from our point of view. You see, sir, the whole thing didn't quite gel. There was Putrey apologizing to Bill for the actions of a DS who didn't, apparently, report to him. I tackled Putrey about this, and it appears that Cheshire is supposed to report to him, but on occasions has bypassed him and gone straight to Shepherd.

"Cheshire, apparently, sometimes worked with Shepherd, and it would seem that the sergeant sometimes took advantage of this relationship. Putrey had tried to put a stop to it and had bawled Cheshire out when it first started to happen, but Shepherd had stepped in to take Cheshire's side.

"That was the real beginning of the chat Putrey had wanted. His reason for visiting us was to get his grievances off his chest and he had come, under the guise of making an apology, to talk to somebody about what he was facing. Shepherd was obviously undermining his authority—at any rate with Cheshire. But there was more.

"Both Bill and I got the impression that Putrey is a conscientious officer. Not a man with great flair, but with enough interest in his job to make him thorough and efficient."

"The sort of chap we need, in fact," suggested Anderson. "Saving your presence, George, and yours, Bill."

"I haven't got flair," grunted Green.

"Maybe not, but you've got a vast fund of useful knowledge. And with that as a foundation you've been able to help build some wind- and weather-proof cases. George is a skilled architect, but you're a skilled mason. No really outstanding edifice is built without both."

"Nice of you to say so, sir."

Anderson turned to Masters. "Go on about Putrey."

"Briefly, sir, he gave us to understand that Shepherd has been causing him some concern. Two or three jobs have been taken out of Putrey's hands. Whether they all had to do with the activities of Dringle and Swabey, we have no means of telling, but we mentioned the death of Stinky Miller to him. He was surprised that we should know of this. We explained away our knowledge by saying that we only knew of it because Mrs Miller had written a letter of complaint to the Yard—to the commissioner, actually—about the way the police had handled the affair. We told him that though the commissioner was, of course, in no position to help her, complaints like that, these days, are noted, because of the public interest in such things.

"Putrey accepted this. We questioned him as closely as we dared about the Miller business without giving anything away of what we had discovered. Evidently it was typical of two or three similar occasions. Putrey learned of the death through the channels and, quite correctly, had set out himself to investigate, taking Cheshire with him. At the end of the first day, Shepherd took him off the case, presumably because he, the DCS, had by then been told by Dringle and Swabey that there was another death the police should not enquire too closely into. Putrey had been annoyed by the whole affair because he doubted whether the falling stone would have killed Miller and he wanted to piece together the bits and pieces that Mrs Miller had told him about the garage doors being shut and so forth. But he wasn't given the chance. Shepherd sent him off on some investigation which turned out to be nothing at all, leaving Cheshire to deal with the Miller business. By the time Putrey had finally proved that the job he had been sent on was a wild goose chase, Shepherd had sent the evidence concerning Miller and the police opinion to Lambourn."

"There were several such cases, you say?"

"That's what Putrey led us to believe. The last of them was the hit and run that killed Pearce. Putrey wanted to sink his teeth into that one, but Shepherd ruled that there were more important things to do, such as investigating a number of break-ins into sea front kiosks."

Anderson nodded grimly. "That the lot?" he asked.

"Putrey, I believe, sir, had his perceptions sharpened quite a lot by Shepherd's treatment. At least he started to notice a number of odd things. Phone calls that the DCS would not answer before clearing his office of any other person there. Failure to inform his staff as to where he was going, and why, on various occasions."

"And a definite deterioration in Shepherd's moods and temper," added Green. "Not that Shepherd had ever been easy, but he grew worse these last couple of years."

"It was to talk about these matters that really brought Putrey to call Bill and ask for the meeting," said Masters. "I felt sorry for the man, because he was near breaking point as a result of the treatment he was receiving, and yet there was still a strand of loyalty for his superior that hadn't yet broken."

"If you hadn't come along, what then?" demanded Anderson.

"Resignation, sir. It's still on, because we were not able to do anything for him except listen. He doesn't know Shepherd will be removed within hours, and we could give him no hint. We did the Dutch Uncles act. Told him not to resign because he never could tell what was just round the corner and so forth. We've probably staved off his decision for a few days and by that time I hope his resignation won't be necessary."

"Good. We don't want to lose trained men for reasons like this."

"That's the lot, sir. Hebditch has prepared a short statement on suspected heroin imports in this area. I think you should have it in your pocket in case of need when you meet Mr Gore."

"Whom I shall ring forthwith. I've got his office and home numbers. Liaison at the Home Office supplied them. I shall insist on seeing him this evening."

"Will you need us any more, sir?"

"No, no. I expect your families will be back by now.

But stay in the hotel this evening, just in case I have to consult you."

Chief Constable Gore was to have chaired a meeting asked for by the Area Conservationists to discuss, mainly, police failure to prosecute those responsible for leaving litter both in the towns and the rural areas under his jurisdiction. The Conservationists, he knew, would be demanding to know why, in face of the statutes permitting heavy fines for discarding litter, few, if any, cases had been initiated by the police under his command.

When Anderson rang and asked to see him, Gore gladly handed over the meeting to his deputy and invited the AC round to his home in time for an early-evening drink.

Gore was a shrewd man. As soon as he heard that Anderson wanted a longish chat with him, he realized that something more than a courtesy visit was in the wind. Besides, he had met the Yard man on one or two occasions, briefly but for long enough to leave him in little doubt that the AC Crime would not, himself, travel from London to Chinemouth to discuss trivia.

Gore had a study. After introducing Anderson to Mrs Gore, he ushered the visitor into this room with its desk and locked filing cabinets.

"Gin and tonic?"

"Excellent. And I should say that I'm pleased you've offered it before you hear what I have to tell you, because after it you may not be feeling quite so generous towards me."

"Like that, is it?"

"Bad."

"Right. Try that for size." Gore handed Anderson his drink. "And to show that whatever happens I shan't begrudge you a refill, I'll put the tray with all the makings on the desk between us, and you can help yourself if I forget my duties as host."

"Thank you."

Gore sat down. "Now, what's it all about?"

Anderson told his long story. He had it all in his head,

but even so, to help him convince Gore, he had the file with the original letter, the photographs, the marked maps, and reports from all the investigating officers.

It took over an hour to tell. Anderson was a skilled raconteur. His facts were marshalled and lucidly put. Gore felt the need to interrupt only rarely. After he had heard Anderson out, however, he questioned him closely for almost another half-hour. At last he sat back and there was a long silence between the two men.

Suddenly, Gore said: "Help yourself to another drink. And while you're at it, pour me one, too."

In silence, Anderson did as he had been asked.

"I can't accept what you have told me," said Gore at last.

Anderson nodded his head slowly a couple of times in mute acceptance of this statement. Then Gore suddenly sat upright as if realizing what he had just said. "I put that badly. What I meant to say was that I just cannot take it in. The enormity of the offences...my own DCS ...of course I believe your report...I wish I didn't..." He stared at Anderson. "I've got to act and act quickly but my mind's like an express train running on the wrong line."

"Have your drink," counselled Anderson.

Gore took a gulp from his glass without, apparently, tasting it.

"The first thing is to arrest Shepherd."

"I'd bring in Cheshire, too," counselled Anderson. "We have no proof that he was actively involved in any of the villainy, but he was Shepherd's man. The chances are that he could be a confederate. Then we shall want to locate and arrest Dringle and Swabey."

"Of course. But I've never had to arrest a senior officer before."

"Anybody can do it. On one of your Chief Constable's warrants. Send a senior uniform man. Chief Super, perhaps."

"I'll do it myself," said Gore quietly.

"In that case, get some back-up. Ring Putrey for instance, and tell him to bring a car with a driver to pick you up."

All the necessary arrangements were put in hand after Gore had made a few phone calls.

"Suicide, sir?" asked Masters.

"In his office. Locked. A bottle of sleeping pills and a bottle of Scotch."

"Best thing," said Green.

"Maybe. By the way, I've had no dinner."

"The dining room is closed, sir. But there's a decent restaurant just down the hill."

"Come and sit with me while I deal with a steak."

As Anderson ate, he talked. "Dringle and Swabey have debunked. The thinking is that they've used that damned inflatable of theirs to get out to sea for a pick up. But we'll have 'em, no matter where they've gone."

"Cheshire?"

"Can't say for sure. A dupe, I reckon. They've got him at the nick. Your pal Putrey is questioning him pretty closely. That young man—Putrey—has got some gall and wormwood in his soul and he's getting rid of it on Cheshire. But I think all we'll find is that Cheshire was teacher's pet. Shepherd needed a second string if he was to ensure protection for Dringle and Swabey. He found a willing ally in Cheshire. Willing because of favoured treatment rather than criminal involvement, I guess."

Masters signalled to the waiter as Anderson pushed his empty plate away. "Coffee and brandy for four, please."

"So," said Green. "No dirty washing?"

"Not at the moment."

"What about Pearce and Stinky Miller's wife?"

Anderson shrugged. "Pearce had no dependents. Mrs Miller will be your pigeon, Bill."

"Mine? In what way, sir?"

"Say you are convinced he was murdered, but you can't get a line on who did it, and after all this time you can see no hope of doing so. The file will be kept open, of course. That being so, she's entitled to compensation from the Criminal Injuries Board. I'll arrange for her to get a decent sum. It's not the best answer, Bill. It's not even a good one, but it's the best we can do in the circumstances. Oh, and swear her to secrecy, will you? This is all strictly illegit."

Green nodded.

"And another thing, Bill."

"What's that?"

"Your old warrior chums—why the hell didn't you drill it into them that they should sign their blasted letters?"

"You know how it is in the army, sir. You have to sign for so many things that it's quite a relief not to sign your own letters."

Anderson looked at him over the rim of his brandy glass.

"The answer to that," he said quietly, "is Bung-ho."

"Talamief," replied Green, raising his glass in response to the implied toast.

THE PERENNIAL LIBRARY MYSTERY SERIES

Ted Allbeury

THE OTHER SIDE OF SILENCE P 669, $2.84
"In the best le Carré tradition . . . an ingenious and readable book."
—*New York Times Book Review*

PALOMINO BLONDE P 670, $2.84
"Fast-moving, splendidly technocratic intercontinental espionage tale
. . . you'll love it." —*The Times* (London)

SNOWBALL P 671, $2.84
"A novel of byzantine intrigue. . . ."—*New York Times Book Review*

Delano Ames

CORPSE DIPLOMATIQUE P 637, $2.84
"Sprightly and intelligent."
—*New York Herald Tribune Book Review*

FOR OLD CRIME'S SAKE P 629, $2.84

MURDER, MAESTRO, PLEASE P 630, $2.84
"If there is a more engaging couple in modern fiction than Jane and
Dagobert Brown, we have not met them." —*Scotsman*

SHE SHALL HAVE MURDER P 638, $2.84
"Combines the merit of both the English and American schools in the
new mystery. It's as breezy as the best of the American ones, and has
the sophistication and wit of any top-notch Britisher."
—*New York Herald Tribune Book Review*

E. C. Bentley

TRENT'S LAST CASE P 440, $2.50
"One of the three best detective stories ever written."
—Agatha Christie

TRENT'S OWN CASE P 516, $2.25
"I won't waste time saying that the plot is sound and the detection
satisfying. Trent has not altered a scrap and reappears with all his old
humor and charm." —Dorothy L. Sayers

Andrew Bergman

THE BIG KISS-OFF OF 1944   P 673, $2.84
"It is without doubt the nearest thing to genuine Chandler I've ever come across. . . . Tough, witty—very witty—and a beautiful eye for period detail. . . ."   —Jack Higgins

HOLLYWOOD AND LEVINE   P 674, $2.84
"Fast-paced private-eye fiction."   —*San Francisco Chronicle*

Gavin Black

A DRAGON FOR CHRISTMAS   P 473, $1.95
"Potent excitement!"   —*New York Herald Tribune*

THE EYES AROUND ME   P 485, $1.95
"I stayed up until all hours last night reading *The Eyes Around Me*, which is something I do not do very often, but I was so intrigued by the ingeniousness of Mr. Black's plotting and the witty way in which he spins his mystery. I can only say that I enjoyed the book enormously."
                     —F. van Wyck Mason

YOU WANT TO DIE, JOHNNY?   P 472, $1.95
"Gavin Black doesn't just develop a pressure plot in suspense, he adds uninfected wit, character, charm, and sharp knowledge of the Far East to make rereading as keen as the first race-through."   —*Book Week*

Nicholas Blake

THE CORPSE IN THE SNOWMAN   P 427, $1.95
"If there is a distinction between the novel and the detective story (which we do not admit), then this book deserves a high place in both categories."   —*New York Times*

END OF CHAPTER   P 397, $1.95
". . . admirably solid . . . an adroit formal detective puzzle backed up by firm characterization and a knowing picture of London publishing."
                     —*New York Times*

HEAD OF A TRAVELER   P 398, $2.25
"Another grade A detective story of the right old jigsaw persuasion."
                     —*New York Herald Tribune Book Review*

MINUTE FOR MURDER   P 419, $1.95
"An outstanding mystery novel. Mr. Blake's writing is a delight in itself."   —*New York Times*

THE MORNING AFTER DEATH   P 520, $1.95
"One of Blake's best."   —Rex Warner

John & Emery Bonett

A BANNER FOR PEGASUS   P 554, $2.40
"A gem! Beautifully plotted and set. . . . Not only is the murder adroit
and deserved, and the detection competent, but the love story is charm-
ing."   —Jacques Barzun and Wendell Hertig Taylor

DEAD LION   P 563, $2.40
"A clever plot, authentic background and interesting characters highly
recommended this one."   —*New Republic*

THE SOUND OF MURDER   P 642, $2.84
The suspects are many, the clues few, but the gentle Inspector ferrets out
the truth and pursues the case to its bitter and shocking end.

Christianna Brand

GREEN FOR DANGER   P 551, $2.50
"You have to reach for the greatest of Great Names (Christie, Carr,
Queen . . .) to find Brand's rivals in the devious subtleties of the trade."
—Anthony Boucher

TOUR DE FORCE   P 572, $2.40
"Complete with traps for the over-ingenious, a double-reverse surprise
ending and a key clue planted so fairly and obviously that you completely
overlook it. If that's your idea of perfect entertainment, then seize at once
upon *Tour de Force.*"   —Anthony Boucher, *New York Times*

James Byrom

OR BE HE DEAD   P 585, $2.84
"A very original tale . . . Well written and steadily entertaining."
—Jacques Barzun and Wendell Hertig Taylor, *A Catalogue of Crime*

Henry Calvin

IT'S DIFFERENT ABROAD   P 640, $2.84
"What is remarkable and delightful, Mr. Calvin imparts a flavor of satire
to what he renovates and compels us to take straight."
—Jacques Barzun

Marjorie Carleton

VANISHED   P 559, $2.40
"Exceptional . . . a minor triumph."
—Jacques Barzun and Wendell Hertig Taylor, *A Catalogue of Crime*

George Harmon Coxe

MURDER WITH PICTURES   P 527, $2.25
"[Coxe] has hit the bull's-eye with his first shot."

—*New York Times*

Edmund Crispin

BURIED FOR PLEASURE   P 506, $2.50
"Absolute and unalloyed delight."

—Anthony Boucher, *New York Times*

Lionel Davidson

THE MENORAH MEN   P 592, $2.84
"Of his fellow thriller writers, only John Le Carré shows the same
instinct for the viscera."   —*Chicago Tribune*

NIGHT OF WENCESLAS   P 595, $2.84
"A most ingenious thriller, so enriched with style, wit, and a sense of
serious comedy that it all but transcends its kind."

—*The New Yorker*

THE ROSE OF TIBET   P 593, $2.84
"I hadn't realized how much I missed the genuine Adventure story
. . . until I read *The Rose of Tibet*."   —Graham Greene

D. M. Devine

MY BROTHER'S KILLER   P 558, $2.40
"A most enjoyable crime story which I enjoyed reading down to the last
moment."   —Agatha Christie

Kenneth Fearing

THE BIG CLOCK   P 500, $1.95
"It will be some time before chill-hungry clients meet again so rare a
compound of irony, satire, and icy-fingered narrative. *The Big Clock* is
. . . a psychothriller you won't put down."   —*Weekly Book Review*

Andrew Garve

THE ASHES OF LODA   P 430, $1.50
"Garve . . . embellishes a fine fast adventure story with a more credible
picture of the U.S.S.R. than is offered in most thrillers."

—*New York Times Book Review*

THE CUCKOO LINE AFFAIR   P 451, $1.95
". . . an agreeable and ingenious piece of work."   —*The New Yorker*

A HERO FOR LEANDA P 429, $1.50

"One can trust Mr. Garve to put a fresh twist to any situation, and the ending is really a lovely surprise." —*Manchester Guardian*

MURDER THROUGH THE LOOKING GLASS P 449, $1.95

". . . refreshingly out-of-the-way and enjoyable . . . highly recommended to all comers." —*Saturday Review*

NO TEARS FOR HILDA P 441, $1.95

"It starts fine and finishes finer. I got behind on breathing watching Max get not only his man but his woman, too." —Rex Stout

THE RIDDLE OF SAMSON P 450, $1.95

"The story is an excellent one, the people are quite likable, and the writing is superior." —*Springfield Republican*

Michael Gilbert

BLOOD AND JUDGMENT P 446, $1.95

"Gilbert readers need scarcely be told that the characters all come alive at first sight, and that his surpassing talent for narration enhances any plot. . . . Don't miss." —*San Francisco Chronicle*

THE BODY OF A GIRL P 459, $1.95

"Does what a good mystery should do: open up into all kinds of ramifications, with untold menace behind the action. At the end, there is a bang-up climax, and it is a pleasure to see how skilfully Gilbert wraps everything up." —*New York Times Book Review*

FEAR TO TREAD P 458, $1.95

"Merits serious consideration as a work of art." —*New York Times*

Joe Gores

HAMMETT P 631, $2.84

"Joe Gores at his very best. Terse, powerful writing—with the master, Dashiell Hammett, as the protagonist in a novel I think he would have been proud to call his own." —Robert Ludlum

C. W. Grafton

BEYOND A REASONABLE DOUBT P 519, $1.95

"A very ingenious tale of murder . . . a brilliant and gripping narrative." —Jacques Barzun and Wendell Hertig Taylor

THE RAT BEGAN TO GNAW THE ROPE   P 639, $2.84
"Fast, humorous story with flashes of brilliance."

—*The New Yorker*

Edward Grierson

THE SECOND MAN   P 528, $2.25
"One of the best trial-testimony books to have come along in quite a
while."   —*The New Yorker*

Bruce Hamilton

TOO MUCH OF WATER   P 635, $2.84
"A superb sea mystery. . . . The prose is excellent."
—Jacques Barzun and Wendell Hertig Taylor, *A Catalogue of Crime*

Cyril Hare

DEATH IS NO SPORTSMAN   P 555, $2.40
"You will be thrilled because it succeeds in placing an ingenious story
in a new and refreshing setting. . . . The identity of the murderer is really
a surprise."   —*Daily Mirror*

DEATH WALKS THE WOODS   P 556, $2.40
"Here is a fine formal detective story, with a technically brilliant solution
demanding the attention of all connoisseurs of construction."
—Anthony Boucher, *New York Times Book Review*

AN ENGLISH MURDER   P 455, $2.50
"By a long shot, the best crime story I have read for a long time.
Everything is traditional, but originality does not suffer. The setting is
perfect. Full marks to Mr. Hare."   —*Irish Press*

SUICIDE EXCEPTED   P 636, $2.84
"Adroit in its manipulation . . . and distinguished by a plot-twister which
I'll wager Christie wishes she'd thought of."   —*New York Times*

TENANT FOR DEATH   P 570, $2.84
"The way in which an air of probability is combined both with clear,
terse narrative and with a good deal of subtle suburban atmosphere,
proves the extreme skill of the writer."   —*The Spectator*

TRAGEDY AT LAW   P 522, $2.25
"An extremely urbane and well-written detective story."

—*New York Times*

Cyril Hare *(cont'd)*

UNTIMELY DEATH   P 514, \$2.25

"The English detective story at its quiet best, meticulously underplayed, rich in perceivings of the droll human animal and ready at the last with a neat surprise which has been there all the while had we but wits to see it."   *—New York Herald Tribune Book Review*

THE WIND BLOWS DEATH   P 589, \$2.84

"A plot compounded of musical knowledge, a Dickens allusion, and a subtle point in law is related with delightfully unobtrusive wit, warmth, and style."   *—New York Times*

WITH A BARE BODKIN   P 523, \$2.25

"One of the best detective stories published for a long time."
                                                    —The Spectator

Robert Harling

THE ENORMOUS SHADOW   P 545, \$2.50

"In some ways the best spy story of the modern period. . . . The writing is terse and vivid . . . the ending full of action . . . altogether first-rate."
—Jacques Barzun and Wendell Hertig Taylor, *A Catalogue of Crime*

Matthew Head

THE CABINDA AFFAIR   P 541, \$2.25

"An absorbing whodunit and a distinguished novel of atmosphere."
                                    —Anthony Boucher, *New York Times*

THE CONGO VENUS   P 597, \$2.84

"Terrific. The dialogue is just plain wonderful."   *—Boston Globe*

MURDER AT THE FLEA CLUB   P 542, \$2.50

"The true delight is in Head's style, its limpid ease combined with humor and an awesome precision of phrase."   *—San Francisco Chronicle*

M. V. Heberden

ENGAGED TO MURDER   P 533, \$2.25

"Smooth plotting."   *—New York Times*

James Hilton

WAS IT MURDER?   P 501, \$1.95

"The story is well planned and well written."   *—New York Times*

S. B. Hough

DEAR DAUGHTER DEAD   P 661, $2.84
"A highly intelligent and sophisticated story of police detection . . . not
to be missed on any account."   —Francis Iles, *The Guardian*

SWEET SISTER SEDUCED   P 662, $2.84
In the course of a nightlong conversation between the Inspector and the
suspect, the complex emotions of a very strange marriage are revealed.

P. M. Hubbard

HIGH TIDE   P 571, $2.40
"A smooth elaboration of mounting horror and danger."
                                               —*Library Journal*

Elspeth Huxley

THE AFRICAN POISON MURDERS   P 540, $2.25
"Obscure venom, manical mutilations, deadly bush fire, thrilling climax
compose major opus.... Top-flight."
                                  —*Saturday Review of Literature*

MURDER ON SAFARI   P 587, $2.84
"Right now we'd call Mrs. Huxley a dangerous rival to Agatha Christie."   —*Books*

Francis Iles

BEFORE THE FACT   P 517, $2.50
"Not many 'serious' novelists have produced character studies to compare with Iles's internally terrifying portrait of the murderer in *Before
the Fact,* his masterpiece and a work truly deserving the appellation of
unique and beyond price."   —Howard Haycraft

MALICE AFORETHOUGHT   P 532, $1.95
"It is a long time since I have read anything so good as *Malice Aforethought,* with its cynical humour, acute criminology, plausible detail and
rapid movement. It makes you hug yourself with pleasure."
                                —H. C. Harwood, *Saturday Review*

Michael Innes

APPLEBY ON ARARAT   P 648, $2.84
"Superbly plotted and humorously written."   —*The New Yorker*

APPLEBY'S END   P 649, $2.84
"Most amusing."   —*Boston Globe*

Michael Innes (cont'd)

THE CASE OF THE JOURNEYING BOY   P 632, $3.12
"I could see no faults in it. There is no one to compare with him."
                              —*Illustrated London News*

DEATH ON A QUIET DAY   P 677, $2.84
"Delightfully witty."   —*Chicago Sunday Tribune*

DEATH BY WATER   P 574, $2.40
"The amount of ironic social criticism and deft characterization of scenes
and people would serve another author for six books."
                    —Jacques Barzun and Wendell Hertig Taylor

HARE SITTING UP   P 590, $2.84
"There is hardly anyone (in mysteries or mainstream) more exquisitely
literate, allusive and Jamesian—and hardly anyone with a firmer sense
of melodramatic plot or a more vigorous gift of storytelling."
                          —Anthony Boucher, *New York Times*

THE LONG FAREWELL   P 575, $2.40
"A model of the deft, classic detective story, told in the most wittily
diverting prose."   —*New York Times*

THE MAN FROM THE SEA   P 591, $2.84
"The pace is brisk, the adventures exciting and excitingly told, and above
all he keeps to the very end the interesting ambiguity of the man from
the sea."   —*New Statesman*

ONE MAN SHOW   P 672, $2.84
"Exciting, amusingly written . . . very good enjoyment it is."
                                         —*The Spectator*

THE SECRET VANGUARD   P 584, $2.84
"Innes . . . has mastered the art of swift, exciting and well-organized
narrative."   —*New York Times*

THE WEIGHT OF THE EVIDENCE   P 633, $2.84
"First-class puzzle, deftly solved. University background interesting and
amusing."   —*Saturday Review of Literature*

Mary Kelly

THE SPOILT KILL   P 565, $2.40
"Mary Kelly is a new Dorothy Sayers. . . . [An] exciting new novel."
                                         —*Evening News*

Lange Lewis

THE BIRTHDAY MURDER   P 518, $1.95
"Almost perfect in its playlike purity and delightful prose."
—Jacques Barzun and Wendell Hertig Taylor

Allan MacKinnon

HOUSE OF DARKNESS   P 582, $2.84
"His best . . . a perfect compendium."
—Jacques Barzun and Wendell Hertig Taylor, *A Catalogue of Crime*

Frank Parrish

FIRE IN THE BARLEY   P 651, $2.84
"A remarkable and brilliant first novel. . . . entrancing."
—*The Spectator*

SNARE IN THE DARK   P 650, $2.84
The wily English poacher Dan Mallett is framed for murder and has to
confront unknown enemies to clear himself.

STING OF THE HONEYBEE   P 652, $2.84
"Terrorism and murder visit a sleepy English village in this witty, offbeat
thriller."   —*Chicago Sun-Times*

Austin Ripley

MINUTE MYSTERIES   P 387, $2.50
More than one hundred of the world's shortest detective stories. Only
one possible solution to each case!

Thomas Sterling

THE EVIL OF THE DAY   P 529, $2.50
"Prose as witty and subtle as it is sharp and clear. . .characters unconven-
tionally conceived and richly bodied forth . . . . In short, a novel to be
treasured."   —Anthony Boucher, *New York Times*

Julian Symons

THE BELTING INHERITANCE   P 468, $1.95
"A superb whodunit in the best tradition of the detective story."
—August Derleth, *Madison Capital Times*

BOGUE'S FORTUNE   P 481, $1.95
"There's a touch of the old sardonic humour, and more than a touch of
style."   —*The Spectator*

Julian Symons (cont'd)

THE COLOR OF MURDER P 461, $1.95

"A singularly unostentatious and memorably brilliant detective story."
—*New York Herald Tribune Book Review*

Dorothy Stockbridge Tillet
(John Stephen Strange)

THE MAN WHO KILLED FORTESCUE P 536, $2.25

"Better than average." —*Saturday Review of Literature*

Simon Troy

THE ROAD TO RHUINE P 583, $2.84

"Unusual and agreeably told." —*San Francisco Chronicle*

SWIFT TO ITS CLOSE P 546, $2.40

"A nicely literate British mystery . . . the atmosphere and the plot are exceptionally well wrought, the dialogue excellent." —*Best Sellers*

Henry Wade

THE DUKE OF YORK'S STEPS P 588, $2.84

"A classic of the golden age."
—Jacques Barzun and Wendell Hertig Taylor, *A Catalogue of Crime*

A DYING FALL P 543, $2.50

"One of those expert British suspense jobs . . . it crackles with undercurrents of blackmail, violent passion and murder. Topnotch in its class."
—*Time*

THE HANGING CAPTAIN P 548, $2.50

"This is a detective story for connoisseurs, for those who value clear thinking and good writing above mere ingenuity and easy thrills."
—*The Times* (London) *Literary Supplement*

Hillary Waugh

LAST SEEN WEARING . . . P 552, $2.40

"A brilliant tour de force." —Julian Symons

THE MISSING MAN P 553, $2.40

"The quiet detailed police work of Chief Fred C. Fellows, Stockford, Conn., is at its best in *The Missing Man* . . . one of the Chief's toughest cases and one of the best handled."

—Anthony Boucher, *New York Times Book Review*

Henry Kitchell Webster

WHO IS THE NEXT?   P 539, $2.25
"A double murder, private-plane piloting, a neat impersonation, and a delicate courtship are adroitly combined by a writer who knows how to use the language."   —Jacques Barzun and Wendell Hertig Taylor

John Welcome

GO FOR BROKE   P 663, $2.84
A rich financier chases Richard Graham half 'round Europe in a desperate attempt to prevent the truth getting out.

RUN FOR COVER   P 664, $2.84
"I can think of few writers in the international intrigue game with such a gift for fast and vivid storytelling."
       —*New York Times Book Review*

STOP AT NOTHING   P 665, $2.84
"Mr. Welcome is lively, vivid and highly readable."
       —*New York Times Book Review*

Anna Mary Wells

MURDERER'S CHOICE   P 534, $2.50
"Good writing, ample action, and excellent character work."
       —*Saturday Review of Literature*

A TALENT FOR MURDER   P 535, $2.25
"The discovery of the villain is a decided shock."   —*Books*

Charles Williams

DEAD CALM   P 655, $2.84
"A brilliant tour de force of inventive plotting, fine manipulation of a small cast and breathtaking sequences of spectacular navigation."
       —*New York Times Book Review*

THE SAILCLOTH SHROUD   P 654, $2.84
"A fine novel of excitement, spirited, fresh and satisfying."
       —*New York Times*

THE WRONG VENUS   P 656, $2.84
Swindler Lawrence Colby and the lovely Martine create a story of romance, larceny, and very blunt homicide.

Edward Young

THE FIFTH PASSENGER   P 544, $2.25
"Clever and adroit . . . excellent thriller. . . ."   —*Library Journal*

If you enjoyed this book you'll want to know about
THE PERENNIAL LIBRARY MYSTERY SERIES

Buy them at your local bookstore or use this coupon for ordering:

Qty	P number	Price
	postage and handling charge	$1.00
	_____ book(s) @ $0.25	
	TOTAL	

Prices contained in this coupon are Harper & Row invoice prices only. They are subject to change without notice, and in no way reflect the prices at which these books may be sold by other suppliers.

HARPER & ROW, Mail Order Dept. #PMS, 10 East 53rd St., New York, N.Y. 10022.

Please send me the books I have checked above. I am enclosing $_____ which includes a postage and handling charge of $1.00 for the first book and 25¢ for each additional book. Send check or money order. No cash or C.O.D.s please

Name_____

Address_____

City_____State_____Zip_____

Please allow 4 weeks for delivery. USA only. This offer expires 3/31/86
Please add applicable sales tax.